MAXIMUM EXPOSURE

Jenny Harper

Published by Accent Press Ltd 2014

ISBN: 9781783752621

Cover design by headandheartpublishingservices.com

Acknowledgements

Daisy Irvine works in a small regional newspaper, based in the fictitious town of Hailesbank. Her paper, *The Hailesbank Herald,* faces the kinds of challenges faced by many similar publications in today's rapidly-changing world. For insights into this, and how a small newspaper works, I'm much indebted to staff at *The Dumfries and Galloway Standard* – though none of my characters is based on anyone I met there and *The Hailesbank Herald* and its news stories and general workings are entirely figments of my imagination.

I enjoyed a long conversation with newspaper veteran Bill Rae, and I would have loved to have been able to include some of his colourful anecdotes in this story. However, the atmosphere he created for me definitely lingers still in the run-down *Herald* offices – no doubt fixed for ever in the nicotine-stained walls!

I have to thank my friend and fellow novelists Sara Bain and Bill Daly for all their help, and Jane Knights for her patient reading of the manuscript. My husband, Robin, has put up with my hours at the computer with great tolerance, for which I thank him. Writing a novel requires a degree of self-belief that has occasionally faltered, and the support of my family and of many fellow authors has been absolutely necessary to drive me on. I am more grateful for it than I can say.

Maximum Exposure is the first of my novels to be published by Accent Press and I'd like to thank Hazel Cushion for showing her faith in my work by signing me to her stable of authors, and her fantastic team for their terrific support.

Note: Hailesbank and the Heartlands

The small market town of Hailesbank is born of my imagination, as are the surrounding villages of Forgie and Stoneyford and the Council housing estate known as Summerfield, which together form The Heartlands. I have placed the area, in my mind, to the east of Scotland's capital city, Edinburgh.

The first mention of The Heartlands was made by Agrippus Centorius in AD77, not long after the Romans began their surge north in the hopes of conquering this savage land. 'This is a place of great beauty,' wrote Agrippus, 'and its wildness has clutched my heart.' He makes several mentions thereafter of The Heartlands. There are still signs of Roman occupation in Hailesbank, which has great transport links to the south (and England) and the north, especially to Edinburgh, and its proximity to the sea and the (real) coastal town of Musselburgh made it a great place to settle. The Georgians and Victorians began to develop the small village, its clean air and glorious views, rich farming hinterland, and great transport proving highly attractive.

The River Hailes flows through the town. There is a Hailes Castle in East Lothian (it has not yet featured in my novels!), but it sits on the Tyne.

Hailesbank has a Town Hall, a High Street, from which a number of ancient small lanes, or vennels, run down to the river, which once was the lifeblood of the town.

In my novels, characters populate the shops, cafes, and pubs in Hailesbank and the pretty adjoining village of Forgie, with Summerfield inhabitants providing another layer of social interaction.

You can meet other inhabitants of the town and area in *Face the Wind and Fly* and *Loving Susie* – with more titles to follow!

PART 1

Chapter One

Outside the offices of *The Hailesbank Herald*, a late frost edged the cobbles with a white rime that glinted and sparkled in the thin early morning light. Daisy Irvine retrieved her camera kit from the boot of her antiquated mud-splattered Suzuki and fumbled for her office key in the depths of her bulky fleece. Being the youngest ever chief photographer at the local newspaper was an achievement she was really proud of, but early-morning call-outs were a definite downside to the job.

She shoved the door open with her shoulder and the heat in the office slapped into her with a force that felt almost physical. She peeled off her jacket, swung her bags onto her desk, and registered that the editor was already in and flouting the law as usual by smoking a cigarette. She was just working out how to frame her request for a pay rise when she heard a strange moan.

She looked up and saw Angus MacMorrow fall, straight as a newly felled tree, onto the shabby threadbare carpet of his smoke-filled lair.

Damn and blast.

The pound signs in her mind popped and evaporated like soap bubbles in the pale February sun. She was sympathetic, but she wasn't unduly alarmed. The old reprobate had collapsed before. Everyone knew his health was dodgy. Only a year ago he'd had a heart attack and spent a week in hospital recovering. Serve him right, the old bugger, for being overweight and seriously unfit.

She marched across the main office to Big Angus's door. Despite his recent health scare, he'd refused to stop smoking, cursed the government for banning the practice in the workplace, and ranted at length to anyone who would listen about the temerity of having his human rights curtailed by small-minded, meddling politicians.

Daisy studied the slumped body. In the heat of the office, she felt as though her cheeks were on fire, yet all the colour had drained from Angus's face. The folds of flesh that sagged from his chin in flabby jowls looked flaccid and waxy. Dammit, he didn't look good. She stooped over him, prised his still burning cigarette from one hand, and stubbed it out in the ashtray he insisted on keeping on his desk. There were already three stubs there and it was still only six thirty. In his other hand he was clutching a sheet of paper. She wiggled it free and stuffed it in her pocket, then set about loosening his tie and collar and rolling his bulk – with great difficulty – round a teetering pile of back copies of the newspaper into the recovery position. His timing was bad. It had been ages since she'd had more than a cost of living increase and she was feeling the pinch.

Still thinking about the negative balance in her bank account, Daisy sighed. Her plea would probably have to wait a week or two now. Absently, she pushed up the rough tweed of Angus's jacket and felt for his pulse. Nothing.

She shifted her fingers and tried again.

No movement, not even a tiny flutter.

She must be missing something. Focusing her attention more sharply, she tried for a third time. She redoubled her efforts. A sense of alarm stirred somewhere near her stomach, which only a few minutes ago had been craving a bacon sandwich.

Still nothing. Rocking back on her heels, she studied the inert form closely, her misty grey eyes widening. She'd seen dead bodies before in the line of duty, but this was the first time she'd been the person to find one. And the fact that the body was her boss, the much satirised, belligerent, annoying, lazy, old-school, cynical, hard-bitten, highly experienced – bizarrely lovable – editor of *The Hailesbank Herald,* made the whole thing much, much worse.

Time to call an ambulance.

Thirty miles away, Ben Gillies woke up in a small guest house on Lindisfarne to a fog so impenetrable that if he hadn't known there was a castle not half a mile away, he could never have guessed at the fact.

He pushed aside one chintzy floral curtain and peered out of the window. Pale grey light filtered through the wet glass but failed to catch the red highlights in his rich brown hair. The mist hung in heavy droplets on the bare branches of the tree outside his room. The garden looked dank and dreary, with patches of sad, limp detritus from last year's growth begging to be cleared and a lawn that was clearly waterlogged. He could just about see the wall at the bottom of the sad expanse of green. He flicked the curtain back into place. Time to get moving.

'So that's it then?' His mind went back again to the last scene he'd played out with Martina. No rows, just a kind of inexorable inevitability about the end of their four-year relationship.

'I guess.' She'd looked pinched and miserable, but there was no attempt at compromise, really nothing left between them. Her jumper hung off her in baggy folds, and her legs looked stick thin and delicate. For a second he felt protective, then he remembered that she didn't want his protection.

He'd picked up the last of his bags and stuffed it into the battered old car he'd bought for this journey.

'Bye then. I'll be in touch.' He bent and kissed her forehead, a melting pot of a dozen conflicting emotions – sad, relieved, angry, empty, exasperated, and liberated.

The idea of the walk – four days from Melrose to Lindisfarne – only came to him when he was already half way up the A1 on the way north to Hailesbank.

'... the reverse of the route of the pilgrims when they fled with the body of St Cuthbert from Lindisfarne at the start of a two-hundred year journey,' said the voice on the car radio. 'This walk has everything. Hills, woods, rivers, moorland, and finally, a walk across the stretch of sand to the Holy Isle itself.'

The programme had held his attention from the beginning. He used to love walking. He had all the time in the world, with

5

no job, no commitments. What better way of marching into a new life than a long walk? Plenty of time to think – or not, as he pleased.

On impulse, he swung off the main road and into Morpeth. There he added to his life's clutter by purchasing stout walking boots, socks, a backpack, waterproofs, a vacuum flask, and a pair of walking poles. He made a few phone calls to arrange accommodation and baggage pick up and headed for Melrose.

Nefertiti, ensconced in the front seat beside him, turned heads at every stop along the way. Ben grinned to himself and thoughts of Martina were edged out of his mind by memories of the day he'd bought the life-size clothes mannequin. He'd walked past a dress shop in Camden Town when it was closing down and the dummy had been mere pennies. He couldn't resist the joke, even though he'd had to carry her along four streets and across a park to the flat he shared at the time with three other blokes. She'd been stark naked, her body a dull biscuit colour, a small bash disfiguring her right hip. She was remarkable for her lack of nipples and – mercifully – of pubic hair, though she sported a fetching black bob above a face that was oddly sweet.

Nefertiti had caused a storm with his flat mates, who battled him endlessly for custody. They dressed her, undressed her, decorated her with police hats or underwear they'd begged, borrowed, or stolen from girlfriends, dates, or sisters. Finally she'd become more or less inseparable from a scarlet negligée and she'd stood in his window, gazing unquestioningly out on the world and causing, from time to time, great amusement to passers by.

Martina had seen the joke, at first. But in time poor Nef became one of the causes for friction and was relegated to a cupboard. On the road, she wasn't too much of a problem, but in towns he'd found that he had to cover her completely with a sheet to avoid unwelcome attention. In Melrose, leaving the car in the care of the guest house where he spent the first night, he took the usual precautions then, leaving even this responsibility behind, set off on his own personal pilgrimage.

6

The four days since then had been the most uplifting, most liberating, most carefree of his life. He'd been blessed with great weather – cold and frosty but clear as a bell. Underfoot, the trail had been springy but passable. Day after day he plodded forward, feeling his lack of fitness at first, then through the tiredness finding new motivation and a sense of achievement. He'd seen buzzards and rooks, peewits and pheasants and even, one day, sitting perfectly still on a rock as day drew to a close, had watched a badger lumbering out of its set in search of food. The sharp edges of Martina's face had begun to blur and fade and the tightness round his heart had loosened. In front of him, like the miles to Lindisfarne, his future lay uncertain but exciting, a path that promised adventure, twists and turns, with long vistas and not a few challenges.

But now the mist had drifted in. Ben dropped the curtain and turned back into the room. His pilgrimage was over, Nefertiti was waiting for him, loyal and uncomplaining under her protective sheet in his rust-heap back in Melrose, and his parents were expecting him in Hailesbank.

Who knew what the future held? Who cared? Ben turned towards the shower, rubbed his hand over the gingery stubble on his chin, and grinned. He felt very relaxed. And there was something exciting about uncertainty.

Chapter Two

Daisy Irvine, dreaming of thumps and bumps, falling timber and toppling editors, woke with tears wet on her cheeks and an empty space in her heart. She wished, more fervently than she had wished over a long year of wishing, that Jack Hedderwick was still by her side.

Angus MacMorrow's death had shaken her more than she cared to admit. So he'd shouted at her and cursed her (he yelled and swore at everybody) but he'd also been her mentor and guide since the day she'd joined *The Hailesbank Herald*, young and green and very unsure of herself. She ventured a pyjama-clad arm out into the cold of her cottage bedroom, pulled a tissue from the box by her bed, and blew her nose noisily. She thought she'd held it together well when Jack left, but maybe she'd just shoved the pain deep down inside her as she'd sleepwalked through the last year. Anyway, it seemed that Big Angus's demise had brought all her insecurities to the fore because in the three days since he'd had that final fatal heart attack, she'd thought of little else but Jack.

Pain sliced through her and came to a juddering halt in her heart. She took a deep breath, but still felt the unavoidable constriction, like a tourniquet tightening. It had been a year now and she still hadn't got over the shock and anguish the break-up had caused.

An image of Jack's familiar features rose in her mind, as real as if he was standing in front of her. He had a sweet, baby face, with clear blue eyes and soft fair hair that curled in wisps round his ears. Jack the lad, with his lean frame and hips so sexy she still felt weak thinking about them –

Beside Daisy's head, her alarm trilled loudly.

'*No-o-o-o.*'

She jumped, unprepared, and fumbled for the off button. It was too early. She wasn't ready to face another day without Jack. The duvet, ice blue and feather-light, billowed above her as she pulled it over her head, then settled around her, snug and warm. Just ten minutes, she allowed herself. Then she'd shower and dress. Just ten minutes to remember all the wonderful things Jack had done for her.

Precisely five seconds later the tumbling electronic notes of her mobile phone repeated insistently from her bag across the room.

'Bother,' said Daisy crossly as she threw back the cover and padded across the room in bare feet, reluctantly obedient to the phone's command. 'Hello?'

'Daisy? We've just had a call from a punter. A lorry's overturned south of Eyemouth and its load's escaped.' Sharon Eddy, the *Herald*'s chief reporter, sounded hideously cheerful for the time of day.

'Escaped?' It seemed an odd word to use.

'Pigs. Big fat porkers. Bacon sarnies to you and me. They're having a hell of a time catching them apparently. See you there soon as? Could make a great picture.'

'OK,' Daisy said resignedly, although she was already turning over the pictorial possibilities in her mind. Escaped pigs sounded like fun and anyway, life went on, with or without Jack, just as the paper had to go on without Angus MacMorrow.

Shivering, she flicked on her one-bar electric heater and started to clamber blearily into her jeans. The shower would have to wait.

Four days later, Daisy pulled on her black trouser suit, the one she kept for posh jobs and funerals. It came to her that today really was the end of an era. Angus MacMorrow was dead and this morning he would be buried.

She flopped down on the edge of her bed to wriggle into her tights. They felt just that – tight. She had to get a grip on her weight or she'd never win Jack back, that much she knew.

Since he'd left she'd overeaten constantly by way of compensation, though it only made her more miserable. On the mantelpiece above the fireplace opposite the end of the bed, assorted cuddly toys were ranged. They surveyed her reproachfully.

'I know, I know,' she sighed. A battered teddy bear looked back at her, one eye lower than the other, but said nothing. 'I'll start next week. But today's the big man's funeral so I can't really be expected to think about lettuce, can I?'

Her gaze moved along the line to Minty, the now grubby polar bear her mother had bought for her sixth birthday, too rich with smells and stains and memories to consider cleaning him. She could remember the day perfectly. The parcel lay by her place at the breakfast table, enticingly mysterious with its crisp, crinkly silver wrapping paper and ice-blue ribbons. She'd been excited. It was a special day and if she was good maybe Daddy wouldn't shout at her. Mummy helped her to unwrap the parcel. The knots were too tight for her small fingers and she couldn't wait to see inside. As soon as a corner of the silvery paper was open, she put in her little hand and felt soft fur and gave a squeal of anticipation. The fur was silky and comforting. She pulled out the toy and fell instantly in love with the round, snuggly bear with its soppily contented expression. She cradled it close to her skinny chest and thought the day was going to be as perfect as she'd dreamed it would be.

Then her father said, 'I do wish you wouldn't buy her these wretched animals, Janet. She's much too old for that nonsense,' and she put it down, slowly, her lips trembling just the tiniest bit. Why did Daddy always manage to spoil things? Later, she found it when she went to bed, snuggled against her pillow, under the blanket. Mummy must have hidden it there for her. She kissed it one hundred times to make up for having abandoned it all day.

She couldn't remember what her father's gift had been. Some educational book or other, long since abandoned, she imagined, designed to fashion her into something she wasn't while Minty the bear lived on in her heart and on her mantelpiece.

'He's really gone, Minty,' she breathed softly to her captive audience while thinking of Angus MacMorrow. 'Definitely deceased.'

She'd never managed to rid herself of the habit of talking to her menagerie. The companionship of her furry animals had always been important to her. When her father had shouted at her, she would run to them for comfort, picking one at random and hugging it close fiercely. Her animals didn't think she was spineless. They didn't tell her to 'buck up and get on with it' or bawl at her when she failed to get a good grade. When her mother, as soft and ineffectual as a waterlogged sponge, failed to comfort her, it was to her animals that she'd reveal her insecurities, trust her innermost thoughts and share her anger.

'Why?' she addressed her menagerie in a tone of deep despair, inviting their views on life in general. When there was no response, she gave a small sniff and put her hand in her pocket to find the comforting presence of Tiny Ted – TT – the smallest of the bears and her constant companion.

'They're not *real,* Daisy,' a voice came from her bedroom door, but gently.

Daisy took a last look at the sheep, the lion, the bears, and the rest of the tattered toys and raised a sceptical eyebrow before swinging round and saying indignantly to the tall figure lounging against her door-post, 'I know that, Lizzie.'

Lizzie Little, lazy-limbed and heavy-lidded, possessed a languorous beauty that she was quite unaware of (which was an important part of her attractiveness). In the cottage that Daisy had shared with her since Jack had left her homeless, Lizzie had the largest room, where she surrounded herself with rich velvets, sumptuous silks, soft woollens in every colour and hue imaginable, the tools of her trade. They lay draped over chairs, hung from tailors' dummies, swathed round the curtain poles, stacked in shimmering layers, skimmed across the radiators, formed pillows and covers on the bed.

Lizzie sat on the bed next to Daisy and wound her long legs into a lotus position. Still in thick brushed cotton pyjamas in a glorious deep purple and a luxurious Carmen red velour wrap, she put her arms around Daisy's shoulders and asked tenderly, 'You OK?'

Daisy nodded, tears coming unanticipated to her eyes. She'd thought she *was* OK until Lizzie's sympathy caught her out. She pulled a tissue from out of her sleeve and blew her nose loudly.

''Course. It's only a funeral. I've done loads before.'

'But not Angus's. Not a friend's.'

Had Angus MacMorrow been her friend? Daisy considered the word. She'd always thought of Angus simply as her boss. When she'd gone to the *Herald*, he'd been the scariest person on the planet. The huge mass of him, bulging and straining above his trousers, the barking intolerance of bad spelling or the misuse of apostrophes, the constant urging to 'Use your *brain* girl, if you have one,' had been overwhelming. At first she'd thought he was just like her father – ordering, criticising, vetting her every move so that she couldn't talk, think, or breathe for herself. But soon she'd seen his humour and his kindness and had come to understand that his carping was driven by a passion for high standards, that Angus would defend his staff to the death, while at the same time shouting at them for their failure to get a story before *The East Stoneyford Echo*.

Fourteen years old. Another birthday – and, for the first time in her life, a gift from her father that she actually liked. A gift that was to change her life.

'Here.' Her father shoved a bag at her. His hands were big and clumsy, strong but lacking in any kind of finesse. They were hands designed to catch a struggling criminal and handcuff him, but never to touch skin and thrill to its human warmth. She could still see the hairs on the fingers, darkly sprouting and could almost smell the rough maleness of him.

'For me?'

He looked around the kitchen before saying sarcastically, 'Is there someone else in here who has a birthday? I don't see anyone, do you, Janet?'

The bag read 'Tibbett's – for all your photographic needs'. She could see the blue and red lettering as clearly now as she had then. Inside, there was a box.

'SLR,' Daisy read, curiously.

'Single Lens Reflex,' her father filled in before turning back to his newspaper. It was the end, apparently, of his interest.

Why a camera? Daisy had never shown the slightest interest in photography. She fingered the box tentatively, turning it round to view the image of the contents. Was this yet another attempt by her father to direct her life? Daisy pushed the box away at the thought. She didn't want it. She couldn't bear to have him looking over her shoulder, criticising every picture she took.

'Thanks,' she said dully, expecting him to demand that she open it. He'd pull out the instruction book himself, take charge, force her to sit and watch while he read through the notes, worked out what to do.

'There's a couple of films to start you off.'

He got up and patted her on the head, then turned and left the room.

She sat staring at her mother. Janet, her eyes grey and wide and so like her daughter's, stared back silently, her small mouth hanging slack. Daisy didn't know who was the more surprised.

Had Eric Irvine been bizarrely struck by prescience? Uncharacteristically infused with insight? Or had he simply been passing Tibbett's and been drawn by a sale sign? Daisy never knew the answer. A week or two after that birthday, she'd finally opened the camera box and lifted out the gleaming black and chrome apparatus inside. From the second she'd touched it, she knew that this was her destiny. She found freedom behind the camera. She cherished the feel of it in her hands, trusty and true. It did her bidding, responded as she demanded, produced results that she could control and that she felt proud of.

Three years later, when she decided on photography as a vocation, she inevitably incurred her father's disapproval – 'Really Daisy, you'll never make any money'. When her mother had diffidently pointed out that it was he who had

14

started her passion for photography in the first place, it silenced him on the matter for long enough to allow her to enrol in college.

Her confidence battered by constant criticism, she discovered (to her astonishment), that people thought her photographs were good – people like Angus MacMorrow who had, in his own inimitable way, encouraged her and helped her to realise her potential. Now he was dead and she had to take pictures at his funeral.

A friend? A better one than she'd ever understood.

'I'll be fine. Thanks Lizzie. Just another job,' Daisy said, moving out of Lizzie's kind embrace and reaching for her camera bag. *Never let your feelings come between you and an assignment.* Angus's words. *Be professional at all times.* Thanks Angus, she smiled palely at the ghost of the big man, I will be.

She checked her appearance in the mirror – black trouser suit, safety pin at the waist to give her another inch of slack, touch of smoky shadow at her eyes to enhance her best feature – and turned to leave. The funeral was in less than an hour and all Hailesbank would be there. Her job was to capture it on camera. The *Herald* had to give its editor a resounding send-off and her role in that was crucial.

'Bye, Dais,' Lizzie unwound her legs and stood to give Daisy a hug. 'I'll be there for you.'

Daisy noted the anxiety in the hooded hazel eyes and was touched.

'Thanks, sweetie. I'll be fine,' she said, and held Lizzie close for a second before heading for her battered Suzuki. *Thank heaven for friends,* she thought as she climbed in. *And teddy bears.*

She fingered Tiny Ted in her pocket for a second, drew a breath, and turned on the ignition.

Just another job.

Chapter Three

The church at Hailesbank was huge. Although the town was relatively small – at least, the old, largely eighteenth-century, heart of the town – its parish church was disproportionately large. A group of monks, finding the loop of the river a convivial place to live and to worship their Lord, had founded a monastery on this site in the twelfth century. This had once been a magnificent complex of buildings, whose crowning glory was the massive, high-vaulted church. Then it had been sacked and ransacked, rebuilt again, desecrated, the stones carried away for other local building projects, the roof stripped of its protective and valuable lead until, by the middle of the twentieth century, all that remained was the nave, a couple of Victorian windows, and the satisfyingly worn stone-flagged floor.

The efforts of Lady Astoria Fleming (who lent her name) and Mrs Doris Worthington-Hitchcock (who gave copious quantities of her deceased husband's hard-earned cash), led to the restoration and opening up of the plundered apse in the 1970s, putting St Andrew's into the guide books as a tourist attraction and putting Hailesbank back on the map.

Daisy set herself up half way between the gateway into the church's grounds and the large, heavy wooden door into the building. As mourners wound their way through the churchyard, they all had to pass this spot, where the light filtering through the massive old sycamores lent a pleasingly dappled effect to her compositions. She knew what the arrangements inside the church would be. Angus's wife and family would sit in the front couple of rows. He'd habitually spent such long hours at the paper that Daisy had almost forgotten he had a family. Local bigwigs, bechained and beribboned, would claim the row just behind them. Daisy dutifully caught them on camera as they went into the church, looking suitably serious and sad.

There was the self-important Provost Archie Porter and his fat little wife Doris, her bunions squashed painfully into a pair of drab courts in honour of the occasion.

Here came a bevy of councillors of all political hues.

There was bald Jimmy Johnston, president of the local Rotary Club and implacable political enemy of Provost Porter, hanging back to avoid sitting near him.

Sir Cosmo Fleming arrived, pushing his mother, Lady Fleming, in her wheelchair. She was still very much in command of all her faculties, though, even in her eighties.

Cosmo gave Daisy a rueful grin as he passed her. 'Didn't predict *this*, did I?' he said.

The cuffs of his tweed jacket were frayed. Daisy thought that what he needed wasn't a trip to the little alteration shop on the High Street, but a woman – and she wasn't thinking of his mother. Cosmo was a mildly eccentric bachelor, but he was also the largest landowner in the district, which allowed him the luxury of pursuing his hobby, astrology. He penned the weekly horoscopes for the *Herald* in return for not very much. It was an activity to which his mother, Presbyterian to the core, was implacably opposed.

'Hold it there … thanks,' said Daisy, flashing off a few shots of the Flemings. She liked Cosmo, even if he always smelled of dog and the state of his car was unspeakable, full of doggie hairs and slaver and possibly worse. 'No one could have predicted it.'

'Get on with it, Cosmo, it's bloody freezing out here,' piped up a voice from the wheelchair. The bundle of blankets moved and a pair of faded brown eyes peered upwards impatiently from below a mauve felt hat that would not have been out of place in a fifties drama.

Cosmo, unseen by his mother, rolled his own brown eyes to the skies before trundling off.

The *Herald*'s staff were all there, that went without saying –
her colleagues, so familiar and frequently so irritating. Daisy
loved them and loathed them in almost equal degrees.

The chief reporter, Sharon Eddy, was blonde, pretty, pert,
and very bossy. 'Dishy' Dave Collins, the junior reporter, was
unkempt as a pop icon, and fashionably cool. Murdoch Darling,
feature writer, took the role of cynic supreme. And Ruby
Spence, of course – 'Ma' Ruby – the receptionist, who had been
at the paper for ever and knew absolutely everyone in town. Ma
was the biggest gossip of all, the best source of information,
nosier than any journalist.

Poor Ruby, she looked devastated. For years they'd all
fabricated stories of a long-lasting affair between her and
Angus, fuelled by the long hours the two of them spent in the
Herald's offices. Daisy had thought it was all just a bit of fun,
made up to amuse the staff and handed down through
generations of reporters – but looking at Ruby's ravaged face,
the chins wobbling as the lip quivered, the bosom heaving, she
wondered if there had been some truth in it after all.

Then, among the throng of townspeople, there was someone
else.

Daisy probably wouldn't have recognised Ben Gillies if he
hadn't been with his parents. It was years since she'd seen him.
She'd been – what, sixteen? – when the Gillies family had
moved down south. And although they'd moved back to
Hailesbank a couple of years ago when Martin Gillies had
retired, Ben had stayed in London.

They'd been such friends, the Gillies and Irvine families.
Her father, so often a bully in private, turned all charm when
gentle Kath Gillies was around. She remembered splashing in
the sea at St Andrews, bolting down the 'shivery bite'
afterwards. At other times they picnicked in Perthshire. She and
Ben had dammed the burn, up to their knees in freezing water.
The sense of freedom generally only lasted so long before her
father, noticing, would raise his voice. 'Daisy, I thought I told
you to stay on the bank? Take hold of her, Ben, and get her out

here at once.'

Had Ben obeyed her father's orders? Probably. But he would have winked at her as he did so, sympathising. He'd been an ally, despite the three-year difference in their ages. That hadn't seemed to matter when they were with their families, but at school it felt like a chasm. When the Gillies family moved to London, they'd simply lost touch.

It must be Ben Gillies. Looking at him through the lens of her camera, Daisy was able to study him for a minute in private. She pressed the shutter. Yup, it was Ben all right, but not the Ben she remembered. Stockier – he'd filled out. He certainly wasn't fat, he was more solid. Strong-looking. But he still had the same brownish red hair, the amazing golden amber eyes and the exact way of holding his head that she remembered. Now, though, he had stubbly hair on the chin, brownish red just like the head.

She clicked again.

'Diz?' It was his old name for her. Daisy – Dizzy – Diz – on account of her general disorganisation.

'Hi Ben.' There was no more hiding. She lowered the camera and took his outstretched hand.

'Sorry about your boss.'

'Yeah. Me too. Thanks.'

And then he was gone, along with his parents, to search for a seat in the rapidly filling church.

Daisy didn't see Ben again for a few days and she didn't really think about him much, because when she got home that night and changed out of the trouser suit into something more comfortable, she pulled on the jeans she'd been wearing on the day Angus died and felt something crackle in the pocket.

She had no recollection of taking the letter from Angus MacMorrow's hand when he collapsed, so the paper held no meaning for her. She felt no sense of importance or impending doom and merely tossed it onto the kitchen table, intent on pouring a glass of wine and joining Lizzie to grab some support for her harrowed emotions.

'Didn't you *lurve* Provost Porter's wife's hat,' said Lizzie, already into her second glass of red.

Lizzie, who loved to mix vintage and casual, was wearing a floppy cotton tea dress in navy with a tiny white flower pattern, pulled over a long-sleeved white T-shirt and navy leggings. Her feet were encased in shaggy sheepskin boots. Daisy had long envied the ease with which Lizzie created a 'look'. She felt boring in her jeans and chalk-blue baggy sweater. If *she* wore shaggy boots she'd look like a woolly sheep, not a trendy fashionista. Still, at least her jumper was comfy and hid the bulges.

She grabbed the bottle and slurped a generous measure of wine into her glass, then made herself comfortable on the carver, curling round and pulling her knees up to her chin. 'She should've bought one of yours,' she giggled, remembering the absurd black construction the Lady Provost had been wearing. She took a couple of quick gulps of the wine and began to relax.

'And what d'you think about Ma Ruby?'

'She was *devastated.* She looked far more upset than old MacMorrow's wife.' They'd had countless animated discussions about the rumoured relationship between Ma and Big Angus around this table. Now there would be no more. Daisy felt the sadness at his death return and with it the doubts that had nagged her for the last week. Could she have saved him? If she'd given him the kiss of life maybe she could have revived him.

'Well, I feel sorry for her.' Today Lizzie seemed inclined to be charitable. 'She can't even talk about it to anyone, not like Angus's wife.' She picked up the paper Daisy had thrown on the table and unfolded it, idly skimmed the contents, then swung her legs of the chair and sat bolt upright. 'Have you read this, Daisy?'

Daisy shook her head. 'What is it? It was in my pocket.'

Lizzie passed it across the table and watched as Daisy read the few lines.

'Oh. My. God.' Daisy's ash-gray eyes widened in shock and one hand flew up to her mouth. 'Ohmigod, ohmigod.'

She stuck her right hand automatically into her pocket and found Tiny Ted. Her fingers stroked the soft fur on his little head. The action, familiar since babyhood, brought a measure of comfort, but the colour was still gone from her cheeks as she blurted out, 'This is what Angus was reading when he collapsed, Lizzie. I've just remembered. I stuck it in my pocket. I wasn't even thinking about it, I was checking on him.'

Her eyes, the colour of the haze over the sea on a winter's day, were still the size of dustbin lids. The smoky eye shadow had blurred, leaving a faint bruise of colour. 'But this is what did it. This is what killed him.'

Chapter Four

Dear Angus

You will be only too aware of the falling circulation of The Hailesbank Herald. *We have been watching this and the increasingly poor quality of the content over the past year with considerable concern.*

Naturally, at the Board of the Havering Group, we are all concerned for your health. However, we view the situation as untenable and unless the circulation and advertising figures are back to their previous levels by the summer, we fear we will be forced to close the offices in Hailesbank and merge the paper with The East Stoneyford Echo, *with obvious consequences for yourself and your staff.*

We await with interest.

Yours as ever

Etc.

'Angus had a heart attack because of *this!*' Daisy was incandescent. 'How could they? They bloody *killed* him, the bastards.' She crumpled the paper in her hands and slammed her fist on the table.

'He was in line for a heart attack anyway, Daisy, you know that,' reasoned Lizzie.

'Six months! My God, Lizzie, they've given us six months. It was up to Angus to save us, and now he's bloody well dead!' Anger was still her foremost emotion but it had swung like a pendulum from the owners of the paper to her recently deceased boss. He'd deserted them in their hour of need. Daisy's mouth, always an indicator of her mood, was twisting and working convulsively. 'Never mind my pay rise, I might be out of a *job*.

23

What am I going to do?' Her mouth came to rest in a small sideways twist but the worried expression in her eyes betrayed her concern.

For all her creativity, Lizzie had a practical bent. Now she deployed the same talent that she used to invent an intricate cloth design, and started to take Daisy through a process of basic logic.

'Right.' She dumped her wine glass on the table and pushed it delicately to one side. 'One, you are under threat of closure. Two, you have no editor. Three, you have six months before a decision will be made.' She ticked off the points on her fingers. 'Yes?'

Daisy nodded, concentrating, still curling her mouth to one side anxiously.

'Let's address them one by one. What do you have to do to avoid closure?'

'Erm … improve our circulation and advertising I guess.'

'By …?'

'Getting more readers … writing more interesting features. Hoping there's some grim news to cover.'

'Steady.'

Daisy managed a rueful smile. 'I know, we're like vultures. But it's true, people love a gruesome murder or a horrific plane crash.'

'OK, so maybe you can't fix that but you could talk to the others about how to improve the features?'

Daisy thought glumly about how Murdoch Darling might take to being asked to write better features. An old hack, he'd been with the paper for ever and was nearing retirement. She could just imagine his caustic response to such a request. The words 'off' and 'fuck' would probably be involved, maybe in a different order.

'Two, you need a new editor.'

'Yeah, like they'll give us one when the paper's going to fold anyway.'

'You never know. What'll happen if they don't? Can you carry on without one?'

Daisy shrugged. 'I guess Murdoch might do it. Or Sharon.'

'Right, so they'll start to pull everything together, yes?'

The only thing Murdoch could pull together was a thousand words and he seemed to find that rather tedious these days. Sharon was different. She'd enjoy more power, no question, but could she inspire them all to save the newspaper? Job risk or not, Daisy was fairly certain that she was not the only one who'd not take kindly to a Sharon Eddy with power.

'I don't know,' she said, her mouth slackening with doubt.

'You're not got to let this go without a fight, Daisy,' Lizzie's voice was encouraging, 'Because three, you've got six months.' She leaned back triumphantly. 'And anything can happen in six months. Anything!'

'I suppose.' The slackness turned into another twist.

Lizzie leaned forward again and took her hands. 'It's not going to happen, Daisy. You can save the paper.'

Hope began a feeble flutter in Daisy's chest, the tentative flap of a butterfly emerging from its chrysalis. Lizzie was right. Somehow, they would do it. After all, Hailesbank without the *Herald* was unthinkable. The information she held in her hand was devastating – but not fatal. She, Daisy, would rally the troops, fight the fires, lead the battle to avenge Angus MacMorrow's death. No way was that shower at *The East Stoneyford Echo* going to steal their paper.

Her hand stole into her pocket, felt Tiny Ted's soft fur soothe her fingertips, and hardened her resolve. Tomorrow. She'd start on it all tomorrow.

Ben Gillies, not three miles away, accepted a second helping of marmalade sponge and custard from his mother and wondered what a spell at home might do to his waist.

'Great turnout for MacMorrow,' commented his father. Martin Gillies, a greyer, more weathered version of Ben, put his hand over his bowl to prevent a further dollop of carbohydrates landing on his own plate. He had fought – and won – the battle of death-by-cooking years ago, hence Kath's eagerness to lavish this visible demonstration of her affection on her one and only son, so long absent in London.

'Everyone knew Angus,' said Kath, pouring extra marmalade sauce over Ben's bowl, unheeding of his protestations.

Martin grunted. 'Not everyone loved him though.'

'He was well respected.'

'Like a Doberman is respected.'

'Martin, it's not like you to be so uncharitable,' Kath said, her round face, still winsome despite the loss of youth, puckering in disapproval. 'He wasn't so bad, the bark was a lot worse than the bite. I do believe he was an old softie under that gruff exterior.'

Martin Gillies grunted. 'That's what Ruby Spence thought, anyway.'

'Martin!' Kath's voice was sharper this time, but she couldn't repress a smile. 'That was just gossip.'

'Do I detect scandal?' Ben, with the glimmerings of a memory of what life had been like living in a small rural town, laid down his spoon and wiped his mouth. He hadn't visited Hailesbank since his parents had moved back up here and he'd spent the last few days reconnecting with his roots.

'Well …' Kath finished rinsing her hands at the kitchen sink, dried them carefully on the bright red towel (carefully chosen to match the feature wall), and sat back down at the table. Despite her protestations at her husband's loose remarks, she was the real gossip queen of the family. She leaned forward across the table, with a conspiratorial air. Martin, his wine glass at the ready, leaned forward too. Ben, feeling his overfed stomach bulging against the waistband of his jeans, made up the tight little circle, three heads close together, as if someone might overhear and report them to the Stasi.

'They did say …'

He listened. Or at least, a part of his brain tuned in to the inconsequential talk. Another part, inevitably, drifted back to the funeral. More specifically, the part of his brain that was wired to women homed in on the photographer, Daisy Irvine.

Diz. He hadn't thought about her for years. She'd changed in

26

many respects, but her eyes were the same – big, expressive, slightly startled – just like they used to be when her bully of a father had shouted at her over nothing. They were grey as rain clouds but much more desirable. The mouth was the same too. Curvy. Mobile. She had lips that trembled and quivered and that you longed to still with a kiss. When they curled into a smile, they transformed the eyes from shadowy to alive.

Stop it Ben Gillies, he chided himself. What's this about? You're heartbroken, remember?

Thoughts of Martina were fading as memories began to flood back. Daisy Irvine had been a skinny little thing. Sixteen years old and never been kissed. He grinned inwardly. *Ben, you liar.* Remember that time they ran for shelter to the bridge over the Hailes? They'd arrived laughing and giggling and already wet and he'd taken one look at her shivering body, slight and slim under her damp shirt, and he'd hauled her into his arms and started kissing the hell out of her. She'd responded too, until some old geezer had come along with a dog. The bloody creature had jumped up on them, barking and spoiling the moment. Ben could still remember the sense of frustration, and embarrassment, and almost relief that they didn't have to draw back from whatever might have happened next.

'… I don't know whether MacMorrow had done anything about it before he popped off.'

Ben had lost track of the conversation, a fact that hardly escaped Kath Gillies. 'Ben?'

'What?'

'You haven't been listening.'

'Sure I have.'

What did I just say?'

'That … er … that...' *That you could drown in that girl's eyes.*

'I knew it! What were you thinking about?'

'Does Daisy Irvine have a boyfriend?' Damn. He hadn't meant to say anything and now of course his mother would make something of it.

He was right.

27

'You fancy her?' Kath was delighted.

'No!' His fair skin coloured easily. It always had done, so not for the first time Ben cursed this easy betrayal. 'I was just trying to catch up with gossip, that's all.'

'He fancies Daisy, Martin! Just wait till I tell Janet.'

'Mother, for God's sake. It was just a question.'

'Don't go spreading rumours, Kath. It'll only backfire,' Martin rebuked his wife, getting up reluctantly to stack the dishwasher.

'You were saying something about Angus MacMorrow not doing something before he died,' Ben dredged up desperately from his consciousness in an effort to distract his mother.

It worked, at least for the moment. 'The *Herald*'s senior sub editor retired a few weeks ago. I know they'd hired someone else but I heard at the funeral that the person was offered a better job and left them in the lurch. So I think they're a bit desperate.'

'And your point is?' Ben, who knew perfectly well where his mother was going, was nevertheless going to make her spell it out. It was a small revenge for putting him on the spot about Daisy Irvine. His father, sensing a minor drama, turned from the sink with soapy hands and watched, grinning.

'Well I thought … I wondered …' Kath floundered slightly, evidently embarrassed to suggest that her son should even consider moving back to small-town Scotland after his big-shot job in London, 'Really, Ben, you know very well what I'm hinting at.'

Ben sat back in his chair, folded his arms and surveyed his mother teasingly. Then he said very slowly, 'You're suggesting that I don't renew my contract at *The Express* and that instead I take a very poorly paid job on a really crap local newspaper – for what reason?'

'You could have a crack at Daisy Irvine,' Martin grunted mischievously, just loud enough for his wife to hear him and explode, '*Martin*!' before he swung back to the sink, chuckling.

'I just thought it would be nice, dear, if you did something a little less stressful for a while – and if your father and I saw a bit more of you. Even just for a few weeks while they find someone? And after all,' she paused significantly, 'you could turn that "crap local newspaper" into something rather better, couldn't you?'

It was, Ben found to his surprise, a tempting suggestion. On the other hand, his jeans were quite tight already.

Chapter Five

Armed with the letter, which felt like an unexploded grenade in her pocket, Daisy was full of good intentions. She'd get in early, talk to one or two people about it, make a plan.

Half way to the office, she discovered she'd left the letter on the kitchen table and had to do a smart three-point turn and wind her way back round the narrow country road to retrieve it. When she finally got to the offices of *The Hailesbank Herald*, they had the air of a guerrilla outpost in Cuba when the news of Che Guevara's death arrived from Bolivia – shocked, gloomy, and not hopeful for the future. The new edition of the paper had just arrived from the printer.

'The funeral's in the centre,' said Ma Ruby, stating a fact that every person in the room knew already. It was still early, before the front door opened to the public. This was the time when everyone met over The Diary, the bible for the day's activity; when news was exchanged, gossip picked over, orders given, plans made.

Sharon Eddy was there, in the smart casual clothes she favoured on working days – neat enough to get by if she had to interview someone important, comfortable enough to allow her to clamber over fences or beard a farmer in his den without having to worry about being encumbered by spiky heels or revealing skirts. Dave Collins, the junior reporter – Dishy Dave – was lounging at his own desk, trying to look cool and uninterested, but sneaking looks across at the group all the same. A freelance sub called Ed Hackitt (whose name had caused considerable amusement and not inconsiderable ribbing) grabbed a pair of scissors off a desk and sliced through the strapping that bound the pile together.

31

Daisy watched, disconcerted. It didn't seem right to drop her little bombshell.

'Give it here, Ed.'

Ma took the paper from the young sub, spread it out on a desk, and stooped over it, the fleshy rolls at her waist plumping into several bulging folds above her skirt. Her purple blouse was rising and falling with a speed that was quite alarming. With a pang of sympathy, Daisy noticed that her grey hair, tinted to blonde, looked drier and more flyaway than ever. She caught a whiff of warm body drenched with Givenchy's Ange ou Démon and moved delicately away. No one ever said anything to Ma about the perfume that mingled with mild body odour. She was, somehow, untouchable.

They all stared at the paper in silence. Ma gave a small sniff and turned away. Sharon, Ed, and Daisy had worked on the spread, choosing the best of Daisy's photos as Ed laid out the pages.

'Perhaps you should've made that pic of Provost Porter bigger?' Dave said. 'The man's got an ego the size of a house. Either he'll be on to us or his wife will. Guaranteed.'

'Sod 'em,' Sharon said belligerently. 'You can bet your life Angus would have vetoed that. He never did have any time for that pair.'

'Still …'

'Still nothing.' Ruby's voice cut across their shoulders as she pushed her plump body back closer to the desk to see the pages better. 'This is a tribute to Angus, not to the likes of Provost Porter.'

Sharon turned and slid her pert backside onto the desk, crossing her slim legs just above her ankles and swinging them lazily back and forth. Her blonde fringe fell forward into her eyes and she brushed it aside in a well-practised gesture. 'Ruby's right. Anyway,' she paused for effect, then said dramatically, 'Angus has gone. And until we hear anything to the contrary, I'll be acting as editor. We've got a paper to publish.'

There was a moment's pause. Daisy seized her chance.

'Well maybe we have got a paper, Sharon, maybe we haven't.' Several bodies swung round to look at her. She brandished the letter in her hand. 'I've got news.'

Sharon's voice was snippy. 'Thought I was the news hound round here.'

Daisy ignored her. 'It's important.'

'Oh yeah? So how've you come by it then?'

Daisy took no notice of the jibe. That was just Sharon. Even though they had to work as a team, she never could bear Daisy to steal a march on her. On this occasion, though, Daisy felt no elation at beating the chief reporter to a story. The discovery of the letter in her pocket had brought with it a whole spectrum of emotions: guilt at having taken the letter in the first place, anger at what the shock of the news had done to Angus and sheer, blind terror about the possibility of losing her job. And on top of all that, the last thing she wanted was to witness the end of a paper that had served Hailesbank for a century or more.

'They're going to close us down.'

'What?'

'I beg your pardon?'

'What are you talking about?'

'It's true. Listen.' Daisy unfolded the letter and read, '*You will be only too aware of the falling circulation of* The Hailesbank Herald ... *increasingly poor quality ... considerable concern ... situation untenable ... we fear we will be forced to close the offices in Hailesbank and merge the paper with* The East Stoneyford Echo, *with obvious consequences for yourself and your staff.*'

There was a short silence, then Sharon said scathingly, 'Don't arse around Daisy, that isn't funny. Give that here.' She jumped off the desk and snatched the letter from Daisy's hand. Her face changed. 'Bloody hell.'

'What?' Ma's chins wobbled and her eyes widened. The blood drained from her face and she looked as though she might be about to faint. Daisy, terrified that there might be a repeat death on her hands, rolled a chair across to her and helped her to sit, grabbing a newspaper off the top of the stack to fan her with. 'What?' Ma repeated, breathing heavily.

'She's not joking. That's what it does say. Where'd you get this Daisy?' Sharon stared at Daisy.

'It's what the Boss was reading when he collapsed,' she confessed shamefacedly. 'I took it out of his hand and stuffed it in my pocket. I didn't mean to,' she added hastily as several faces stared at her in horror, 'honest I didn't. I wasn't even thinking about it, only about trying to revive Angus. Then I just forgot about it. I didn't even find it till I got home last night.'

She thought back to the bold ambitions she'd had yesterday evening. She was going to save the paper single-handed. Right. Only now she was in the office, and everyone was looking at her, she knew she didn't have the courage, or the skill, or the experience.

'What are we going to do?' she asked in a small voice.

And for once, even Sharon couldn't find an answer.

Three things happened at once. The doorbell rang. The telephone trilled. And Ed Hackitt stood up and reminded them that he'd only come in to collect his last pay cheque. They sat for a few seconds, frozen in time, a grotesque tableau, staring at each other in shock. Then Ma Ruby heaved herself off the chair and said, as if nothing had changed, 'I'll open up, shall I?' and Sharon reached across the desk to answer the phone. Ed bent down to retrieve the small canvas rucksack he carried in lieu of a briefcase. 'I'm off then,' he said as he swung round to the door. 'Good luck. Sounds as though you'll need it.'

Sharon waved at his departing back and spoke into the phone. 'Hello, *Herald* offices, news desk.'

Another phone call, another story. Business as usual. Only, of course, it wasn't. As Ed waved a hand above his head and closed the door behind him, Sharon came off the phone and announced with an edge of annoyance mixed with a tinge of excitement, 'Well guys, we've got a new editor apparently. He's arriving on Monday,' and Ma, pushing open the door from Reception, stuck her head round it and said, 'Seems like we've got a replacement for Ed already.' Heads swivelled, jaws dropped. They looked at Sharon first then, like well-trained dancers in a minutely choreographed ballet, followed her gaze and stared at Ma. Things at *The Hailesbank Herald* were moving mighty fast. Behind Ma, Daisy could see a head. Short brown hair with a faint tinge of red. Eyes the colour of amber. A shadow of beard, more red than brown.

Ben Gillies, right on cue, smiled slowly at the shell-shocked team and said, 'Hi everyone. I'm Ben. I think you're looking for some help?'

Tiny Ted had never been busier. There was a serious threat to his remaining fur as Daisy spent most of the day reaching for her comfort bear and stroking his familiar fuzz. No one knew where to start – Ben Gillies or the new editor. Ben, being present, won.

'Hi!' Sharon, a natural predator, sized up the newcomer with a practised eye. 'Where've you come from? Are you agency?' She was always direct. Tact and diplomacy were not her strong point.

Ben shook his head. 'I've been working in London. On *The Express*, *The Independent*, and other dailies too. I'm a sub.'

'National dailies?' Sharon looked stunned. 'So why would you want to work here?'

Ben shrugged. 'My folks are here. I need a break. I'm tired of London. Whatever. If you need me, I'd like to give it a shot.'

Sharon's gaze was calculating. Daisy could almost see the wheels turning. Would the new guy steal her thunder – or could he be her next catch? Turning thirty and still single, Sharon was never backward in coming forward where an eligible man appeared on the scene.

'We've just heard we've got a new editor starting next week,' she gave him the fact with apparent reluctance, 'So I guess you'll have to persuade him to hire you. He'll be watching pennies, so what'll happen is anyone's guess. But, hey, we need a sub, so as far as I'm concerned, you should go for it.' She remembered her colleagues belatedly and looked round at them, her green eyes cool, cat-like. 'What d'you think, guys?'

Daisy eyed Ben again. He'd certainly changed from the gawky schoolboy she remembered, but then, she'd filled out too. He was nice looking. You might almost call him handsome, not like Jack, of course, but if she wasn't still in love with Jack, Ben would be the kind of guy she'd go for.

To be perfectly honest, though, she was pretty fed up with hearing about the guy. It seemed to Daisy as though her mother had talked of nothing but Ben Mr-Paragon-of-Virtue-and-Success Gillies ever since Martin and Kath had moved back from London and the friendship of years ago had been resumed.

'Ben's working on a national.'

'Ben's won some award or other.'

'Ben's doing some amazing thing for charity.'

Since she and Jack had split, the drip, drip of information seemed to have become more of a spate and in the last few days, since Ben had miraculously appeared back in Hailesbank, her mother had hardly stopped talking about him. But Daisy had had other things on her mind. Like Jack, for example.

Jack, Jack, I need you back.

If she said it in her head often enough, it would come true. She dived into her pocket for TT, as she did every time she thought about Jack Hedderwick – and since Big Angus's death, that had been every hour, on the hour, and then some.

'What do you think, Daisy?' Sharon was saying.

'Huh?' Daisy pulled her hand away from Tiny Ted guiltily and tried to refocus.

'About Ben here joining the team.'

'Oh. Sure. Great. Yes. Great.' Daisy flashed a smile at Ben, but her mind was still on Jack. Jack and Iris. It sounded really yucky. Jack and Daisy, now that had a real ring to it. That's what people had said for years. Jack and Daisy. *Jackanddaisy*. One word, one person almost. Inseparable – until Iris Swithinbank had come along. A clerk in the bank. A bank clerk with a cheap bank mortgage and a home big enough to share. With Jack.

Sharon looked at Ma. 'Can we sneak an appointment into the

36

new ed's diary for Monday?'

Ma nodded. 'I don't see why not.'

'Thanks.' Ben's smile was warm.

'What's the guy's name?' said Dave from his dark corner. Daisy glanced over at him. He was tapping out a story on his computer, a pen behind his ear, his hair fashionably tousled as if he'd just got out of bed.

'Whose?'

'The new ed.'

They all looked at Ma. The attention appeared to revive her and she confided, 'Jay Bond. He's from London and he'll be here first thing Monday.'

'Jay Bond,' Ben looked thoughtful, as if the name was somehow familiar but he couldn't quite place it.

Daisy was puzzled. How could they have got someone so quickly? Surely any editor worth the name would have to serve notice in his existing job?

Sharon just giggled. 'Yeah. "The name's Bond, Jay Bond." He'll be some kind of hot shot, high-flying, self-regarding wanker, bet you.' Her voice changed and took on a note of bitterness. 'But he's in for a shock. He's not coming for some easy ride. We've been given six months to sort ourselves out or we're done for.'

That, Ben thought, sounded like the kind of challenge that might make a stay in Hailesbank worthwhile – which, unless he could do something to attract her attention, was more than Daisy Irvine was likely to do. She'd not shown the slightest flicker of interest in him.

As the team continued to speculate about their future, he observed them all quietly. Sharon Eddy, blonde and confident, was a type he'd seen all too often. Pushy, a little brash, the kind to keep your distance from, unless you fancied a quick shag, but probably good at her job. Murdoch Darling, serving his time. A journalist from another era, possibly competent but perhaps unwilling to put in the extra effort required to transform copy from acceptable to great. The young reporter – Dave? – cocky, self assured, untested. The sort who knew it all – until his first rotting corpse or traumatised car-crash victim. And Daisy Irvine. She looked as delicious as she did in the dreams he'd starting having since he saw her again. Maybe he would ask her out, but right now was not the time.

He seized a lull in the conversation to escape. 'See you then.'

'Right. Cheers. See you.' Murdoch swung back to his computer and thumped out some more copy.

'Bye Ben. Do come in on Monday, won't you?' Sharon shone her charm on him full beam.

'Bye Ben.' Daisy added absently, checking the diary for her next job. 'Christ, I've got to get going.' She swung away from him with barely a glance.

Ben smiled to himself. If he was going to think about asking her out, he'd have to make more of an impression on her. It was just as well that he enjoyed challenges.

'Ben Gillies? Was he the nice-looking guy with the reddish brown hair?' Lizzie was full of curiosity over the spaghetti.

'Nice looking? I guess,' Daisy said, helping herself to more parmesan.

Ben, grown up and filled out though he was, was just Ben to her. Ben who had buried her up to her neck in the sand on the beach at North Berwick; Ben who'd gone mushroom picking with her in the woods, daring her to eat some disturbing-looking specimen then defended her against her father's wrath when they'd arrived back ten minutes later than the deadline he'd set; Ben who'd helped her with her homework when she couldn't, really couldn't, remember her table of elements or the French for 'impecuniary'.

'I thought he was quite cute,' said Lizzie, shovelling her pasta into her mouth with a speed that was almost indecent. Daisy was used to the spectacle. Lizzie Little, unfairly slim, ate impossibly fast and had a surprising appetite. It was as if every inch of her height required endless nourishment.

'By cute you mean beddable, I suppose,' snorted Daisy,

38

remembering gloomily that she hadn't been bedded herself since she and Jack had split up.

'So?' Lizzie liked men. She brought them home with her, rather as if they were lost dogs she'd found roaming in the street looking for someone to love. Daisy was all too used to meeting some half-clad stranger emerging from the bathroom on a Saturday morning, or sharing her late brunch on a Sunday with the most delicious-looking youth Lizzie had befriended on one of her sales trips to Edinburgh and invited to visit. Half the time she'd have forgotten she'd done so and had to get to know them all over again when they appeared at the door.

They certainly liked Lizzie. What's not to like, Daisy thought, eyeing her friend with well-accustomed envy. It wasn't that she was jealous of Lizzie – she wouldn't have been comfortable with the relaxed casualness of Lizzie's approach to life, men, and love affairs. But if she only had a tenth of her sex appeal, what couldn't she do with it? Get Jack back, for a start – and that was all she wanted.

'Well hands off Ben,' she said without really knowing why, except that for some reason she couldn't bear the idea of Lizzie sneaking her childhood friend into her room.

'Ooh. Could Daisy Irvine be getting real about Jack Hedderwick at last?'

'I *love* Jack,' Daisy said crossly. She did, she really did.

Lizzie sighed, but she left it at that.

Chapter Six

'Hello Daisy!'

'Oh hello, Hammy.' A weekend is never a weekend for a newspaper photographer. Rugby wasn't Daisy's thing, but at this time of year, the rugby ground was often where she found herself on a cold Saturday afternoon, with her warmest fleece and a long lens.

'Good game.'

'For some.'

Hamilton MacBride, *The Stoneyford Echo*'s photographer, was one of the old school. He'd been snapping since the days when you had to take magnesium flares with you on a shoot – or so, at least, it seemed to Daisy. Now, she noticed, he had the latest camera, the one she craved with the auto voice over for recording captions. With the Hailesbank Hawks currently 14-3 down to the Stoneyford Saints, he was looking disgustingly smug.

'Yaaaay!' A roar went up from the crowd at the Stoneyford end – or what would have been a roar at Murrayfield Stadium. The ragged crowd in Hailesbank managed a small cheer. It was another try.

At least, Daisy thought glumly, she'd managed to get a good shot of the Stoneyford forward who'd just thrown himself showily on the ground behind the posts.

'Heard about your new editor.'

'Oh yes?' Daisy's attention was caught. 'What?'

Hammy looked sideways at her, his fat round face smug about his scrap of information. 'Sacked from some trendy TV programme. Caught sniffing the white stuff. So I heard.'

'Yeah?' Daisy tried not to look shocked, or indeed,

interested. 'We knew that. Just a one-off.' She was making it up as she went along. 'He's OK though. Great editor. '

Hammy laughed. 'Good try, Daisy my dear. But you can't fool me. The *Herald*'ll be closed within a year, mark my words.'

The action had moved towards the Hailesbank end of the pitch and he moved off, chuckling.

Drugs, thought Daisy dully. Shit. That was all they needed. She thought of the letter with a shudder. '*We will be forced to close the offices in Hailesbank and merge the paper with* The East Stoneyford Echo ...' Unthinkable.

She watched Hammy MacBride climb into his smart 4x4 and head back to the office as she wrenched open the door of her old run-around. Smug bastard. Just like all that lot at the *Echo*. How come he could afford a posh car and all she could manage was a bashed old work-horse? She turned on the ignition and prayed, but the car started first time and she sighed with relief. She still had to go back to the office to download the pictures.

A couple of streets from the office she found a parking space – the town was busy on a Saturday afternoon – and grabbed her camera bag from the back seat.

'Hi Dais.' She glanced up, startled at the sound of the familiar voice. It was Jack. And Iris. Hand in hand and looking as though they'd been together for always. *Jackanddaisy*, it should be, not Jack and Iris.

'Hello.' Irritated, Daisy realised she must be looking her frumpiest, in her old jeans and fleece, still smeared with pig shit from the celebrated 'bacon sarnie' shoot she'd done last week. Belatedly, she wished she'd thrown it in the machine before pulling it on again. She sneaked a glance at Iris. What did Jack see in her? He couldn't admire her for her looks, surely.? Her lank mousey hair was badly cut and much in need of a wash, her round face was devoid of any particularly pleasing feature, but she was still hand in hand with Jack. It wasn't right. That was her place.

One morning a year ago Jack had taken her for a walk by the river and said the words that inevitably presage disaster: 'We have to talk, Daisy.'

No we don't. We don't have to talk, Jack. You just have to look after me, for ever and ever.

He'd found someone else. Someone who, apparently, was more organised than she was, less dependent. Jack hated her messiness, apparently. Not that he'd ever told her that before. Not that he'd ever given her the chance to change.

'Been working?' Jack gestured at the camera. He was looking drop dead gorgeous, wearing a cord cap she'd given him for Christmas, the year before last. The blonde tendrils of his hair drifted out from the bottom of the cap and wound themselves endearingly round his neck. Daisy's heart twisted as she remembered that Christmas. They'd been happy then. Jack had still been taking care of her and Iris smugsy Swithinbank had been minding her own business.

She nodded and forced a smile. 'Yup. Rugby.'

Jack laughed. 'Poor Daisy,' he said. He knew she wasn't interested in the sport.

'I don't mind. I like it,' Daisy protested, defending her career, not wanting him to feel sorry for her. She felt like saying 'Better than sitting counting money all day,' but managed to restrain herself. The effect of counting money all day was manifest in the spread of Iris's large bottom, she thought with a thread of maliciousness. Then, thinking of her own battle of the bulge and acknowledging that her own backside could benefit from a little toning, she determined to find time to go to the gym, soon.

'Who won?' It was Iris this time.

Daisy avoided meeting her eyes and shrugged, still looking at Jack. 'The Saints, I'm sorry to say. Listen, I must go.' *Don't let me go, Jack. Tell me to stay.* Daisy's hand stole into her pocket. TT was there at the ready. She felt his nose nuzzling against her pinkie then saw that Jack had noticed the gesture and drew her hand out hastily. He knew her too well – and her attachment to her menagerie was one of the many things he'd called 'childish'.

'Yeah. So must we.' Iris was smiling up at Jack, her plain

43

face shining with adoration. 'We've still got to get eggs for tomorrow's breakfast.'

Why couldn't Jack have put his money in a building society? Recognising the cashier at his local bank one evening at his Introduction to Cookery class, they'd apparently got talking and something about Iris's way with a whisk had obviously appealed to him. For the thousandth time, Daisy cursed herself – she had been the one to suggest that Jack learned to cook. Why the hell couldn't she have suggested an art class, or French lessons, or Bridge for Beginners?

'Bye,' she said, making her voice sound casual.

She watched for a minute as they made their way down the High Street, past the pastel-painted houses, the laundry, the Chinese take-away, the Post Office, into the butcher's. Sometimes the prettiness of Hailesbank irritated Daisy beyond measure. It looked cosy, orderly, perfect – but when your heart is broken other people's cosiness and orderliness can be infuriating. She yearned for the dismal stone and ragged broken harling more typical of other Scottish villages – miserable, out of sorts, dour.

Turning, she walked the last few yards to the *Herald* office and punched in the code for the door. The office was empty, but she was used to that. She was often in here alone. As she booted up her computer, it occurred to her that she might like to work with Ben Gillies. He was still, after all, the same Ben she'd watched *Dirty Dancing* with when their parents were out, sharing a Hawaiian pizza and fighting over the pineapple, sneaking vodka from the booze cupboard and topping it up with water so that no one would notice.

The rugby pictures were safely uploaded. She shoved her camera back in its case and picked up her bags. On the whole, she was glad Ben was back – but there was something in Jack's eyes when he looked at her …

He still cared, he definitely did.

Ben Gillies slipped from her mind as she started plotting, yet again, about how she could win back Jack Hedderwick's love.

Chapter Seven

Sir Cosmo Fleming abandoned his Volvo estate about two yards from the pavement outside the *Herald* offices, stuck his mother's disabled sticker in the window, reached across to the passenger seat for the envelope containing his horoscopes, and opened the door. There was an angry shout and a cyclist, clad in skin-tight Lycra shorts and fluorescent jacket, swerved and shot past, missing the door by a fraction of an inch.

'Oh. Sorry!' Cosmo waved a tweed-clad arm at the youth apologetically and was rewarded with a torrent of abuse, which mercifully faded into the distance as the cyclist resumed his frenetic pace. Perhaps he'd thought about stopping for a confrontation, but he could not have failed to hear the chorus of barking from the back of the estate car. Three dogs can make a sensational amount of noise and Leo, Airey, and Gem, his cosmicly-named Labradors, were upset. They could see that their master was going to leave them in the car, and black Labs, bred for the countryside, don't take kindly to confinement. They had not yet had the long riverside walk they were expecting.

Across the road Kath Gillies and Janet Irvine were about to go into Nuggets, the local café-cum-gift shop. They stopped on the threshold, their attention attracted by the commotion, and stared at him.

'He's away in another world half the time, that man,' Janet said, shaking her head in despair.

'Can you blame him?' said Kath, 'with a mother like that to handle?'

'He needs a wife,' said Janet.

'He's not the only one,' said Kath wrinkling her nose and trying not to look at Janet. She might have her ideas, but it was too early to talk about them.

'Indeed,' Janet mused thoughtfully. 'Coffee?'

Oblivious, Cosmo Fleming made his way into *The Hailesbank Herald* offices.

'Hello Ma,' he greeted Ruby cheerfully, 'bearing up?'

'Oh well, you know,' Ma Spence winced, then looked brave. She was still the face of the *Herald* and now that Angus was gone, she believed it was up to her to defend the paper and its place at the heart of the community. 'You?'

Cosmo, leaning on the counter in the pokey front office, glanced at the display board where a selection of photographs from the week's paper was always pinned up. Today, of course, the funeral of the *Herald*'s esteemed editor was predominant, with a portrait of Angus MacMorrow, taken by some chief photographer at least forty years ago, right at the centre.

'That wasn't taken yesterday,' Cosmo observed.

If he'd been looking at Ma he might have observed the tiniest stiffening, a slight intake of breath, a pursing of lips – all the signs of indignation. But even if he had been, Cosmo might not have noticed these signs. Stars he was good with. Dogs he adored. Women … well, it wasn't that he didn't like women; actually he admired many women enormously. One in particular, though he was too shy to admit it. It was just that he hadn't had a lot of experience with women – which might have been the fault of the Dowager Lady Fleming, who gathered her son's attention jealously to herself – or it might have been down to Cosmo's deep shyness. At any rate, he didn't notice Ma's indignation and prattled on regardless.

'Fine looking man in those days, wasn't he?'

Ma said, 'He was always fine looking.'

Even Cosmo noticed her tone and though he was not a man for gossip, some memory deep inside him stirred – Ma Spence and the Big Boss – the Big Boss and Ma Spence – and he hastily improvised, 'Highly respected of course, Boss MacMorrow, highly respected.'

Ma softened visibly. 'You've got the usual weekly then, Sir Cosmo? Anything exciting in store for us?'

46

Cosmo couldn't remember what he'd written for Sagittarius, but as he always tried to get something tantalising for every star sign, in order to keep people reading, he wracked his brains and was about to declare 'Venus rising, Ma,' when he realised the timing would not be good. Instead he reached for the vague, 'Conjunction of the planets at the cusp, good sign, good sign,' and elicited a small smile.

'You'll be wanting to go through I suppose,' she said, unlocking the small door that separated the public from the staff at the paper.

'Thank you, Ma, that's awfully decent of you,' said Sir Cosmo, courteous as ever in his well-groomed public school way. He took off his tweed cap and revealed a thick mop of fairish brown hair.

'Hi Cossers,' Murdoch Darling, the feature writer cum columnist greeted him genially. 'Got any Outlook Towers for me?' 'Outlook Tower' was the title given to the news in brief column they usually dropped in on page five, after the main news stories, the page three attraction – usually a fresh-faced teenager model wannabe (no topless girls in *The Hailesbank Herald* of course), and the less prominent local news stories. Outlook Towers were small items worthy of passing mention.

'Well d'you know,' Cosmo knitted his brow and thought hard, 'my mother did tell me … it sounds a bit strange though …'

'Spill the beans, Cosmo, there's a darling,' Sharon Eddy emerged from behind her computer as Cosmo's already ruddy face seemed to grow ever ruddier. She grinned disarmingly at him and he looked away, flustered. 'We're a trifle thin on toothsome gossip and weird miracles at the mo. Disaster's more the thing, alas.'

'Well, our cleaning lady, Mrs Parson, told Mater that her daughter has a friend who knows someone in Stoneyford who swears she sees the shadow of Jesus Christ on her bedroom wall when the light is right. Can you make anything of that?'

'Jesus Christ? *Jesus Christ*,' said a voice behind them, 'Is that the best this paper can come up with?'

As one, they swivelled round and stared at the newcomer. Tall, thirty-something, he had jet black hair, male model looks with eyelashes that swept on for ever above piercing blue eyes, and a chin with a pronounced cleft, adding sharpness, symmetry, and focus to something that already approached perfection. Beautifully cut denim jeans, well-polished brown leather loafers, an open-necked crisp white cotton shirt and a navy jacket that was clearly expensive completed a look that might have marched straight out of the pages of a fashion magazine.

There was silence, as the presence of this idol registered.

'My name's Jay Bond,' said the man, his voice attractively throaty, 'and I'm your new editor.'

The silence was so profound for some moments that they could almost have been in a nuclear bunker, post holocaust.

Jay, apparently oblivious to the impact he had made on his new team, scanned the office. What he saw clearly didn't impress him. 'Jeez, what a hole. When was the last time this place had a coat of paint?'

They all looked around, taking in their daily working environment for the first time. They were in the main office. Once it had been the drawing room in what would have been a rather grand Victorian house. Above them, there remained an elaborate central ceiling rose, though there was a ragged black hole where once a chandelier might have hung. Instead, fluorescent lights had been suspended at intervals along the ceiling to illuminate the room more evenly. The light they emitted was harsh and unattractive. The cornice work matched the design of the rose. Leaves wound round each other and supported small flowers – lilies? – in what might have been a pleasing design had the paint not been so grimy. Years of cigarette smoking by generations of reporters and subs had left the once white paint a disagreeable yellow. Their desks looked as though they'd come from a salvage yard, the carpet was threadbare to the point of being dangerous. Only the computers on each desk indicated that the room had a place in the twenty-first century, and even the computers looked as if they might be steam driven.

Daisy saw it as if for the first time. It had always been, quite simply, the *Herald* office. It wasn't the environment that mattered, it was what happened in here. What mattered was the way they worked as a team, how they reported the news, supported the community, told stories of suffering, of anger, of heroism, or good fortune, or despair. This was simply where, week after week, they produced the miracle of a newspaper.

The room was undoubtedly scruffy, but Daisy couldn't help herself. Not normally courageous, she felt compelled to defend it. 'We're always so busy,' she started, 'No one's ever noticed.'

Jay Bond turned his blue-eyed gaze in her direction. Why had she opened her mouth? Cursing her stupidity, she was prepared to quail. Instead, unexpectedly, Jay smiled, and she wished she had the nerve to reach for her camera. Who could not want to photograph Jay Bond, Editor? He was, quite simply, idol-icious. 'Well,' he said, 'perhaps it's not our first priority –'

Most women would have melted under the full heat of that smile. He was accustomed to that, it was obvious, but for some reason, Daisy resisted his charm. Years behind a camera lens had taught her to read nuances of expression.

' – and you are…?' His eyes lit up the room, but Daisy saw disdain there, mixed with something else. Arrogance? Condescension? Boredom? They were unattractive traits, and she'd seen them all before he'd switched his mood. Or was it merely defensiveness? At any rate, her guard went up. This man had power over her future – over all their futures.

'Daisy Irvine,' she said as confidently as she could. 'Photographer.'

Sharon Eddy, bubbly and blonde, but by no means dumb, had been uncharacteristically quiet. Now she uncrossed her long legs and stood, tossing her hair back from her face to reveal her high cheekbones and wickedly curvaceous mouth. Daisy realised with a wild feeling of hilarity that the man-hungry reporter was making the first pitch for the newcomer. Ben Gillies, her prey just a few days ago, had already been supplanted by a bigger and better quarry. 'Welcome to *The*

Herald, Mr Bond. I'm Sharon Eddy, chief reporter. Perhaps I can introduce you to everyone?'

And then the phones began to ring, the tableau unfroze, and the deadlines that govern every small newspaper office became pressing. Cosmo Fleming, muttering something about 'Mother, urgent, must dash, sorry,' cast a faintly harrowed glance in Sharon's direction and edged towards the door. Murdoch grunted, '... dog poo ... devilish stuff ... up in arms ...' and swung back to his screen. And Daisy realised that she was due at a photo shoot in the High Street, where the local butcher was finally being forced to close his shop, a victim of the credit crunch and the new supermarket on the outskirts of Hailesbank. Jay Bond, in all his glory, would have to take a back seat while she figured out how to frame a photograph that told the shop closure story without being too grisly. New editor or not, the day had to go on.

As she grabbed her camera gear and headed for the door with Dishy Dave, who was down to interview the butcher, it occurred to Daisy that redecoration was the last job on the list of priorities for the small staff at *The Herald*. But their new editor would be aware of that, surely?

Chapter Eight

It was not an easy day. Jay Bond spent most of it closeted in the glass enclosure laughingly called the Editor's Office – the space where Angus had toppled majestically to his death. Daisy wondered whether he was aware of that. Did he have any sense at all of the Big Man's feisty spirit still lingering in the air? There was still a faint odour of cigarette smoke, that was for sure.

For most of the morning, so far as they could see, he had his feet up on the desk and the phone clamped to his ear, though it was impossible to tell who he was talking to or what about. He emerged at lunchtime, asked where he could get a sandwich, and when Sharon immediately offered to show him the local offerings, smilingly accepted.

Everyone was unsettled. They were still reeling from Big Angus's death and no one had yet got the measure of Mr Jay Bond. What would he do to start turning the fortunes of the paper round? Were their jobs safe? At least no one got fired and Ben, coming in for the appointment Ma had put in the book last week, was duly hired on a short-term freelance contract. By six they were all ready to escape and by common assent they migrated, as one, to their favourite watering hole, The Duke of Atholl.

Young Dave was still high on the butcher closure largely because, thanks to Daisy's ingenuity, the photo was probably good enough to get his story onto the front page. 'We'll headline it "The Last Link in the Chain",' he said, carrying four pints and trying not to spill them.

'Good one, Davy,' Murdoch grunted. 'Except, of course, he was a sole trader, not part of a chain.'

'Sausages, mate,' Dave explained. Murdoch just grinned.

Competition for the front page was always strong. Sharon liked to reserve the honour for herself but it would be Ben, in his new role as chief sub who would make the final decision – unless Jay overruled him.

'Last Link?' Sharon scoffed.

Davy's confidence was undiminished by these criticisms. 'Honest Shar, you should see Daisy's pic, it's brilliant.'

Daisy blushed. Mindful of Lizzie's three points, she was doing her best to do her bit. The shoot had worked out well, even though it had all seemed a bit desperate at first. Knives were too graphic, Bert had been determined to look jolly in the face of adversity, which was not the image she wanted, and she'd been almost at screaming point when one of the other butchers had emerged onto the High Street with a large hamper of best pork sausages and started giving small bundles of them away.

'Got any more of those?' Daisy had asked, 'Unpackaged?' She captured her shot at last, a great image of Albert Harvie clasping a string of sausages. She'd got as low as she could and shot straight up, picturing him against the blue sky.

'You should've seen Daisy,' Dave was still in full flow, 'Lying on the pavement.'

'Just like every Friday night,' said Sharon, grinning.

'Thanks.' Trust Sharon to prick her bubble.

'What did you make of our Mr Bond?' Murdoch, returning from the doorway, where he'd retreated for a quick ciggie, still reeked of smoke. Daisy fanned herself and made a face at Ben.

'I got the impression he feels he's arrived at the arse end of the world,' said Ben, drawing a shamrock with his finger on the top of his pint of Guinness, 'but for my money, he's lucky to be in a job.'

'Really?' Everyone looked at him. 'How come?'

'I thought his name rang a bell, so I Googled him.'

How sensible, thought Daisy, remembering Hammy MacBride's comments and praying there was no truth in them. 'And?' she prompted.

Ben leant forward over the chipped wooden table. The Duke of Atholl, though the *Herald*'s local pub, was not the most salubrious in Hailesbank. It might have been smart enough in the 1960s, which was when it probably got its last makeover, but since then it had endured years of heavy local use and long neglect by its owners. The customers rarely noticed this, though, thanks to the fact that the lighting in the pub was, at best, dim. This dimness enfolded them all, providing a conspiratorial cloak of a kind as Ben's voice dropped half an octave. 'Jay Bond was a presenter on Channel 69,' he said, 'You know, that one that was launched last year.'

Daisy, who seldom watched television and didn't possess a digital set anyway, had never seen it.

'Full of arty farty stuff, avant garde music, reports from exhibitions, South Bank style shows without the top drawer contributors, chat shows with wannabe literati and glitterati.'

'Poncey southern tosh,' Murdoch, who had never been south of the Border in his life, grunted disparagingly.

'Jay Bond was one of their "star" presenters,' Ben went on, 'tipped for better things once he'd served his apprenticeship there.'

Daisy pictured Jay Bond. Cool, cleanly-carved good looks, clear, penetrating eyes, a good voice. The sort of man, her professional eye told her, that the camera lens would love. She could see him as a television presenter. Ben's story was making her feel depressed. She remembered Hammy McBride's jibe and had a horrible feeling she knew what was coming next.

'If he was that hot, what's he doing in Hailesbank?' Dave asked.

'I followed the links to some of the redtop archives for last month,' said Ben. 'Seems he was caught sniffing a line of coke in the Gents' bog just before going on air. A young college student, in on work experience, got lucky and snapped him. It caused a hell of a stink.'

Daisy sat back in her chair with a thump. In the dim wattage of the wall light behind her a small cloud of dust was clearly visible, rising from the padding and settling again, with fascinating slowness, onto the dark fabric of her sweater. Her worst fears had been confirmed. 'So he had to leave?' she asked, subdued.

'Quit before he was sacked, according to the reports I read.'

'So what?' Sharon sprung to his defence. 'Everyone does it. In London, I mean.'

'If you say so,' Ben drained his pint. 'What they don't do is get caught doing it. Not at your place of work, not when you're about to go on air.'

'So how come he's ended up in Hailesbank?' asked Murdoch, pulling out his cigarettes and shuffling restlessly. He'll be off outside again in a second, Daisy realised, he just wanted to hear the end of the story.

'That's the odd bit. I can't figure it out. So far as I could find out, he started his career with a short stint at a local paper in Surrey, then moved on to half a dozen other jobs before landing the contract with Channel 69. He had an import business for a while, then dabbled in finance, without progressing far, married some society beauty called Amelia –'

'He's married?' Sharon's disappointment was predictable.

'Well, he was. They split up rather publicly after he lost his job. It was only a couple of months ago, by the way. But how he got from London to Hailesbank remains a mystery. Connections, I suppose.'

'Does he know about our sentence of death?' It was Murdoch who, pushing his chair back, put the question.

They looked at each other in silence. If he didn't know already, he soon would.

'Jay Bond. Licensed to … to what do you think, Diz?' Ben turned to her, one eyebrow raised quizzically.

Daisy shrugged and stuffed her hand in her pocket where Tiny Ted was nestled. She hated uncertainty.

An hour later and Ben was on his own, nursing the remnants of his third pint and thinking about having to face yet another home-cooked dinner with his parents. He was too old for this. He'd have to find himself a flat if he was going to stay here for any length of time.

Daisy Irvine. There was something completely artless about the woman. She was hardly the skinny girl he remembered, but he found himself deeply attracted to the curves that the shapeless garments she was wearing couldn't really hide. Martina had been thin almost to the point of anorexia. Her refusal to eat anything except raw vegetables and fruit became one of the many issues that began to lie between them, great shadowy unspeakable obstacles whose presence gnawed away at what had once been a passionate relationship. She couldn't talk about it – refused absolutely after one violent argument.

'It's my body! And I choose to eat this way. I feel good like this.'

'It's not healthy, Teeny. And it's no fun. We never go out any more.'

'We do go out. We walk. We went to the cinema last week.'

'You know what I meant. We never eat out. We never see friends any more because you're scared of being invited for supper. What kind of a life is this?'

She'd clammed up, defiant, angry, closing in on herself, shutting him out. He'd stuck it for a year or more, but at the end it became too dispiriting. What had once been a lively relationship turned into something under constant tension. He had to watch every word, measure every response for fear of sparking another outburst or a withdrawal that became, by the end, intolerable.

Ben scratched the short reddish stubble on his chin and rubbed his hand round the back of his neck restlessly. Thinking about Martina was still difficult. It hadn't ended in a big row, more in a kind of mutual regret. But even mutual regret can be painful. No, maybe not that; maybe the ache came more from the loss of a way of life, a habit, the rituals built up and shared over the years. It was like stopping smoking. You knew it was bad for you, that you had to be firm with yourself, just walk away, but you missed getting the cigarette out of the packet, tapping it on its end, lighting up, missed the comfort of holding it between your fingers, using it to make a gesture, underline a point.

It hadn't taken him long to gather his belongings together. He'd never hoarded material possessions. A few clothes, his iPod and laptop, the Delia Smith How to Cook books his mother had given him when he'd left to live on his own, that was about the size of it. He could get the whole lot into two suitcases and a few small bags. Apart from Nefertiti, of course.

Now that he thought about it, he knew what Daisy's appealing curves reminded him of. He grinned to no one in particular. No wonder she seemed so delightfully familiar.

Chapter Nine

Morning arrived reluctantly, as it always did at this time of year, breaking through the darkness in dribs and drabs, peeking out from behind thick cloud cover until the forces of light could no longer be thwarted. Daisy rolled over in her bed and reached out, vaguely, to the side where Jack slept, before remembering, through the blur of half sleep, that she was a year and more out of date. Wrenching her mind from the same old feelings, she tried to visualise The Diary for today.

The Diary, filled in by the reporters to book her time, was what dictated her every move. Short of fire, flood, murder, pile-up, or other disaster, The Diary sent her to this school for nine, that meeting for eleven, down the High Street by two for a photo opportunity with Provost Porter and his dumpy missus or across the county to snap some lucky lottery winner by four. What did it hold for her today? More of the same, undoubtedly. Unless editor Bond had other ideas, of course. If she had a job at all this morning.

'I am not happy,' she said to her menagerie. They looked steadily back at her, their loyalty unwavering. 'Not happy at all.'

Having got that off her chest she felt well enough to swing her legs out of bed, use her feet to find her slippers, wrap herself up in her old candlewick dressing gown, and shuffle through to the kitchen. She hoped Lizzie might already have made coffee, then remembered that she had disappeared into her room with a new man last night and hadn't reappeared.

Lizzie had a relaxed view of relationships. Undemanding and happy, she attracted men like bees to nectar, waving them adieu with such sweet grace when she tired of them that they left uncomplainingly, each feeling that he had been the luckiest man in the world. It was a gift that Daisy had dissected endlessly in her mind, wishing she could emulate both the ease with which Lizzie attracted men and the facility with which she moved on, untouched by sorrow, from each.

It put her in a class quite different from Shagger Sharon.

'Shagger Sharon?' Daisy swung round. Damn. She must have been mumbling out loud. Lizzie had appeared, her thick brown hair lying untidily round her shoulders. Uncombed, unwashed, her face completely without make up, she still looked gorgeous. 'What's she up to now?'

Behind her lurked a man, unashamedly naked to the waist. Tattoos adorned his upper arms and he boasted a six-pack any gym-goer would be proud of. Grinning at them from the shadows, he pulled on a sweatshirt and emerged into the kitchen.

'This is … er … meet …' Lizzie waved at him vaguely.

'Dougie,' the vision supplied, grinning from an attractively unshaven face. 'Hi.'

'Hi,' Daisy said dutifully as Lizzie made coffee.

'You were saying …?'

'About?'

'Sharon Eddy?' Lizzie loved getting the gossip from Daisy's office.

'She's after the new editor. At least, I think she is.'

'Will she get her man?'

'You know Sharon,' Daisy said dismally.

Where Lizzie was kindly, generous in bestowing her favours, Sharon's sexual rapacity had a more desperate edge to it. With Lizzie, sex was simply something she needed to do as part of her work-life balance, like cleaning her teeth or washing her hair. Sharon, by contrast, generally flaunted her conquests triumphantly before, for one reason or another, each moved – or was moved – on.

'Poor Mr Bond,' said Lizzie, but despite a twinge of sympathy, Daisy couldn't really bring herself to feel sorry for him.

'Apparently dog poo doesn't do it for our swanky new editor,' Murdoch muttered to Daisy as he drifted over to join her by the kettle.

'Really?' said Daisy, her mind half on how she could get from Hailesbank to Jordanbank to catch the local Member of Scottish Parliament's visit to a recycling plant, then back to Hailesbank in time for the photo shoot with the cleaners who were stripping the graffiti off the public toilets in town. The reporters on *The Herald*, in her opinion, never made enough allowance for travel, especially at harvest time when the combines were all out or in winter when the roads could be lethal.

'He's axed the story I was working on.'

'No, really?' Daisy said sympathetically, working out that she'd have to take the shortcut via Heriton and pray there were no tractors to slow her down.

'And there's no way your butcher shop photo's going to get front page.'

Now he'd caught her attention. 'What?'

'"Stupid trivia. We must do better." I quote.'

'You're joking!'

He shook his head. 'Would I joke about something like that? No, you'll find out soon enough. He wants "real news". "A big story." "Less of this provincial nonsense."'

'Like what?'

Murdoch shook his head. 'Sharon's in with him just now, discussing it.'

'They can't make up news. If it happens it happens.'

'Maybe he wants something international. A take on Obama. The state of the yen. Famine in Africa.'

'*The Herald*'s a local paper, for Chrissake.' Daisy's jaw had dropped. 'We publish local stories. Stories that interest people locally. That's the definition of a local newspaper.'

'Tell me something I don't know.' Murdoch grimaced. '"Drama. Something hard-hitting",' he went on in a reasonable approximation of Jay Bond's cut-glass tones.

'Blimey,' said Daisy. 'Where are we going to get that?' She was cross about her sausages. How was she going to top that as an image?

Dishy Dave, seeing their huddle, joined them.

'Heard about the sausages, Dave?" Daisy asked.

'What about them?' said Dave, who had just filed the story.

'Axed. Well, butchered at least. Relegated to inside.'

'You're kidding. Why?'

'Not hot enough,' said Daisy.

'You should've griddled them,' grinned Murdoch. 'Very funny.'

'So what's hot?' asked Dave.

'Not the public toilets anyway,' Daisy conjectured, thinking of her Diary.

'Meeting's over,' warned Murdoch, seeing Jay's door open and Sharon emerging.

'Time out, everyone,' Sharon called, slapping her file onto her desk and waving her arms, beckoning. 'I need to brief you all.'

It was unusual, to say the least. Being a small office, they were all pretty much aware of what was going on and Sharon normally kept tabs on all the stories simply by keeping her ears open and wandering round chatting to the reporters. Formal meetings were a rare event.

'New priorities. More punch. Bigger stories. Less trivia. Murdoch, you're to make Westminster, the Scottish Parliament, and international affairs your priorities –' Murdoch gaped, his fading eyes round with surprise, 'Dave, you'll concentrate on the prison, the hospital, and the Council, taking over my responsibilities, and I'll be doing more investigative work.'

They all stared at her before Murdoch, a cynical hack to the core, challenged, 'Investigating what, precisely?'

Sharon was evasive. 'Whatever comes up. I'll get leads. We're looking for big stories.'

Dave asked tentatively, 'What about the small stories? The school plays, the local WRI meetings, the charity stuff?'

Sharon waved an airy hand. 'We'll use fewer of those, of

course. We're going to pull this paper up by its bootstraps.'

'Jesus,' said Daisy, stunned.

'But what about ...' Murdoch started before Sharon cut in again, 'It's about standards, Murdoch. We've let them slip. We're going to be a campaigning newspaper. We'll take up big issues. The economy. The environment. The health service.'

'What?' said Daisy.

'And in the meantime,' Sharon rounded on her, 'you'd better get out there and get a big picture. We need a front page.'

'Big picture? Of what, precisely?' Daisy felt panicky. She glanced over to where Tiny Ted was sitting on her desk, surrounded by coins and sweets from her pocket.

'I dunno. Use your imagination, Daisy. Surely you have one?' snapped Sharon.

'Do I still do the Member of the Scottish Parliament at the recycling plant?'

Sharon sighed. 'I suppose so, yes. We'll need to cover it.'

'And the toilets?'

'We can do without toilets, surely,' Sharon said crossly. 'They're not exactly big news, are they?'

'There's lots of people feel they can't do without them,' muttered Murdoch.

'We're on to bigger and better things than toilets,' snapped Sharon.

'Thrones?' said Murdoch as everyone – except *The Herald*'s chief reporter – laughed. But nervously.

Ben, watching the scene quietly from his desk, put the final touches to the back page (sports) and mentally shook his head. Jay Bond hadn't a clue. That was obvious. What he did have was delusions of grandeur. But if he wanted to get *The Herald* closed down, he couldn't have picked a quicker way of doing it.

Local papers sold on local news. People bought them to see their friends, to read about what was happening in the neighbourhood, to get the results of the local darts league or find out who won the best apple tart category in the WRI. Public toilets were important. A local shop closing was important. These were issues that affected them all and which they got involved in. No one cared about the Scottish Parliament, still less about what was happening at Westminster, unless it was fiddled expenses, higher taxes, schools, or hospitals nearby closing, or local lads being sent to war. Then they were interested all right. How long would Jay Bond get before sliding sales forced him to realise how wrong he was? And Daisy, standing there looking as though she was about to burst into tears over her sausage picture being made into mincemeat – how would she cope?

The truth was, Daisy didn't cope too well. Distracted by events, she forgot to pick up the brief for the Jordanbank assignment, couldn't remember where the recycling plant was, and phoned Ben in a panic just a few minutes before the photo shoot was due to take place.

'Ben? Ben, I need help.' Her voice, though lowered conspiratorially, sounded anxious.

'Oh hi, Diz, what can I do you for?' he said cheerfully.

'I'm lost,' she hissed down the line, 'Listen, don't tell anyone, they'll just laugh at me. Just find my sheet, can you, it's got the directions on it.'

'Right. Hold on.' He placed the receiver on his desk, found the missing instructions, and read them down the line to her. 'Got it now?'

'Yes, left, right, then third left. Thanks Ben, you're a star. I'll love you for ever.'

If only that were true, thought Ben, replacing the receiver slowly.

'Ditsy Daisy lost again?' said Murdoch, dropping a printout of a page plan on his desk.

Ben grinned at him. It was impossible to keep secrets in an office like this.

The challenge of getting a big story was mercifully solved that week when some poorly stored fertiliser exploded in a barn next to the main road south to England. The incident not only sparked a major blaze at the farm and its outbuildings and killed two workers, but also caused smoke to billow across the carriageway, with an inevitable multiple pile-up and further deaths.

Sharon was happy. 'It's not my way to be pleased at the misfortune of others,' she said sanctimoniously amid barely suppressed sniggers, 'and I'd really prefer to get a thorough investigative story on the front but –' she held out the paper at arm's length and admired it. '– it's not bad, is it? And we did get there before *The Stoneyford Echo.*'

Daisy had surpassed herself with an image that captured the full drama of the incident taken from Tarbert Knoll, a small hill near the scene. She'd reached the spot before any other photographer was in the vicinity, realised she wouldn't be able to get a good photo from ground level, and had puffed her way up the hill, cursing her extra pounds and general lack of fitness, until she could get a decent view.

It was a stunning shot. The flames from the farm were clearly visible, the smoke was drifting away from where she stood, carried by a light breeze, and the carnage on the road was crystal clear. Only the nationals, fielding helicopters, got anything better, and in some ways Daisy's image, taken from closer, had the advantage of a riveting kind of intimacy.

She was proud of the photograph. She'd run down the hill and managed to sneak in close to the accident by dint of pleading with one of the policemen at the scene, an officer she'd dealt with before. Daisy might be disorganised, but she could be very determined. The advantage of local knowledge and local contacts paid off – the officer turned his back for just long enough for her to do her job. The heart-wrenching photos of crunched metal she managed to snatch before she was shooed away complemented her main picture perfectly.

'Not bad,' said Jay, admiring the front page. 'Well done, Sharon. Fancy a drink?'

'Sure. Thanks.' Sharon smiled up at him, flicking her hair back self-consciously and twisting her body towards him in a come hither pose.

As the door closed into the silence behind them, there was an explosion of indignation.

'Bloody hell, Daisy, that front page was all yours!' said Dave.

Murdoch concurred. 'Sharon's copy was fine, but a bit on the sensational side for my taste. Your photos now, they told the story brilliantly.'

'They're right,' said Ben. 'Fancy a drink, Daisy?'

Daisy, who'd been hurt by Jay's lack of recognition, was slightly mollified by the support of her colleagues, but turned Ben down unthinkingly. 'No thanks, Ben,' she said, 'I've got other things I have to do.'

Heading for the door, she missed the look of disappointment on Ben's face.

The first edition of *The Hailesbank Herald* under the editorship of Jay Bond rolled off the presses and out to the shops the next day. Jay called his staff together. They clustered apprehensively round the water cooler.

'Congratulations,' he said, looking from face to face and smiling. Daisy, observing, was forced to acknowledge that he had charisma, when he chose to use it. Today he was wearing a checked shirt in crisp cotton and smart navy trousers, their creases like knives. He'd rolled up the shirt sleeves – to look more like one of the lads maybe? She watched Sharon, too. The chief reporter's face said it all; she was smitten.

Who could blame her, thought Daisy. If you disregarded the cocaine story and the fact that he was married, it seemed that Jay Bond had it all; a great body, money, style, looks, charisma.

'It's not there yet, not by a long way,' Jay was saying, 'But at least we've made a start. Axing those little fillers – the WRI column, the reports from the local history society, bird watchers, ramblers, and such societies has opened up space for more in-depth journalism.' He picked up a copy of the paper and flicked through the pages. Ben had worked his own miracle. Using the same template, he'd somehow managed to make the paper look smarter, more contemporary. Study it as she might, Daisy couldn't work out how he'd done it. There was something about the white space? Maybe the font? The way he'd put in the headlines? She'd have to ask him what his secret was.

Daisy looked at Sharon again. She might like the idea of 'in-depth journalism' in principle, but they really didn't have the resources for it. She and Dave – Murdoch too – would have to half kill themselves to fill the pages if they got rid of all the bits people sent in. And besides, Daisy was pretty sure that the members of the aforesaid societies would not take kindly to their news disappearing from the pages of *The Herald*.

'The horoscopes will have to go – I mean, nobody believes that stuff any more, do they?'

Oh *poor* Sir Cosmo.

'But that was a great front page – Sharon, Daisy.' The full beam of his smile was directed at her. At last her efforts had been recognised – but it had taken ten dead on the roads and a major fire to achieve it. What a price.

'So congratulations, team. A great start. Let's hope we can even better it next week. Sharon? A bit of corruption on the local Council perhaps?' Sharon smiled bravely. 'Everyone likes a good scandal.'

Except those exposed by it, Daisy thought grimly. How could he *say* that when he'd just been the centre of a scandal himself? And was this really the way to save the paper?

Ten minutes later, they received the first phone call and from then on, it was madness. Ruby, fielding calls feverishly, was getting increasingly upset. Daisy got so distressed by the complaints that she stuck a made-up appointment in The Diary and headed out. The rest of them, she learned later, had had to cope as one by one every member of every club, group, society, and association in the neighbourhood rang to protest indignantly that the report of their meeting seemed to have been missed out this week.

Chapter Ten

On Monday evening she walked into the kitchen in her new jeans wailing, 'Look! Look at this!' She'd bought the same size as always, but they simply wouldn't zip up.

'Lie on the floor and tug,' advised Lizzie, ever practical.

Daisy lay down and tugged. The zip eased up an inch and stuck.

'Here, let me,' Lizzie pulled on the slide. It refused to budge. 'Nope. No good. You'll have to change them for the next size up.'

Daisy sat up, horrified. 'No way! Jeez, what am I going to do? Horrible, horrible, horrible!'

'Oh for heaven's sake, Daisy, the world is not conspiring against you. If your jeans are too small it's because you're too fat. Do something about it.'

Daisy stared at her, her mouth sagging open. Where was the laid-back, gentle Lizzie she knew and loved?

Lizzie drew a tired hand across her forehead, gathering her thick hair back and twisting it into a scrunchie she found round her wrist. 'Sorry Dais, didn't mean to snap, I slept really badly last night.' She gave an apologetic smile, then went on, 'but to be honest, it is down to you. Go on a diet, go to the gym, preferably do both. The jeans'll soon fit.'

Daisy scrambled up from the floor, reeling from the shock of Lizzie's outburst.

'Right,' she said, and padded back into her bedroom to find her old jeans.

But Lizzie's words stuck and she made a resolution to rejoin the Hailesbank Fitness Centre. On Wednesday, between filing her last photographs and covering an important presentation by

Provost Porter to a delegation of Russians visiting from the twin city of Uskbegost, she snatched a break and headed off to an appointment with Markie Moss, a camp young fitness instructor who'd been assigned as her 'friendly personal trainer'.

Now, self-conscious in lycra leggings and a baggy old T-shirt that she'd optimistically thought might cover the worst of her bulges, she was standing at the door of the gym. There was no escaping her fate.

It was like an alien world.

'Height? Weight? Waist, hip, thigh measurements?' Markie, fired personal questions at her with no sense of embarrassment or discretion. Daisy was unable to answer most of them – she'd steered clear of scales for years. She was forced to succumb to the indignity of being weighed and measured and was shocked at the results, which she could hardly dispute.

'Medication? Heart problems? Breathing difficulties? Back problems?'

This was worse than school medicals and heaven knows they'd been embarrassing enough.

'No, nothing. I'm fine. Really,' she stammered, already wishing she hadn't come.

'What kind of regular exercise do you take?'

'Erm, I … well I have to walk a fair bit in my job.'

'How far?'

'Well, across fields, that kind of thing.'

'How many fields? How big?'

Daisy stared at Markie. Was he being serious? She glanced at his biceps, bulging beneath his sleeveless purple vest, and saw that he was. 'Well, usually just one at a time. And back to the car of course. Not every day. Sometimes there's no fields, of course. But I did climb a hill this week.'

'Which hill?'

'Tarbert Knoll,' she murmured shamefacedly, aware that it was a very small hill. 'But I did have my camera gear with me.'

'Right.' Markie laid down the file and studied her. 'What are your objectives in coming here?'

'Oh, I'd like to get fit, of course. And lose weight.'

'And how committed are you?'

'Very,' said Daisy staunchly, wondering what other answer she could reasonably have given.

'OK. I think we should do some tests, work out a fitness routine for you, test your heart rate afterwards. I'll reassess you in, say, four weeks. You should be ready to step up the repeats by then, but of course, you may feel able to do it much earlier. Let's go.'

Daisy followed him meekly, tugging her T-shirt down over her bum as she went. 'Thanks very much, Lizzie Little,' she thought morosely as Markie led her into the gym, which was full of strange contraptions that seemed to resemble medieval torture devices.

'Hop on here, Daisy,' Markie indicated an exercise bike. Daisy hopped. Markie punched a series of numbers into some gadget and said, 'Right. Off you go.'

Daisy began to slip off the bike. 'Off you go, *pedalling*,' said Markie, shoving her back on firmly.

Daisy pedalled. Within sixty seconds she was puffing, by two minutes she was bright red, and when the resistance increased, she slowed down pathetically.

'Keep going,' said Markie relentlessly.

She thought she'd die. Christ! They *were* medieval torture machines. Daisy's calves screamed, her thighs ached, and sweat ran down her face. It only stopped after six endless minutes and she had slowed to a pitiable speed. But the respite was brief. 'Put your feet here,' commanded Markie, indicating two large paddles on another machine.

'What is it?'

'It's just steps. Here, I've made it easy for you. Now step.'

Easy? To keep the machine going she had to push down hard on the paddles otherwise she sank ignominiously downwards, and every time she thought she'd got the better of the machine, the difficulty seemed to increase. Then it was on to another beast, which stretched and pulled at her inner thighs. By the time she got to the treadmill, her legs were wobbling dangerously, but still there was no let-up in Markie's torment.

'Run.'

She ran. After that it was shoulder and arm work and finally, abs. Lying on the floor felt blissful, but as soon as Markie had shown her how to hold her hands to her ears and keep her elbows back, he made her start sit-ups.

'So just do that set of exercises for a start. Don't do them every day – every other day is better. If you need me, give me a shout, otherwise I'll see you in a month.'

Daisy, her eyes clenched tight shut as she concentrated on the searing pain in her abdomen, merely grunted. Thirty-five, thirty-six … nearly there … thirty-seven … Sweat was pouring down her face. She was scarlet with effort, her features contorted with pain. Her T-shirt, an emerald affair sporting the legend 'Organic spuds – you know they make sense' (it had been given to her on a photo shoot at an agricultural show last year) was clinging to her soaking body. Thirty-eight …

'Daisy?'

She knew that voice. In a cloud of pain, Daisy half-registered, half-blanked it. Thirty-nine …

'Are you all right?' The voice was amused.

Her exhausted brain made the connection. 'Jack!'

Her last excruciating repeat abandoned, she made up for it by sitting up abruptly and staring through a veil of perspiration at the unexpected sight of Jack Hedderwick, looking cool, trim, fit, and sickeningly sexy in figure-hugging lycra, standing above her and staring down in surprise.

'I didn't know you were a member here.'

'I didn't know you were.'

'Sure.' The boyish grin flashed. 'I joined in January. Iris said I wouldn't last a month but here I am.'

Daisy was conscious that she was hardly a picture of elegance. Blast and bother! Why did Jack have to come across her looking like this? Once this man had known every inch of her body, known how to make each hollow and bump tickle and tingle and yearn for more attention. Now lumps had replaced hollows and the bumps had multiplied. Embarrassed, she tried to conceal them.

'Well done, you,' she said. 'I thought you were looking in good shape.' She squirmed round painfully and struggled to her feet.

'Have you finished your routine?' Jack asked. 'Fancy a drink?'

'Is there a bar here?' Daisy asked, surprised. A pint would slip down rather well.

Jack laughed. 'A coffee bar. See you there in fifteen minutes?'

Showering, thought Daisy, had never been such a pleasure. And as she dried her hair with the super fast driers, it came to her like a streak of lightening out of a blue sky that if Jack came here regularly, she could get him to herself, just as regularly. Then she could find out how he really felt about Iris, because surely – heavens – surely he couldn't really be in love with her, not in the way that *they* had been in love for all those years?

Her insides melted with joy at the thought of Jack. Schoolgirl love. Wow. Finding Jack down by the river one glorious May day when she'd been skiving had been something else. A happiness explosion. Never mind that she was just seventeen, never mind that he was five years older and already finishing training college – they were destined to be together.

Just two weeks after that first meeting, unable to explain her long absences without inventing lies that were more and more implausible, she'd taken him home to meet her parents.

'Mum's all right. Dad will probably be difficult,' she warned Jack as they neared the house.

'Difficult? Why?'

Daisy shrugged. How to explain her father to Jack? Eric Irvine with his strict sense of duty and his need to control her life. Her nervousness increased with every step. Every pebble on the garden path gleamed and winked and tried to warn her to stop. The wobbly stone at the end – the one that looked like a dog crouching low – stood like a sentinel before the door. *Friend or foe?* What would her father say?

Ten minutes later, she thought she was going to get away with it.

'Jack. Right. Yes.' He shook Jack's hand, briefly, then turned his attention back to the news on the television and for the rest of the evening he was silent.

Supper over, the excruciatingly stilted conversation at an end, Jack finally took his leave, with a whispered, 'Call you later,' as he left. It was not until he'd closed the garden gate and his shadowy figure had moved out of sight that the explosion happened.

'And what in hell's name do you think you're doing, young lady? Did I give you permission to start seeing someone? Did I?' He pushed his face, florid with fury, into Daisy's.

'I'm ... I ... don't you like him, Dad?'

'Like him? Bloody smart-arse. Pah! And anyway,' Daisy watched a vein in his neck throb as his face grew redder, 'he's far too old for you and you, young lady,' he grabbed her by the wrist and swung her close to him so that she couldn't escape his glare, 'you are too young to be dating at all. Especially with your exams coming up.'

Daisy glanced helplessly at her mother. Useless to hope for support from there. Janet was clutching the back of a chair, her whole frame shaking, the gold shards in her eyes dulled and shadowy.

'Eric, darling, she's only ... she did bring him home so that ...'

'So that what?' He rounded on her, his face puce. 'Did he think that cosying up for an evening would make everything all right? Huh? Well, did he?' He was snarling now. Daisy thought she'd never seen him so angry. 'And as for you,' With a sharp shove he released her wrist and started moving threateningly towards Janet. 'Why didn't you tell me about this earlier? Thought if you sprung it on me I wouldn't be able to do anything, huh?'

This was new, this shadow of violence. Eric Irvine had always been a bully, but it had all been words. As Daisy saw for the first time a streak of raw viciousness – triggered, she could only suppose, by her bringing a competing male into the house – she reacted, instinctively and uncharacteristically.

'Stop it!' she said, her voice low and urgent, but controlled and commanding. 'Just stop!' For a second he did stop, astonished. In two words, she had reversed their roles and taken control. She took a deep breath and instinctively tried to cool the atmosphere down a fraction. 'I really like Jack.' Her voice was low. Soft but steady. 'I want to carry on seeing him. Please, Dad.'

Be nice, her instincts told her, *appear to submit. Find a way of getting him on your side. You've got to.* But she saw at once that Eric was not to be diverted. She quailed at the fury in his eyes and was forced to drop her gaze. Her father kicked a chair out of his way. It skidded and scraped on the floor, teetered on one leg, tumbled and fell on the tiles with a clatter. Janet, still gripping the back of the chair near the sink, uttered a low moan.

'You're not to see him, Daisy.' The rage made his voice rough. 'You're not old enough to date anyone. And that's final.'

'But …' The word escaped before she could bite it back.

He turned savagely. 'I don't want to hear another word, Daisy. And if I find you've defied me …'

He left the words hanging as he left the room.

Helplessly, Daisy looked at Janet.

'Sorry, love,' she whispered.

Sorry wasn't enough. Sorry was hopeless. This time, Daisy thought as she silently helped to tidy the kitchen, she had to find courage from somewhere, because she had to be with Jack Hedderwick, she just had to.

Daisy finished drying her hair and assessed her reflection in the mirror. Maybe there was something about this exercising lark after all, she thought. The scarlet had subsided, leaving a glow that was actually quite flattering. Her eyes looked brighter than usual too – or maybe that was just the thought of the coffee with Jack.

'I got you a latte as usual. That's right, isn't it?' he waved at her as she entered the bright brasserie.

'Fine, yes, thanks Jack.' She wouldn't tell him she'd switched to black in an effort to trim the calories – just knowing

73

that he remembered the past was sweetness to her soul.

'Great front page this week, by the way,' he said as they placed their cups on a small table near the window. The brasserie was well situated, in a loop of the river not too far from where they'd first met all those years ago. The town had grown outwards, reaching stony tentacles across the fields into the rural heart of the area.

'Thanks Jack.' He'd noticed! He liked her photographs! He still cared! Daisy's mind hopped and bumped along a path of logic uniquely designed by some inner conditioning of her brain to reach the conclusion she wanted. 'Of course, no one wants something like that to happen, but ...'

'But news-hounds are vultures of the worst kind,' Jack grinned.

'I was going to say, but at least if it does, we like to be able to handle it sensitively,' Daisy said primly, conveniently setting aside the fact that emblazoning graphic images across the front page of a newspaper for all to ogle at could hardly be labelled 'sensitive' behaviour.

Jack refused the challenge. 'So how are things otherwise, babes?' he asked. 'I gather that guy you used to be so friendly with is back in town.'

'Do you mean Ben Gillies? By "friendly", I take it you're thinking of "friendly" activities such as stream-damming and apple-chucking, or maybe the intimate little activity of snowman-building,' Daisy said, keen to remind Jack that Ben Gillies had been nothing more than a kid when he'd moved to London.

'Apple-chucking, right.' Jack's mouth twisted in amusement. 'What are the rules of that again?'

Daisy put on a superior look and started to reply, 'First one person grabs an apple ...' when she suddenly remembered the Provost's presentation. 'What's the time?' she interrupted herself.

Jack glanced at his watch. 'Nearly seven-thirty. Why?'

'No-o-o!' Daisy wailed, snatching her bag and hopping to her feet, 'It can't be! I'm late, I'm late, Christ, where's my key?'

Jack, watching her fumble through her pockets and shook his head ruefully.

'Not here … or here. Where …? Must be … no …' she turned to Jack, as she always had, for help. 'I've lost them! And I've got to get to the Town Hall! Now!'

Jack sighed. 'OK. Think. When you came into the gym, what did you do with them?'

'I put them in my right hand pocket. I always do,' said Daisy, her mouth quivering. She was demonstrating how disorganised she was again and she knew he'd hate it, but she had to find her keys, and quickly. 'They're not here!'

'Sure?'

She turned the contents out onto the table. A crumpled tissue, a lip salve, a few coins. 'Nothing. No keys.'

'OK. Left hand pocket.'

Sweeteners. A Werther's Original, still wrapped. A wrapper from a Kit Kat, contents eaten. Tiny Ted. No keys.

'Jeans' pockets?'

Daisy looked at him and shook her head, unwilling to admit that her jeans were too tight to allow her to put anything in the pockets. 'I've lost them! And I'm late! What am I going to do, Jack?' She turned to him helplessly, as she always had, for answers.

He thought for a second. 'What was your locker number? Perhaps they fell out there?'

'How do I know?' Panic was rising to a dangerous level. 'No wait, I remember, 608.' She'd chosen it particularly. Sixth of August of course. Jack's birthday. 'I'll run and look.'

The gods were smiling on her. No one had taken her locker and the keys, which must have fallen out of her pocket when she'd thrown the coat in, lay glistening on the wood at the back corner. She grabbed them and ran.

'Got them! Jack, you're a genius.' She reached up and kissed his cheek, her stomach flipping at the familiar touch of him, the never-to-be-forgotten smell, the way his hair grew in a fine down in front of his ears. 'Must run. See you soon.'

As she fled the brasserie, she was already planning her next visit. Knowing she could get Jack to herself made the thought of doing the ghastly fitness routine just slightly less painful.

Chapter Eleven

'Handsome is as handsome does, runs the old saying. Listen to the wisdom of times past and don't allow yourself to be seduced by the false gods of youth, good looks, and flashy attire. Your destiny lies elsewhere.'

'Huh!' Sharon, reading the Cancer predictions that Cosmo Fleming had just handed in for the new edition, shoved the sheets of paper back in the envelope and tossed it on the desk in front of her. 'He never did know what he was talking about.'

Her eyes followed Jay Bond as he walked past her into his office and closed the door. *Good looks and flashy attire*, thought Daisy, amused, though Sharon's look was more of desire unfulfilled than love requited. She checked her camera batteries, pushed the camera safely into its case, then reached for the horoscope envelope Sharon had discarded. Pisces. *'Never look back. Look for the better self within you and remember the commandment, Thou shalt not steal.'* What did that mean, for heaven's sake?

'Got your investigative masterpiece sorted out yet, Sharon?' Murdoch asked disingenuously, as his fingers pattered across his keyboard. He pushed his half-moon specs up onto his forehead and blinked at his screen, then replaced them on the end of his nose and continued to type.

'Of course.' The pertness of Sharon's little upturned nose, Murdoch always maintained when out of the chief reporter's earshot and the possibility of a sexual harassment suit, could only be matched by the cuteness of her backside.

'Good for a front page?' Ben asked from his desk in the corner.

Daisy glanced across at him. He's turned rather quiet in his

77

old age, she thought. The Ben Gillies she remembered had been livelier, more fun. What had happened to him in all the years he'd been away?

'Sure, Ben,' Sharon was saying. 'I've been looking at the failure rate of the surgeons in Hailesbank Hospital. I'm going to name and shame.'

'Bloody hell, Shar,' said Murdoch.

'What?' She rounded on him.

'What do you think that'll achieve?'

'It'll get them to pull up their socks.'

'It'll get excrement dumped through their letter boxes. Then they'll move away and we'll be left with no surgical facilities in Hailesbank and you'll end up having to run a campaign to get the NHS to send some raw junior surgeon down here, with the end result that our surgical records will be poorer than ever. People are too well known here for that kind of exposure. Not unless they really warrant it. And you can't say whether an operation should have been successful unless you have all the facts of the case at your fingertips. Which you don't.'

'Rubbish, Murdoch,' Sharon retorted, but with less than the usual conviction in her tone. 'I'll check it out thoroughly. Anyway, what are you working on, Mr Feature Writer Superior?'

'Rubbish,' said Murdoch curtly, returning to his tapping. 'Or to be more precise, wheelie bins.'

Sharon looked aghast. 'But that's just the sort of trivia that Jay doesn't want in the paper. I thought we'd agreed on a feature on that retired professor living out at The Hazels, the one who played a key role at Bletchley Park during the war.'

'Done it,' said Murdoch without looking up. Actually, as Daisy well knew, he'd done the interview three times over the past twenty years and had simply telephoned The Hazels to ensure that the old professor was still alive. She was booked in to visit the old folks' home that afternoon to take the photograph.

'So what's with the wheelie bins then?'

'There's a protest on this morning. The good citizens of

Hailesbank are furious with their Council for moving to fortnightly collections. They've all painted protest slogans on their wheelie bins and are going to march through the town. Daisy's off there now.'

Sharon would have remembered, thought Daisy, if Jay hadn't distracted her.

'Well I guess you'd better cover it, Daisy, but I can guarantee that it won't get space, or not much, anyway. After all, people's lives sacrificed on the altar of our aging surgeons' golf handicaps are much more important than wheelie bins.'

Ben raised an eyebrow. Murdoch grunted softly and swivelled his chair fractionally away from Sharon. Daisy hoisted her gear onto her shoulder and started limping stiffly towards the door. The session at the gym had left a crippling legacy. Tiny Ted, evacuated from her pocket when she checked for some change, lay sadly on her desk.

She remembered him half way to the car and turning, hobbled back. Going on a photo shoot without TT was unthinkable.

Jack, Jack, you must come back.

This was the third time this week at the gym and she hadn't seen Jack again. Daisy finished her cycling and moved on to the abductor machine. At least the stiffness had worn off and an odd side effect she'd noticed was that her appetite seemed to have dropped. Simply by making herself drink lots of water after her sweaty exertions, she felt quite full and having done all that work, it did seem a pity to undo it all by chomping on chocolate.

'Hi.'

'Oh, hi Jack.'

Yes! He was there. He'd seen her. He was talking to her. He'd come because he'd known she'd be there. Daisy finished her last few exercises slowly and watched him. God, he was just as gorgeous as he'd been the day she met him. He didn't look a day older and his body was fantastic. She watched as he took to the treadmill. He was fit, a natural athlete. She went to the treadmill next to him and started the machine. He turned and smiled and her day lit up.

'Not given up yet then?' His arms were pumping as he jogged, but he was barely out of breath.

'Me? Give up? Never.' Daisy's treadmill was picking up pace. She hated this machine. It seemed to have a life of its own. Her legs were moving faster. They had to or she'd fall off. Her breath began to get ragged. 'Fancy a coffee?'

Jack was running now, not jogging, but still he looked comfortable.

'Just started my routine, Daisy.'

'Oh. Me too.'

He looked at her and grinned. Daisy was sweating so much she had to wipe the back of her arm across her eyes to clear them. The move unbalanced her and she wobbled and yelped. 'Aargh! Help!'

Quickly, Jack jumped off his treadmill and hit the red emergency button on her console, steadying her with strong hands. 'Take it easy, kitten.'

Kitten. His old loving name for her. A sense of foolishness mixed with delight. *He called me kitten!*

'I'm OK. Thanks. So you will have a coffee?'

He glanced at the clock on the wall. 'I'll be another forty-five minutes in here.'

'Me too.'

'OK. Catch up later then.'

Forty-five minutes. Bloody hell. She'd be crippled, but she'd do it. To see Jack at the end of it all, be with him, alone, she'd pay any price for that. Walking heavily, she went back to the cycling machine, set it on its lowest level, plugged her iPod into her ears, and started her routine all over again.

'What the hell's happening at the *Herald* then, Daisy?'

Jack, showered and fresh-smelling, accepted his coffee and sat down opposite her. She'd lasted twenty minutes before conceding defeat and retiring to the pool. A dozen slow, laboured lengths later, she called it a day and took her time in the changing room.

'What d'you mean?'

'It's crashingly obvious that the new guy's got ambitions. Doesn't like local news, that's clear. It seems a bit odd for a local paper. Is he trying to drive it into the ground?'

'He's just got new ideas, that's all,' Daisy said loyally. Even to Jack, she didn't want to run down the *Herald*. Rumours of the threat of closure didn't seem to have circulated round Hailesbank yet, but if things went on like this, they wouldn't need to. It would fold well before the six months were up.

'Everyone at the school's fizzing.' Jack blew aside the foam on his coffee. 'The Local History Society news has been dropped, the Drama Group couldn't get their announcement of auditions for the Easter show in, the home ec teacher's complaining because the notice of their next Quilter's meeting has been returned.' He picked his cup up. 'Frankly, Dais, it all seems headed for disaster.'

Daisy's eyes filled with tears. She felt deeply torn between wanting to defend her paper, feeling desperate for Jack's sympathy, but at the same time wanting to show him she could cope on her own.

'Jay's keen to raise the standards of the paper,' she tried to hold her ground.

'To what? It's a local rag.'

'We all want it to be the best local paper around,' Daisy said staunchly.

'I'll give it a month, then I bet the advertising will drop and everyone will simply buy *The Stoneyford Echo*.'

'Oh Jack.' Daisy put her own cup down. She couldn't hide her worries any longer. 'I don't know what to do. We're under threat of closure as it is and this just seems to be making it worse. Don't tell anyone, will you?' She looked up at him pleadingly. He looked shocked.

'Threat of closure?'

She nodded. 'I saw a letter. Angus was reading it when he died. Things haven't been going well for us recently anyway and they want us to merge with *The Echo*. And now it seems to be all slipping away.'

'What does the new guy say?'

Daisy shook her head. 'He's not said anything. I'm beginning to wonder if he even knows.'

'Surely he does.'

Daisy shrugged miserably.

'Then someone has to tell him.'

Tell him? She thought of Jay Bond and his utter conviction about what he was doing. How could she tell him anything?

Jack smiled and put his hand on her arm. 'Don't worry, Dais. I'm sure it'll be fine.'

She felt the touch like a flame. The warmth of his hand burned through her sweater and spread up and down her arm until it seemed to reach her face and she felt herself blush with the intensity of her delight. She willed him to reach down and take her hand as he always used to. She longed to feel his fingers curl round her own, stroking them with the old familiar touch.

He took his hand away, reached for his sports bag, and stood up. 'Must go. Iris will have the supper ready. See you, Dais. It'll be all right.'

She felt the absence of his hand like a void in her soul. *Don't go, Jack*. She willed him to turn but he met a friend near the door, exchanged a few words then left. *Kitten*. He'd called her kitten. Her heart swelled and glowed as she remembered how he'd come to her aid on the treadmill. Her man. She stood up, picked up her bag, swung it onto her shoulder, took two steps, then came to an abrupt halt.

'Aargh!'

Heads swung round in alarm. She grinned vaguely at the concerned faces. 'It's OK. I'm fine.'

But she wasn't fine. The rest had caused her to stiffen up after her double session on the exercise machines and the pain in her legs was excruciating.

Chapter Twelve

<Miss you babe.>

Ben got the text from Martina early one Sunday morning. For the past month, there had been nothing. He'd wondered, daily, how she was doing. Now, out of the blue, this. Shit.

Ben's room, at the top of his parents' house, was essentially an attic conversion. Through a small window he had fine views of the Hailes River. Although it was part of a small new development, the plot was on the edge, giving open access to the river and clear vistas across to fields and woods on the far bank. He liked it, although he didn't plan on getting too comfortable here. He was thirty, for God's sake, far too old to be living with his parents, however easy they were to get on with. At the far side of the room, next to the window, Nefertiti stood, mistress of all she surveyed. Kath Gillies had enjoyed the joke and popped in from time to time to change her outfit or add an accessory or two. Currently, Nef was wearing a pair of cropped navy linen trousers, a red and white striped Breton sweater, and a jaunty felt hat – from Nuggets on the High Street made, he'd been told, by one of Daisy Irvine's friends.

Daisy Irvine. God, she was ditsy. Ditsy Daisy. It could be frustrating sometimes, but it was also very appealing.

Ben rubbed his hair, itched his belly, scratched his balls, and began the process of waking up properly. Daisy was a great photographer and she had the kind of charm that everyone responded to, from tiny tots to crumblies in care homes. She could persuade people to do anything for the camera – so what was it that stopped her from believing in herself? She was like a kid. Except that she was a very attractive young woman.

'What do you think, Nef? Might Daisy Irvine be the girl for

me?' he asked the model. She stared blankly back across the room at him, her eyes wide and unblinking, her perfectly smooth face beautifully framed by her red wig. 'Thanks. You're no bloody use at all.'

His mobile beeped again.

<And I'm sorry.>

This was a little worrying. He glanced at his watch. It was really early. Six thirty. Christ, he hoped she was all right. If she was up at this hour she must have had a bad night. What could he do? What *should* he do? Text her back? Phone her for a chat? Let her stew? What was she trying to achieve – did she want to reopen their relationship? He sincerely hoped not. He didn't feel strong enough to start wading through the thick, sticky treacle of their involvement. But on the other hand, he didn't like abandoning her if she was really down. He owed her more than that.

'Sod it, Nef, I'm off out.' He swung out of bed, pulled on his clothes, found his walking boots, and padded downstairs quietly with them in his hand. He opened the front door, sat on the top step, and put them on. It was a great morning, cold but clear. Since his walk along St Cuthbert's Way he'd found that the exercise was a great way of chilling out, thinking, seeing the countryside, and keeping fit all at the same time. He could shower later.

'Later' turned out to be much later than he'd anticipated. Barely thinking, he turned onto the path that led to the coast and found himself at the sea before he realised how far he'd walked. Seven miles at least. He stood on the sand dune and felt the wind lift his hair. God, it was great. Scotland was great. There was no way he could get this kind of walk anywhere round London, not without travelling miles out. Maybe he should settle back here – not as a sub with *The Hailesbank Herald*, though, that was too uncertain and too poorly paid. He was only there because of Daisy. The irony was, she barely seemed to notice him. He should say something. Ask her out. How could he know if she was interested if he didn't even try?

The wind was bitter here, down on the coast. Exhilarating though. Impulsively, Ben threw up his arms and ran down to the edge of the sea, his boots dragging in the sand where it was soft and loose, then moving more easily as it dampened and firmed. At the edge of the water, where the waves lapped in, silver and ephemeral, he stopped, breathing heavily. He felt elated by the exercise, by the clean, fresh air, and the beauty of the scenery on every side. He felt as he had at Lindisfarne, where life had seemed to hold so much potential. All things were possible.

His route back home took him through one of the small villages that edged this stretch of coast prettily. In one of the roadside cottages, crisply whitewashed and roofed with rust-coloured pantiles, a café was advertising 'Full Scottish Breakfast', 'Coffee and muffins' and 'Great home baking'. Ben was ravenous. Half past nine. He pushed at the door more in hope than expectation of it being open so early on a Sunday, but was rewarded with an easy swing, a sensation of warmth, and the smell of freshly brewed coffee. The café was empty. He sat down at a small table in the window and stretched his legs out in front of him luxuriously.

'Hi.' A young girl appeared from a door at the back. 'Can I get you something?'

'Please,' Ben smiled. 'Coffee? And a cake?'

'We just have filter, is that all right? It's freshly made.'

'My favourite.'

She set a cup in front of him. 'Do you mind if I leave you for a bit? Just call if you need something. You can help yourself to more coffee,' she indicated the jug on the hotplate, 'and choose a cake.'

'No problem. Thanks.'

Bliss was a coffee, some delicious baking, the sun filtering in through the window and the absolute, perfect stillness of the day, broken only by the soft tick tock of an old school room clock on the wall across the room. Outside, a stretch of coarse grass ran down to a pebbly beach. Seaweed had been washed in with the tide and lay in great curving loops along the strand.

The sea was a pale, shimmering ribbon that joined seamlessly into the sky somewhere on the far horizon. He could see some large black and white birds dipping and scuttling and busying themselves along the edge of the water, looking for food he presumed. They had red beaks with legs to match.

He let out his breath contentedly. Perfect.

Diddly dah. Diddly dah dah dah.

The harsh electronic notes of his mobile broke into the silence with shocking brutality. He reached into his pocket with resignation. His mother, probably, wondering where he was. He should have had the sense to leave a note for her.

'Hello?' He fumbled for the green button without looking at the number that came up.

'Ben. Hi.'

Feeling his body tense, he sat up straight. Martina. 'Hi. How are you?'

'Did you get my texts?'

'Yeah. You OK?' It was odd hearing her voice again. It had been how long – a month? And yet the tones were so familiar.

'Yeah. You?'

'I'm good. Great.'

Please God, she doesn't want to try again.

'It's been a month. I miss you,' she said.

'Yeah.' God, he'd become inarticulate. 'How's things? Work going well?' Martina was a lawyer, working in a large global firm in the City. Her hours had always been long, but she thrived on it. Her work, like her eating habits, was a form of self flagellation. Quite what she was punishing herself for, Ben had no idea.

'Challenging.'

'Good challenging?'

'Yes and no.'

There was a silence. Again Ben could hear the tick tock of the clock. Down on the shore, the large black and white birds had gone and a flock of smaller birds had replaced them. The sea was looking rougher now and a large dark cloud hung over the horizon. The fine weather of the early morning looked as if it was moving away. He should really get going.

'Ben, I just wanted to say I'm sorry. I wish we could have done it all differently.'

'Me too.'

'I am trying with the food, really I am.'

'Good. I only wish the best for you, Teeny.'

'I know.'

Again there was a short pause, then she said, 'I do miss you, Ben.' His heart sank. 'But only in a good kind of way. Actually, I've started seeing someone else. I wanted to tell you.'

The words were shocking. He'd never imagined that she would start dating again so quickly.

'He's a lawyer at my firm. Nothing started before we split, Ben, honest. But he's fancied me for some time, apparently. We headed out for a drink one night and it went from there. Are you OK about it? I want you to be OK, Ben.'

Ben twiddled the teaspoon in his saucer. It made a small chinking noise against the cup. Martina and someone else. It was an odd thought and underlined their separation in a way he hadn't managed to in the past month. It gave him permission, he realised, to move on. Perhaps it was what he'd been waiting for.

He smiled. 'Babes, I'm delighted.'

'Really?'

'Really. It'd make me feel very good to know that you've found happiness.'

'Thank you, Ben. I do miss you, you know. Really. I'll never forget what we had.'

'Nor me.' He meant it too.

'Is there anyone else for you, Ben?'

Was there? He would like to think so but wasn't at all sure. 'Maybe,' he said slowly. 'I don't know if she cares for me though.'

'Go for it Ben. You're a great guy. Go get her.'

The sun through the window picked out the rich deep amber of his eyes as he rumpled his hair and grinned. 'Thanks, Teeny. Be happy.'

'You too, babes.'

He flipped his phone shut and looked out. It was starting to rain. He'd better go. But his heart felt light, whatever the weather could throw at him.

Chapter Thirteen

'Ben, you're dripping! For heaven's sake, let's get your things off.'

Kath, greeting him at the door a good three hours later, spotted her son coming into the hall and dodged out of her living room to intercept him. Daisy, feeling prim and proper and dressed in her Sunday best, was uncomfortable – more than uncomfortable, seriously awkward. Only her mother's pleading and the knowledge that with Kath present her father would be on his best behaviour had finally persuaded her to accompany them to the Gillies's for lunch. That and the oddest feeling that she shouldn't pass up the opportunity to see Ben somewhere other than work. Now, though, sitting on the chintzy sofa, waiting for Ben to appear, she felt crucified. What would he think when he found her there? Too late she realised that there should be a separation between work and not work. Sitting in his house, with her parents observing everything, she just wanted to bolt.

'We've got guests, love,' she heard Kath Gillies say. 'I've asked Janet and Eric round for lunch.'

'Oh? Right.' There was a rustle (a jacket being shaken out?) and a couple of clunks (boots?), then she heard him say, 'I'll just go for a shower first, will I?'

'Fine, just pop in and say hello before you go.'

Ben's head appeared. It had been raining for the past three hours and he looked as though he'd been out in every minute of that time. His thick browny-red hair was plastered to his head and his fair skin looked flushed.

'Oh! Hi Daisy. Hi.' Surely his face had gone a deeper shade of pink? 'Hello Janet, hello Eric. Good to see you. Listen, I'm dripping here, I won't come in and spoil Mother's carpet. I'm going to nip up for a shower.' His head disappeared for a moment, then reappeared suddenly. 'Good to see you,' he repeated, weirdly, before Daisy heard the soft thump, thump of him bounding up the carpeted stair in bare feet.

She stared at her skirt. It was an ankle length, swirly affair in dusky blue, with huge diagonal patchworky type squares and raggy bits. Why she'd let Lizzie persuade her to buy it she couldn't imagine, it wasn't really her thing, and she felt like someone else in the skirt.

What the hell was she doing here, thinking about a skirt, for God's sake – and on her day off? She could be at the gym. She twisted her mouth pensively. No, no point in going to the gym today. Jack would be with Iris, though not for much longer with any luck. *Kitten.* He'd called her *kitten.*

Purrr.

'Hey.' Ben was back. Christ that had been quick. Men seemed to get through the shower-and-change thing so fast.

Daisy smiled. 'Hey.'

'Remember I was telling you about that old Cream album? Want to hear it?'

He dressed casually in the office, but he looked even more relaxed now, standing there barefoot in cotton joggers and a soft zipped cardi over a white T-shirt, clean and scrubbed like a small boy just out of the bath – a big version of the Ben she used to play with all those years ago. And abruptly the girl Daisy had been was there with him again, running barefoot off to his room with smuggled treats to play board games or guessing games or just lie on the carpet staring at the ceiling and listen to music. She realised with surprise that she really liked Ben – more than just liked in a 'He's all right' kind of way. He was easy to be with, really comfortable. And actually, it occurred to her, looking like he did right now he was really rather sexy.

'Daisy? Cream? Crossroads? Baker, Bruce, and Clapton?'

She'd been drifting. She blinked, grinned and said, 'Sure. Love to. Have we time?'

Kath nodded, smiling. 'Want to take a drink up with you?'

'What, you mean legally?' Ben laughed.

He had the same memories.

They chose white wine, took a bottle and two glasses and pinched a couple of bags of crisps for good measure. It was funny how she was remembering – little things, like how he used to dance like a maniac whenever she put Abba on. God, he'd lacked co-ordination. She looked at his sturdy legs, the broad shoulders, the comforting solidness of him as she followed him up the stairs and wondered whether he'd changed.

'Do you dance these days?' she asked as they reached the door to his room on the top floor. A week or two back she would have been puffing but now, she was pleased to note, the long climb hadn't troubled her.

'Are you asking?'

She laughed. 'I'm supposed to say "I'm asking," huh?'

'Then I say, "I'm dancing".' He turned inside the room and stared at her for such a long moment that she felt uncomfortable. She blushed and turned to pretend to admire the view, then saw that there was someone else in the room. 'Hi,' she greeted the dummy involuntarily, then laughed at her mistake. 'My God, Ben, what's that?'

'Let me introduce Nefertiti, my constant companion and chaperone.'

'Delighted,' said Daisy, crossing the room to inspect her. 'Heavens, my friend Lizzie would just *love* her.'

'She's a dummy fetishist?'

'Nope. She's a textile designer. That looks like one of her hats.'

'Ah. Got it now. You share a house with her.'

'More of a tiny cottage, and a cold one at that, but yeah. You'd like her, she's gorgeous.' The heavy beat of Ginger Baker on drums filled the room and she closed her eyes to listen to Bruce and Clapton on guitar with the old classics she remembered from her parents' collection. 'Jesus, it's years since I heard this. Fabulous.'

Ben tossed her a pillow on the floor for her to sit on. She

subsided onto the floor and leaned back against the bed. Ben screwed the top off the wine, filled her glass, took his own and sank down to the floor with a practised ease, his toes splaying slightly to aid his balance.

Distracted by the sight, she said, 'You know those tickets that came in to the paper, the ones for the *X Factor* tour concert at Braehead?'

Ben's foot was tapping the carpet to the strong beat. 'Sharon won them in the draw, didn't she?'

'Yeah. But afterwards she told me she'd realised she had a diary conflict and can't go that night. She gave them to me.'

'What, just gave them away? And why you? Pardon me for making the observation, but I hadn't thought you were the best of mates.'

Daisy grinned. 'I know it's not saying much, but I'm as good as she's got there.'

'Hmm, you may be right. Sad.'

'I was wondering if you wanted to come with me?' The idea had just occurred to her. She would normally have invited Lizzie, but Lizzie was away next week. There was no point in asking Jack, not yet anyway, and Ben was cool, easy to be with.

'Are you on?'

'Are you asking?'

'I'm asking.'

'Then I'm on.'

Fucking magic. Ben sank back into the pillow he'd grabbed from the bed to lean against the wall in his lowly position on the floor and closed his eyes. *'Goin' down to the crossroad …'* He was at a crossroad all right. Before him lay all sorts of possibilities. The day, which had started early and had looked rather unpromising, had got better and better.

'Crossroad, crossroad, crossroad.'

He didn't need to worry about how to ask Daisy Irvine out on a date.

She'd just asked him.

Sales of the *Herald* had slumped. Chantelle in advertising was finding sales harder than ever. Sharon seemed to be constantly grumpy and Daisy guessed things weren't going too well with Jay because he was irritable most of the time and they hadn't been spotted in each other's company.

Out together on a story, Sharon chose – unusually – to confide in Daisy. 'It all started so well, Dais.'

Daisy, driving to the school in the small rural village of Main where parents were staging a protest against the decision not to exclude a very troublesome pupil (aged six), negotiated a tight bend in the narrow road, squeezing past a tractor coming in the opposite direction. That corner was dangerous. There'd be a serious accident there one of these days. The villagers had organised plenty of protests about it but the Council's attitude seemed to be to do nothing until there was a fatality to prove the villagers right. 'Yeah?'

'I mean, he's just *gorgeous*, don't you think?'

'Jay?'

'Of course, Jay. And he really took to me, I mean *really*.'

Daisy glanced across at Sharon. 'Not surprising. You're very pretty, Shar.' She was too. If she could just curb her bossiness she'd be a much more attractive person, but she had looks all right.

'Thanks.'

Sharon sounded surprised. Maybe she didn't get too many compliments. Was she aware of Sir Cosmo, finding every excuse to come into the office, standing in the corner eyeing her up like a loyal Labrador, his tongue practically hanging out? Daisy thought not. And even if Sharon was aware of Cosmo's unspoken passion, she'd probably be dismissive of it. He was, perhaps, a bit on the crusty side, but a good scrub and an airing, plus a bit of TLC, and Cosmo would probably come up shining in unexpected ways. He was too much under his mother's thumb and that was his biggest problem.

'But it's a bit difficult. He's kind of all over me one minute then looks at me like I'm a complete stranger the next. What can I do?'

Daisy passed the small, isolated church that marked half way to their destination. She picked her words carefully. 'Shar, is it the best idea to be trying to date the boss? You know what they say.'

'Yeah, yeah, I know, don't shit on your own doorstep. But I can't help it Dais, I'm smitten. And to be honest ...' she hesitated.

'What?'

Sharon's hesitation, uncharacteristically, continued. 'Well, to be honest, I don't like what he's doing to the paper. I want to leap on the guy and shag him to death, but professionally ... I'm worried.'

Daisy, taken aback, admitted, 'I know. Me too. What can we do?'

'That's the problem. I haven't a clue. I can't do a thing. If I tell him, I'll certainly lose him. I'm sure he's capable, but he's just getting it so wrong.'

Daisy thought about it. She had to slow down to pass a horse and rider. It gave her time.

'I think he's doing it with good intentions. He wants the paper to be great. He's just made a wrong judgement about how we can achieve that.'

'Can you help Daisy? Please? You're so good with people.'

A compliment? From Sharon Eddy? Was the world turning upside down? They had reached the edge of the village. The school was yards away. Daisy could already see the small gaggle of protesters, women mostly, carrying placards. She'd have to concentrate now on the job in hand.

'I'll try Shar. I'll think of something.'

Chapter Fourteen

As it happened, an opportunity to talk to Jay presented itself remarkably soon.

It was April Fool's Day and Daisy woke to a white world. She opened her curtains and looked out on the snow with astonishment and delight. The cottage didn't have a garden, as such, it was more of a small field, marked out from the farmland beyond only by a low dry stone wall that had deteriorated into ragged humps and bumps over the years. The view out to open countryside, therefore, was a long one. Daisy could see across several fields to a small wood at the foot of the hills that rose beyond. They were all white. Everything glinted and shone in the brightest of sunshine from a clear blue sky. She thought she had never seen anything quite so beautiful.

Hea-ven-ly, she thought, before recalling that she had to drive down to Kelso and negotiating the roads wouldn't be easy, even in the 4x4. To make matters worse, she couldn't find Tiny Ted. She spent a frantic ten minutes searching the cottage before realising that she must have left the bear on her desk. She felt naked and vulnerable without him in her pocket. Idiot. She swallowed some coffee and cursed her own scattiness. She really must concentrate instead of letting her mind wander.

Lizzie was away, she had the cottage to herself, and the task of digging the car out of the drift that had built up round it was all hers as well. When she'd finally managed to clear enough space between it and the road to get started, Daisy felt as though she'd had another full workout in the gym. Thinking about the gym naturally sent her mind spiralling to Jack Hedderwick, her beloved Jack. Surely it wouldn't be long now before they were back together? They'd fallen into a pattern of being at the

Fitness Centre on Monday, Wednesday, Friday, six thirty sharp unless work prevented her getting there. She'd upped her repeats several times (which Markie took the credit for) and she actually found that she had begun to enjoy the exercise for its own sake. Sometimes she ran alongside Jack on the next treadmill and even found breath to talk. They almost always had a coffee afterwards. Over the past few weeks they'd fallen back into the kind of closeness they used to have, before the cracks had begun to show. Cracks caused by Iris up-herself Swithinbank. Well, the woman would soon know what a rift between you and the man you loved felt like.

She felt close to Jack again. Only yesterday, she'd asked his advice about Jay. 'What can we do, Jack? We've got to save the *Herald*.'

'Have you tried talking to him?'

She shook her head. 'I think he still sees us all as hicks from the sticks. He doesn't get it.'

'What does he say about the threatened closure?'

She pondered that before answering. 'You know, he's never mentioned it. Not once.'

'Does he know?'

'Know? Surely he knows.'

'Try to find an opportunity – informally if you can – to talk about it, huh? Soon.'

'I will. Thanks Jack.' She tried to put all her love into her eyes when she looked at him. Did his clear blue ones show the same? She held his gaze for a long tingling minute and felt the thrill of it lift the hairs on her neck. Talk about a meaningful look! He hadn't said anything yet, but that didn't signify anything. He would soon, it was just a matter of time. Their reunion was inevitable. *Jackanddaisy. Daisyandjack.* They were meant to be together. The gym was just a start and it wasn't really the place for romance, she had to find a way of meeting him somewhere more intimate. And she would.

On the road to Kelso, she began to think. Jay Bond was playing with the *Herald* like a new toy, not handling it like a fragile one. She had to find out how he was planning to rescue the paper. Maybe she could work in a word for Sharon at the same time. Why not? It could be her good deed for the day.

The conference she was photographing turned out to be dull in the extreme. The paper was doing a special supplement about the day-long meeting. It was good money and heaven knows they needed the income, but finding ways to make groups of people talking or keynote speakers speaking look interesting was always a challenge, and it was not one that Daisy felt particularly inspired by today. She did her best though, and at four, packed her cameras away and stepped out of the hotel for the first time since she'd arrived at nine. The sunshine had gone and the sky was heavy with the threat of more snow. Across the square, she could see her car. There had clearly been a heavy fall at some point during the day and she had to spend five minutes scraping the windows. As she swung the car out of the square, the first flakes drifted down from the grey skies and two minutes later the snow was swirling down heavily. At home, in the cottage, she'd have watched it with childlike pleasure. But now, all she could think about was getting back to Hailesbank in one piece.

Three miles up the road, the snow developed into a blizzard and she was struggling to see through the windscreen. The car felt steady enough, but a van, coming the other way, slid and skidded towards her and she turned the wheel in alarm. A second later, she was in the ditch, cursing.

'Sod it!' She stuck the car into reverse and revved up. Nothing. The wheels were simply spinning. Daisy peered out of her window. There was no sign of the van, she was on her own. Cautiously, she opened the door and hopped out. There didn't seem to be any damage but the angle of the car had left one back wheel in the air, leaving the other to take up the traction and the soft snow was compacting into a mass of ice as she tried to rev, making it impossible to get out.

'Shit! What am I going to do?' she wailed uselessly up into the swirling snow. Ben. He'd know. Stumbling back to the car, she found her mobile and dialled the office.

'*Hailesbank Herald*, how can I help?' Somehow she'd got straight through to Jay Bond.

'Oh Jay. Hi. Hi, it's Daisy,' she was flustered. 'Is Ben there please?'

'Sorry, Daisy, I sent everyone home early. The snow's pretty bad here. You OK?'

Bother, she'd have to tell him, she didn't really have any other option. 'No. Not really. I'm stuck in a ditch. Well, in a snowdrift in a ditch, I guess.'

'Where?'

'Just outside Kelso.'

'Can you leave the car there and walk back in?'

'When I say just outside, I mean four or five miles. I don't fancy walking in this blizzard.'

'No. Wouldn't be sensible. Can you hitch a lift?'

Daisy looked out at the road dubiously. 'Apart from the van that forced me into the ditch, there's not been anything past for ages.'

'OK, Daisy. Listen, I'll come and get you.'

'Yes?' Daisy's heart lifted at the thought of rescue. 'That's really kind, Jay, but how will you get here? I mean, the weather's totally rubbish.'

'I've got my Discovery. I've been dying to give it a proper test.'

'Oh. Great.' How Jay had managed to blag a really smart vehicle in the current economic climate, heaven knows. 'Well, if you're sure, Jay, that'd be brilliant.'

'I'll be there in half an hour. I just need to close everything up here and I'll be with you. Keep warm, won't you?'

'Will do.'

Daisy looked around. The snow had stopped and a break had appeared in the clouds. Now that she'd stopped panicking about being stranded, she realised that there was something magical about the view. If she walked another thirty or forty yards up the hill, she'd have a spectacular line of sight right across to the countryside. It was too good to miss. Grabbing her camera, she rammed a woollen hat on her head and climbed out of the car.

Twenty minutes later, it didn't seem like such a great idea. The snow was up to her knees and her jeans were soaked. The climb, though, proved to be worth it. Although the light was grey, the scene was majestic. She lifted her camera, photographed the gnarled tree at the top of the hill, its branches laden with snow. A few forlorn sheep stood and stared at her. Black and white, on white. She took pictures of them too. Below her, in the distance, her car, its rear end in the air, half buried in snow, looking like a wreck. Who could have guessed that the scene of desolation would offer so many fantastic opportunities?

By the time she'd finished, the snow had started again, but even so, getting back to the car was easier than the climb had been. It was downhill and she had already beaten a kind of a path that she could follow. There was still no sign of Jay. She turned the engine on. At least she'd had the sense to throw an old wool coat in the back, as well as one of Lizzie's fabulous silk and velvet scarves. It didn't matter that it was red, a colour she never dared wear, it felt luxurious and cosy. She huddled behind the steering wheel, listening to the radio and rubbing the steamed-up window from time to time to peer out.

Jay arrived shortly before six, inching along the road with great care. Road? She could hardly see it. The edges had long since disappeared. White lines? The only white line visible was the broad swathe of snow between the tops of the walls that marked the edges of the fields.

'Hi! Thank God you're here.'

'How much further to Kelso?' Jay looked strained.

'Not more than four or five miles. I did it in ten minutes on the way out.'

'We'll have to head for there, Daisy. There's absolutely no way I'm going back the way I've come. Grab your camera gear and hop in.'

They rolled slowly down the hill. Half a mile on, they wound their way between a thickly wooded stretch of forest. Here the way was clearer and, fifteen minutes later, the first houses on the outskirts of Kelso appeared. They might even be able to walk now if they had to.

It didn't come to that. They crawled back into the square at a quarter to seven, nearly three hours after Daisy had left it.

'We'll have to hole up for the night and hope it's cleared a bit by morning,' Jay said, switching off the engine. He looked exhausted. His shoulders had slumped and he no longer had the arrogant air that she'd so disliked when she'd first met him.

'OK,' she said. 'I don't have any clothes with me though.'

'Nor me. Never mind. Let's find somewhere to stay.'

They tried every hotel, but with no success. Other travellers had beaten them to the accommodation. At the last hotel they picked up a local tourist brochure with the telephone numbers of a dozen or more guest houses and phoned them all, but with no luck.

'Right,' said Jay determinedly. 'We'll go back to the hotel in the square. I'll insist we camp down in the lounge if we have to.'

When they returned to where they'd started, their luck turned. 'Someone's just phoned to cancel their reservation, sir,' said the clerk on the desk. 'Seems they can't get through. The snow's quite bad, I believe.'

'Tell me about it,' grunted Jay. 'Can we take the room?'

'Certainly sir.' He signed them in and handed them the key.

A room? One room? Just one room for her and for Jay? Christ. She'd have to share a room with her boss. Perhaps he would offer to sleep in the lounge.

'Can we help with your bags?'

Jay laughed. 'Bags? I don't think we need help. Can we purchase a couple of toothbrushes?'

'I'll put them on the bill, sir.'

They made their way upstairs. Daisy prayed that the room would, at least, be a twin and in that her luck held out, but as the door swung to behind them, she stood inside, gripped by unaccustomed shyness and embarrassment.

'Looks all right,' Jay flicked a switch and twin lamps came on at either side of the two beds.

Daisy stood, still rigid. Turning, he caught sight of her face.

'You all right?'

Then, the situation he'd put her in evidently dawning on him, he said hurriedly, 'Hey Daisy, I'm sorry. I should have asked. Are you OK about this? I promise you, absolutely, I have no agenda here, but ... listen ...' he stepped away from her hastily. Maybe he had had a sudden vision of a sexual harassment suit, or even worse, a rape charge, '... you can sleep in here. I'll grab some rest downstairs. It would be nice to be able to snatch a quick shower before I decamp, though?'

Daisy's hand stole into her pocket for the comfort of Tiny Ted's presence, but of course it was empty. 'It's all right,' she said in a small voice. 'You can stay.'

Chapter Fifteen

Daisy had never spent a night in a hotel with anyone other than Jack. If she was honest, she'd never slept with anyone but Jack. Of course, she'd been very young when she'd fallen in love with him. Reflecting on it, she began to realise just how young she'd been. A schoolgirl. She'd thought she was so grown up, but she'd known nothing. Jack had enfolded her in his arms and in his care and for ten glorious years she hadn't had to worry about anything. She walked nervously across to the bathroom and looked in. It was large, solid, and had a lock on the door.

'Is it really all right, Daisy? If you're at all worried –'

'It's all my fault, Jay. You being here at all, I mean. If I hadn't gone into that ditch you wouldn't have had to bail me out. There's no reason why you should have to sleep on a sofa.' She flashed a brave grin. 'So long as you don't snore.'

He laughed and slumped down in an armchair. 'Can't promise but I've never had any complaints. Look, freshen up a bit and we'll go find some food.'

She picked up one of the toothbrushes and her handbag and closed the bathroom door behind her. Out in the bedroom, she heard him turn on the television and was grateful for the noise.

The dining room was busy. Daisy recognised quite a few faces from the conference earlier in the day. No wonder they'd had so much trouble finding accommodation. It was also warm. Fortunately, she was a dab hand at layered dressing and that morning she'd pulled on a grey T-shirt under her woollen sweater. At least it looked presentable and, worn with Lizzie's pretty velvet scarf, she felt half respectable. Her jeans were still sodden, but the shower and hair wash had transformed her into a different person from the Daisy who'd shivered in the car wondering if Jay would ever find her.

'What do you fancy? I think I'll have the beef.'

She studied the menu. 'The fish for me. Thanks.' A whole evening with Jay Bond. Jeez. And a night. She still didn't want to think about that bit. She'd have to slip into bed while he was in the bathroom. And despite all his promises, she'd be leaving her underwear and T-shirt on. 'Thanks for coming for me, Jay.'

He smiled at her and again she understood the force of the charm he could exert. The lines of his face were sculpted and sharp, his mouth shapely, his face perfectly symmetrical, his hair thick and beautifully cut. In the flickering flame of the candle on their table, he looked very attractive indeed. Funny that. How you could be dining with the most handsome guy north of the Border and still not fancy him one bit?

'That's a nice scarf.'

Daisy had looped Lizzie's red creation round her neck. Its folds fell softly below her chin and the ends draped in long tendrils down her back. 'It's not really my colour.'

'It suits you.'

'Thanks.'

'What do you think of the paper now?'

'What? Sorry …' The question took her by surprise.

'Do you think it's improved?'

Daisy gulped. What could she say? She thought of Sharon. *'Do something, Daisy.'* She thought of Jack. *'Talk to him. Be honest.'* When would she ever get another opportunity like this? And Christ knows, her job was on the line. What did she have to lose? On the other hand, she didn't want to make things difficult for herself if they *did* manage to save the paper. Again, she felt paralysed by indecision.

'You can be honest,' said Jay, clearly catching her mood.

'Well,' she began cautiously, 'yes and no.'

He put down the large menu and stared at her. What on earth was she doing? Criticising him would be sheer foolhardiness. He was her *boss*. She backtracked hastily. 'I think Ben's done a great job on the layout. And the headlines.'

As her courage slipped, an image of Angus MacMorrow rose up in front of her. Angus, falling like a tree, shocked to death by the threat of closure. Angus, who'd taught her so much and been so passionate about the *Herald*. She owed it to him, she owed it to all of them at the paper. To Ruby, who'd obviously loved the old reprobate. To dear Sir Cosmo, who relied on the horoscopes to allow him to come in and drool over Sharon. To Murdoch, who deserved better than to be made redundant just before the end of his career. To young Dave, who wasn't experienced enough to find another job easily. To herself, damn it. And to all the people of Hailesbank, who were missing the news of the clubs and societies that made up the beating heart of the town.

'But on the other hand ...' she started. And by the time the wine came, a few minutes later, she felt as though she'd written her own dismissal.

The waiter splashed the rich ruby liquid into Jay's glass. He swirled it around, inhaled, and nodded. 'It's fine,' he said. 'Which is more than my editorship is, it appears,' he added to Daisy.

'There've been lots of good ideas, Jay,' she said, belatedly trying to sugar the pill, 'and we appreciate you're trying to bring up the standards. I know we'd all got a bit lazy in the last year or two while Angus was ill.' She sighed. 'That's something none of us is proud of. It's just that it isn't really the best time to be experimenting with new ideas. With the threat of closure hanging over us and all.' She took a big swig from her glass. There. She'd said her piece, just as she'd promised Sharon and as Jack had suggested. For better or ... 'What's wrong?'

Jay's jaw had slackened and his eyes had grown round. 'What did you say?'

'Which bit? The club news? The horoscopes?'

'About closure.'

'That's what killed Angus. I think so anyway. He was reading the letter from the Chairman when he had his heart attack.'

'Letter?'

'About the proposed closure.' She remembered what Jack had said – '*Does he know?*' But it was unbelievable that he would not know. 'Surely you were told?'

'Are you telling me that *The Hailesbank Herald* is being threatened with closure?'

So he really hadn't known. That seemed unfair. Surely someone coming into a new job should be told about something as critical as that?

'I don't believe it. Just wait till I see Uncle Oliver.'

Uncle Oliver? At last she made the connections. Sir Oliver Wyndham, Chairman of the Board of the Havering Group of Newspapers. Uncle Oliver. It explained how Jay had arrived so speedily in the post after Angus's death. It explained the smart car – a small sop, no doubt, for what was likely to be a very short-term job. And it explained how Jay had managed to land the post despite leaving Channel 69 under a cloud.

'What did the letter say, Daisy? Tell me. Tell me exactly.'

The fish was delicious. She hadn't realised just how hungry she was. The wine was the best she'd ever tasted. And Jay Bond, once they'd let down the defences between them, turned out to be far more approachable than she'd ever imagined he could be.

'About Sharon,' she ventured, dipping her spoon in the delicious pudding and sucking a small mouthful off the end of it. To hell with the healthy diet. She'd earned this treat.

His face stilled. 'What about Sharon?'

'She … she really likes you, you know.'

Jay laid down his spoon on his plate. His chocolate crepe was only half eaten.

'You know I'm married,' he said.

Daisy blushed. They had known, of course. He saw it at once. 'And I guess you also know about my ignominious departure from Channel 69.' Her blush deepened. 'I guess I'd be rather disappointed if you hadn't done your research. You are journalists, after all.' He finished his crepe quickly, set his spoon down again, and went on, 'I'd like to put the record straight. The newspaper reports were overblown, as you might expect from the redtops concerned. I'm not an addict, Daisy. I was mad to take drugs in the studio before going on air. But everyone did it, you know. A couple of snorts sets you up, focuses the mind, gives you an edge, sparkle, confidence. At least, that's what it feels like.'

He glanced at Daisy. She tried to look non-judgemental.

'That was all it was,' he went on, 'Unfortunately, I got caught. The channel didn't like it. My wife didn't like the subsequent publicity and I found myself out of my lovely home on my ear, no job, amazingly few friends, and a marriage on the rocks. I tried everything, but I was getting nowhere, fast. In the end, I had to resort to calling Uncle Oliver and he sent me up here. He gave me a chance – or so I thought.'

He paused and held Daisy's gaze.

'By the way, for the record, I'm still in love with my wife.'

That was plain enough. Sharon wouldn't be happy, but she couldn't accuse Daisy of not trying on her behalf. The fate of *The Herald,* though, was another matter. Maybe she could do something about that.

'Jay,' she began slowly.

'Daisy?'

'Could we all try together? To save *The Herald* I mean? I'm sure if we all put our heads together, we could turn things around.'

Jay picked up his glass. 'There's nothing I would like better. Let's drink to success.'

'To success.'

Chapter Sixteen

By morning, the temperature had risen, the blizzard had turned into rain, and most of the snow had disappeared. It was hard to believe that the day before had been so wintry. Back in Hailesbank, Daisy had to go straight to her first assignment. She parked her rescued car near the office and met Sharon at a bleak-looking warehouse across the river.

'Could you squat down here,' she indicated a spot on the floor of the warehouse to the young man she was trying to photograph, 'and look through the spokes of the bicycle, like this.' She demonstrated. It was hard work. She'd tried a few different poses, but the guy was one of the shy ones.

'So how many bikes are you sending out to Africa?' Sharon asked from somewhere behind her.

'Three hundred, first off,' said the man, Bob Sampson, curtly. He might be charitable but no one had schooled him in media relations.

'Three *hundred*?' Sharon was incredulous. Pedal People was a charity set up to provide unwanted bikes so that poverty-stricken Africans could make the long commute, see family, get into the towns more easily, but Sharon had been pretty bored by the story – until she heard the figure. 'Where're you going to get them all from?'

Bob shrugged. 'Round and about. The church has put out an appeal. We go out in the van and collect 'em. Do 'em up a bit. Check the brakes 'n that.'

Daisy leant forward and moved the bicycle a fraction so that the wheel spokes, rather than the frame, were in front of Bob's face.

Click. Click click. She snapped away as Sharon talked to

him, eliciting the facts she needed for the story. It didn't take long and within half an hour they were on their way back to the office. The warehouse where they'd been interviewing Bob Sampson was a short walk across the river, in one of the unlet units the charity had managed to secure for the project. They were strolling back into Hailesbank across the picturesque old sixteenth-century pedestrian bridge when Sharon raised the question of the paper again.

'Ma Ruby was telling me there've been more complaints. Some guys wanting to set up a fiddle band tried to get a piece in and were told they'd have to place an advertisement.'

Daisy, not thinking, said, 'Don't worry, Shar, it'll be all right now. I had a really good chat with Jay over dinner last night and he ...'

'Over dinner?'

'Yeah, he came to fetch me from Kelso 'cos I got stuck in the snow and we got stranded.' She giggled. 'We ended up sharing a room, it was so funny ...'

Sharon stopped dead. 'You shared a room with Jay Bond?'

Daisy, still giggling at the memory of pulling her jeans on under the bedclothes in case Jay came out the bathroom before she'd got them on, looked at Sharon, saw her face, and came to an abrupt halt.

'It wasn't anything, Sharon. Honestly. It –'

'Fucking hell, Daisy Irvine, you know how I feel about Jay. I *told* you. And yet just a few days later you go and try to steal him from me. "Wasn't anything"? Christ! The oldest excuse in the book. "It didn't mean anything". Do you think I came up the Clyde in a banana boat? Dinner for two, sharing a *room* for God's sake! What a bitch you are, Daisy.'

'I didn't ... we didn't ... It wasn't like that.'

'No? So what was it like? You shared as room with Jay Bond and you just *looked the other way*? Christ Almighty, Daisy, you expect me to believe that?'

Daisy frowned. 'Just because you wouldn't, Sharon, you've no right to think everyone else is the same as you.'

'Fucking *preaching* now are you? What a sodding hypocrite

you are.'

Sharon's face was contorted with anger, the clear green eyes were blazing, her usual prettiness turned ugly by seething emotion.

'Listen, Sharon, nothing happened. Honestly. Anyway, he's still in love with his wife. He told me so.'

Designed to take the edge off Sharon's anger, her words had exactly the opposite effect. Sharon started towards Daisy as if she was going to attack her, then she stopped short, opened her bag, rummaged inside, and pulled something out.

'Well fuck you, Daisy Irvine. I *trusted* you. I fucking *trusted* you!'

She was holding the object high in the air, her fist tight round it, she was shaking it around. Daisy, looking upwards to see what she had in her hand, caught a glimpse of it a second before she threw it into the river.

'Noooo!' The scream wrenched out of her in a long, high-pitched wail that sounded unlike her own voice.

The object was Tiny Ted. Her beloved bear. Her comfort bear from the days of her childhood. The bear she kept in her pocket, whose presence soothed her and calmed her. The bear that had protected her from her father's wrath for as long as she could remember. Her amulet, her talisman, her good luck charm. Carelessly, she'd left him in the office – and Sharon had obviously spotted an opportunity to wreak revenge. So now all she could do was watch helplessly as he arced high into the air and fell with barely a splash into the fast-flowing waters of the Hailes far below them.

Daisy stared at Sharon, too shocked to speak. Even through the reporter's fury, the horror on Daisy's face seemed to register.

'Well,' she muttered defiantly, snapping her handbag shut and slinging it back across her shoulder, 'you can't fucking blame me.'

There was no time for recriminations, no time for tears. Daisy simply turned and sped off the bridge and down to the path by the river bank. Tiny Ted. She had to find him. She simply *had* to. Running along the path, she scanned the waters for signs of her precious bear. He was nowhere to be seen. A mile. Over the stile that marked the end of the tarmac, where the path turned onto the edge of the fields. Nothing. Stopping every few yards to scan the water, Daisy stumbled on. Tears were coming now, streaming down her face, blurring her vision. She dashed them away with the back of her hand, ran on.

After twenty minutes, she had to admit defeat. Tiny Ted was gone. It was crazy, but her heart ached for her little bear. There had never been a time in her life when she couldn't remember having Tiny Ted near her. She could almost feel his little nose under her finger now, sense the softness of his fur. Except that her pocket was empty. An essential part of her life had gone. Simply vanished – and all over nothing.

When she finally got back to the office a couple of hours later, still trembling, a paper bag lay on her desk. Dumping her camera bleakly on the table, she twisted it open. A small golden bear nestled inside. She glanced over to Sharon's desk, but the chief reporter was obviously out on another story. Daisy shoved the bag into a drawer in her desk and closed it. The bear was worthless. Nothing could make up for the loss of TT. Except Jack perhaps. More than anything, she longed to feel Jack's arms around her. He'd understand. He knew how she felt about Tiny Ted. Only Jack could help to make up for this loss. Mechanically, she downloaded the images from yesterday and from this morning's shoot. Ben, passing behind her desk as she brought the snow pictures up on screen, stopped.

'That's good.'

She glanced round, her eyes red and the lids heavy. 'Thanks.'

Was it? Yesterday she'd felt perhaps she was capturing something special, but now she wasn't sure she could make a clear judgement. Nothing seemed to matter to her any more. Maybe they were good. She hadn't taken pictures like this in a long time.

'No, I mean really good, Daisy. Fabulous.'

She brought up another image. Looking back the way she'd struggled up the hill. In the distance, behind the wall she'd stumbled over, she could see her car, its back end in the air, half smothered by snow. It was a scene of utter desolation.

'Perfect,' Ben said approvingly. 'I'll put it on the front page.'

'Really?' His praise distracted her momentarily.

'And Dais – '

'Yeah?' She swivelled round to look at him.

'You should have an exhibition sometime you know. Show these.' He waved at the screen. 'Work on some others. You've got real talent.'

'Do you think so? Thanks, Ben.' His unexpected words brought a small feeling of warmth into one corner of a very chilled heart.

Daisy's mobile trilled. She picked it up and Sharon's voice hissed in her ear. 'Dais?'

'What?'

'I'm in the car park. Can you come out?'

'Why?' She was suspicious. What else could Sharon do to her now? She'd hurt her to the core already.

'Please?' Sharon sounded agitated.

'You destroy the one thing that really mattered to me and now you …'

'Please, Dais. I need to talk.'

Reluctantly, Daisy pulled on her jacket. Sharon was standing out of the chill wind in the far corner of the car park, next to the recycling bins. She was drawing heavily at a cigarette. Daisy saw the smoke first, Sharon's blonde head a second later, and finally, the bright pink of her jacket.

'Hi.'

'Hi.' She stared at Sharon curiously. Her face was streaked with tears and her hands were trembling. 'You OK?'

'You didn't sleep with Jay, did you, Daisy?'

Daisy shook her head. 'No. I told you.'

'Fuck. Listen, I'm sorry. Honest. I should've believed you. I

113

was just *mad*. You know, that you'd spent all that time with him when I've been fantasising about it for ages.' The cigarette glowed red again. 'I lied about him, Daisy. He never was all over me. I just wanted him to be. And when you told me … I thought. Shit.' She tossed the stub away and fumbled for the packet in her bag so that she could find another cigarette. 'I'm pissed off, Daisy, that's the truth of it. His wife you say? He's still in love with his wife?'

Daisy nodded. 'Amelia. Yes. That's what he said.'

'Shit. I can't believe it. The first guy worth making a play for in Hailesbank for years and he's still fucking hung up on his wife.'

'Sorry.'

She looked up at Daisy and flashed an apologetic smile. 'No I'm the one who's sorry. I know how much you loved that fucking bear, Daisy. I shouldn't have thrown it in the river.'

This time she stamped the cigarette out under her heel, grinding it to and fro on the tarmac.

'I am sorry. Really.'

She buried her face briefly in her hands then rubbed it roughly with her sleeves. A smudged streak of mascara betrayed her earlier tears, but Daisy didn't have the heart to tell her about it.

Tiny Ted. Gone. She still couldn't believe it. This must be how people felt when a favourite dog died. She remembered Cosmo last year when one of his labs had pegged it. He'd been inconsolable, wandering around town with a face so long you could trip over it. She should still be furious with Sharon. Throwing TT in the river had been an act of pure malice – but looking at Sharon's face, still twisted with emotion, Daisy couldn't help but feel sorry for her. In all the years she'd known her, Sharon Eddy had never managed to settle into the kind of loving relationship she'd had with Jack. Despite her sexiness, she'd always flitted from one man to another. Daisy had always thought she was simply sexually voracious, but another explanation occurred to her. Was Sharon Eddy just lonely, hungry for love?

Impulsively, she reached forward and hugged her. 'It's OK,' she said. She could feel Sharon's body trembling and for the first time in all the years she had known her, she felt as if she were the stronger person.

In the afternoon Jay called a staff meeting. They were all present, clustered round the water cooler, notepads and pens at the ready.

'Right.' Jay began, his voice very firm, his arms crossed defensively.

What was coming? Nervously, they looked at each other, each surreptitiously trying to gauge the feelings of the others.

'I have three things to say. First, I have only ever had the interests of the *Herald* at heart. Second, I knew nothing about the threat of closure that I believe has been made. And third ...' He glanced around them all, engaging each with his glance before moving on to the next. Then he reached his arms out in front of him, spread his hands wide in broad appeal and said, 'third, I'd like to ask if we could start again. As a team this time. If you're willing.'

'Christ,' Murdoch muttered.

'Holy shit,' Dave hissed.

Sharon gave a small moan.

Ben, sitting passively at the back, lifted one reddish-brown eyebrow and Ma Ruby, in a cloud of Givenchy and hair spray, burst into tears.

The plan they agreed on was simple. The clubs and societies would be reinstated immediately. Sir Cosmo would not only keep supplying the horoscopes, they would add a photograph of him, and Sharon would write a full feature of the local toff with a gift for astrology. To get more local faces in, they would do a 'personality of the week' – any age, any gender, any walk of life – and they'd talk to all the schools in the area about sponsoring a special social responsibility prize. 'Maybe something for the team who come up with the best ideas for reducing their carbon footprint?' suggested Sharon. 'Or recycling?' came from Murdoch. 'Or charity venture?' – Ma Ruby. The competition could run for a few weeks so that they could up the interest, week on week.

They discussed the work Sharon had been doing on the investigative side. Clearly, they didn't have enough resource for proper investigative journalism, but Sharon had news. 'I might be on to something with Provost Porter.'

'Really? What?' Murdoch was agog.

'Can't say yet. But let's say Fat Doris won't be too pleased if I'm right.'

'No!'

'Christ! He's not screwing around?'

'Who'd have him? Yeugh.'

Sharon looked important and pursed her lips. 'I'm saying nothing. But if I'm right, we might have a great story sometime soon.'

'That'll sell papers,' said Murdoch, rubbing his hands at the thought of it. Provost Porter, for all he had been re-elected, had his party sewn up, but was not generally popular in Hailesbank. No one quite understood the hold he had on his people, but Daisy suspected that even some of his own might rejoice in his downfall.

'So we're all agreed? Chantelle –' Jay turned to the head of the advertising team '– will you be able to get the advertising back up, do you think?'

Chantelle, a sharp-faced, lank-haired bony woman who'd been at the paper for years, shrugged. 'I'll try, of course. Might need to get an issue out first, give everyone a taste for the new *Herald*. Make it a corker, can you?'

'Good issues 'r us. Corkers take a little longer.'

'We'll see what we can do.'

'OK, team?'

'OK,' they chorused, grinning.

For the first time since Jay Bond had arrived, they felt inspired to work with him for the benefit of the paper.

Chapter Seventeen

Ben, happily crushed close to Daisy by the crowd, watched her crooning out the words the band was singing, swaying to the seductive beat of the music, her arms above her head, waving in time with the rest of the concert goers.

He wasn't really listening to the lyrics. Something about school … ?

School. The smile on his face grew even wider. Daisy Irvine as a schoolgirl had been the bonniest thing that walked the planet, so far as he could remember. You didn't see it, of course, when you grew up with someone. He'd been – what – seventeen when the hormones had kicked in and he'd realised that his fourteen-year-old companion had something to recommend her other than her ability to hopscotch across a burn on wobbly stones without falling in.

Blue spotlights arced across the skies then swept over the crowds. Daisy was momentarily bathed in the rich deep colour. He saw her like a blue angel, her dark hair bouncing round her face, sapphire glinting in every strand. Her eyes, usually so strikingly pale and grey, seemed to absorb all the colour of the beam and assumed for a few seconds the hue of velvet, rich and sumptuous. She looked brilliant. He put his arms around her and hugged her close. For a moment she melted happily into his embrace, then pulled away and continued to dance, in the dark again, one among thousands.

'Enjoying it?' she shouted at him, the whites of her eyes and the gleam of her teeth the most visible part of her as the song died and the *X Factor* runner-up segued into the final part of the concert.

He nodded and grinned. Enjoying it? The music was good,

yes, but being here with Daisy, so comfortably, so happily together – yes he was enjoying it. And the rest.

'*You know I love you ...*'

Love? Hard one, that. He'd loved Martina, or he thought he had. But it had faded, over time, among all the pressures of life. She'd changed. People changed. Why would it be any different with Daisy, if he could ever move this relationship on?

Love. Yes. 'Whatever love means.' Who'd said that? Of course. Prince Charles. Famously, on getting engaged to Diana Spencer. What an odd thing to say. It had jarred at the time and had come back to haunt him. But he'd been right, in a way. Love was many things to many people, something quite different, no doubt, to a prince of the realm. He was no prince, though, and Daisy no princess.

The band struck its last chord, the cheers were deafening, the calls for encore even louder. Ben put his hand under Daisy's elbow and began to steer her towards the exit.

'Must we go?' He could sense, rather than hear the words.

He nodded. They had to make their way back to Queen Street Station in time for the last train so it was essential to beat the crowds out of the stadium.

'Pure, dead brilliant,' Daisy muttered sleepily as Ben's car hiccupped cheerfully along the road from Edinburgh station back towards Hailesbank.

'My ears are still humming.'

'Pardon?' She peered at him through the darkness. 'I didn't hear you, my ears have gone a bit deaf.'

Ben laughed and steered the car onto the city bypass. Soon they were speeding along the empty road. They'd be home in twenty minutes at this rate. Would she ask him in? Could he kiss her tonight? Much as he longed to, the transition from work-mate to lover was not an easy one.

'Fancy a coffee?'

'Sure. Quick one. Thanks.' Quick? He hoped not. It just sounded polite. Late though it was, inside the cottage the lights were still ablaze and he could hear music. They stepped straight into the kitchen.

'Have a seat.' She pulled a chair out from the table, folded a newspaper that had been left open, tidied a pile of paperwork and moved some dirty plates across to the sink. 'Coffee? Tea? Glass of wine? Whisky? I think we've got some whisky,' she opened a cupboard and peered into it hopefully.

'Tea would be good. A large mug with milk and lots of sugar. Thanks.' God, she looked delicious from behind. She'd lost weight recently. When he'd first seen her, at Angus MacMorrow's funeral, she'd looked a bit on the dumpy side. Not that he'd minded, but she did look better without the love handles. She'd ditched the baggy sweaters too. Her jeans fitted in all the right places.

'Let's go and sit in front of the fire. I think Lizzie's still up.'

He felt a surge of disappointment. He wanted Daisy Irvine all to himself. But he rose obediently, mug in hand, and followed her into a small room where a fire flickered feebly in a black grate. He had the impression of red walls and richly swathed curtains and big comfy chairs before he saw that there was indeed someone lying across one of the chairs. He saw long legs draped across a plump, overstuffed arm and a pale hand trailing near the floor, then a cascade of light brown hair.

'Lizzie, this is … Oh. I think she's asleep.'

'Perhaps we should sit in the kitchen.' Ben started to retreat.

The body moved luxuriously, a log collapsed in the grate, and a pair of hazel eyes opened.

'Hi.' Lizzie swung her legs off the arm of the chair and stood up in one easy, graceful movement.

'I've brought Ben in for a cuppa,' Daisy said. 'You know Ben?'

'Hi,' Lizzie said again and held out her hand.

Ben shook it and smiled. Despite wanting to be alone with Daisy, he couldn't deny that this was one attractive woman.

'I'll cheer the fire up a bit.' She swung round, crouched down in front of the embers, poked, prodded, added some small kindling and a few coals, and watched as the fire leapt into life.

'Would you like some tea, Lizzie? There's some still in the

pot.'

'Thanks. Yes please.'

Ben, seated in a low chair next to the fire, felt the warmth of the flames against his legs.

'Good concert?'

'Brilliant.'

'Daisy enjoy it?'

'What do you think?'

Lizzie's gaze washed over him lazily. This girl is luscious, Ben thought appreciatively, taking in the fine oval face, the generously curved lips, the sheer self-confidence with which she was looking at him. Without even trying, she was reeling him in with a brand of sexuality he hadn't come across in a long time – and most attractive of all, she appeared to be completely unconscious of it. As he looked at the softness of her mouth, the lips curled upwards at the ends, lifting into the prettiest of smiles. 'I'm sure she did. I think going to the concert with you was probably the best things she's done in a long time.'

'Best thing who's done in a long time?' Daisy asked, re-entering the room with a mug for Lizzie.

'You, sweetie,' Lizzie smiled up at Daisy's face. 'I've been telling you for ages that you need to get out more and now you have.'

'I'd go out every night if every night could be like that.' Daisy settled herself down next to Ben. 'Wasn't it fantastic, Ben?' she appealed to him.

'Fantastic,' he agreed, feeling the warmth of her thigh close to his and trying to ignore the effect it was having on him.

'How's the challenge coming along?'

'Challenge?'

Lizzie's brain had clearly jumped to another place and he hadn't followed her.

'The paper. Can you save it? Daisy told me about the meeting.'

'Ah, the paper.' He considered the matter for a second. Switching into professional mode wasn't easy while he was sitting in this richly seductive room. 'Yeah, that is a challenge.'

'Don't talk about it,' Daisy groaned, 'you'll spoil my evening. I'll only get stressed.'

Lizzie swung her feet to the floor and stood up in one fluid movement. She lifted her mug and took a couple of steps towards the door. 'Sorry. Listen, I'm knackered, I'm off to bed. You two love birds need to be alone anyway.'

'No, it's OK, don't go,' Daisy protested.

'Night night, sweetie,' Lizzie blew her a kiss from the doorway. 'Nice to meet you, Ben.' She closed the door behind her, taking her sensuality with her.

'Gorgeous, isn't she?' Daisy said.

'Who?'

'Lizzie, of course. She can't help it. All the guys fall under her spell.'

'Not me,' Ben said, meaning it. You could appreciate a fine work of art without wanting to possess it.

Daisy said nothing, she just stared into the fire.

Ben closed his eyes. Outside, an owl hooted softly in the still of the night. The snows of earlier in the week had vanished and the temperature had risen perceptibly, but he was still grateful for the warmth of the fire. Inside the room, the only sound was the soft cracking of a log as it burned. Daisy was still sitting very close to him on the small sofa. Encouraged, he lifted his arm and put it round her shoulder, pulling her even closer. Her head dropped onto his shoulder and he could smell the fragrance of her hair.

'Thanks for coming with me, Ben,' she mumbled drowsily. 'I had a great time.'

'The pleasure was all mine,' he said, resting his cheek on top of her head. He'd make a move soon. Turn her towards her. Lift her chin so that he could see right into those eyes. Kiss her gently, take his time. He was looking forward to it, treasuring the moment. No need to rush. She was within his grasp now. He could see the soft rise and fall of her breasts and longed to reach his hand forward and cup one, feel its soft warmth, steal under the thin fabric of the T-shirt and stroke the smooth skin until the nipple stood erect. He would trace the dark valley between her breasts with his fingers. Take his time. They had all night.

'You two love birds.' Daisy giggled and sat up, swinging round towards him out of his embrace. 'That's funny,' she said. She swung herself off the sofa and threw another log on the fire, then poked it and nurtured in back into flames. 'Do you remember that time we snogged, Ben? Under the old railway bridge? Then that man came along with his dog.'

Shocked out of his fantasy, Ben could feel his jaw tighten with disappointment. She didn't come back to the sofa, but sat on the floor, her back to the overstuffed chair where Lizzie had been lying. She reached out for her tea, rested the mug on her knees, studied him, the firelight playing on one cheek, throwing her small nose into sharp relief.

'What a laugh. You know,' she sipped her tea thoughtfully, 'I'm really quite glad he did come by. I mean, it was great fun, but I'd've hated to lose you as a friend and if we'd got it together, I probably would have.'

Ben didn't respond. Fuck, he thought, looking at her. Fuck, fuck, fuck. She didn't think of him the same way he thought of her. How had he misjudged it so badly? How had he allowed himself to think of tonight as a beginning?

'D'you know,' she was still prattling on, 'that was my first kiss?' She laughed. 'I really liked it, Ben. You were a great kisser. I didn't realise how good you were, of course, till a few other boys had tried it on.' She grinned brightly at him. 'In fact, till I met Jack, you were definitely the best.'

She had plunged in the knife and now she was twisting it. He felt pain. Actual pain. It surprised him. He hadn't thought he was this keen on her. Or maybe it was just his pride that was wounded. Was he smiling? He hoped so. His mouth felt as if he was smiling, but all sensation was fading fast. He wouldn't be feeling any kisses tonight, that was now obvious.

'Jack's going to come back to me, Ben.'

'Yeah?' He managed to get a word out.

She nodded. 'I'm sure of it. I've been seeing him a lot, you know.'

'Have you?'

'Yup. Down at the gym. Iris doesn't go there so I get him all to myself. He's been so supportive. About the paper, I mean. And he's helped me in the gym too. He's just like he used to be, before that woman got her claws into him.'

'Has he said anything?'

She shook her head, almost imperceptibly. 'Not as such. He doesn't need to. But I can tell. He sometimes uses his old pet name for me, it's just like the old times.'

'What about Iris?'

She shook her head dismissively. 'He can't love her. Not in the way he loved me. In the way I think he still loves me. He *can't*. We had such a huge thing going. Earth shattering. Monumental.'

'Daisy ...' Ben's heart was twisting within him. She was making a terrible mistake here. Couldn't she see it? 'Don't you think that maybe he's moved on?' he asked gently.

Daisy stared at him. 'Moved on? Maybe, for a while. But he's regretting it. I know he is. We were made to be together. Daisy and Jack.' She rolled the words round her mouth. 'Jack and Daisy. Sounds right, don't you think?'

Ben stood up. His legs felt like lead, but he had to leave. He had to get out of here. He felt sick with disappointment. What a fool. He'd come through the door a mere hour ago so full of expectation and hope. And now he was leaving, weighed down by self-pity and helplessness.

Daisy uncurled herself and stood up. 'You're very special to me, Ben. We'll always be friends, won't we?'

Friends? No actually, that wasn't what he wanted. He moved to the door. 'Good night, Daisy. I'll see myself out.'

'Night, Ben. See you Monday.'

Monday. In the office. Right.

Ben sat in his dented, rusty bucket-heap of a car and watched the lights go out in the cottage, one by one. The euphoria he'd felt during the evening had evaporated and he felt tired to the bone. She was so wrong about Jack Hedderwick. She was fooling herself. But why? What kept drawing her back to this

123

guy? Why look back into a past that hadn't worked when there was a whole world to look forward into. A world with other men, guys who were solid and caring and who wouldn't let her down. Like him, for example.

Sod it. Maybe it was time to move on somewhere else. He'd put out some feelers for work in Edinburgh, for starters. He turned the key in the ignition. The engine tried to start, but simply wheezed and died. Damn. He gave it a moment, then tried again. Nothing. Feeling for the headlight switch in the darkness with his fingers, he realised that he must have left the lights on when he'd gone inside with Daisy. He'd been so excited that he'd forgotten to check – and there was nothing as sophisticated as an alarm to remind you, not on this old bone-shaker. The battery was flat. Shit.

Tired, irritated and generally pissed off, Ben clambered out of the car and kicked the door shut behind him. He had two options – knock on the cottage door and ask Daisy for some floor space for the night, or walk home, five miles in pitch darkness. Well, he liked walking, didn't he? Turning, he hunched his shoulders, set his head down to check where he was putting his feet, and started on the long road home.

Chapter Eighteen

Daisy saw Ben's car outside the cottage when she left to go into Hailesbank. Strange. She walked around it a couple of times, puzzling, then gave up and got into her own car. She'd call him later. It was well after midday already and she'd promised her mother she'd be at the house by twelve thirty for lunch. As usual, she was dreading it. For a start, her mother would try to feed her pudding. It remained to be seen whether she'd be able to resist it, though she'd got a lot better in the willpower stakes recently. She was almost back at the weight she'd been when she'd started seeing Jack all those years ago.

All thoughts of Ben were banished as she turned the ignition and began to reverse into the lane. If she was honest, her reluctance to visit the home of her childhood went much deeper than the bottom of a pudding bowl.

She was still scared of her father. Eric Irvine. Policeman, father, charmer, bully, good man, bad man, golfer, chief. She'd substituted her own words years ago for the traditional 'Tinker, tailor' rhyme and chanted them in her head any time she had cherry stones, prune stones, fish bones – or anything you left at the side of your plate. There had to be one or two or three or five, but never four or six or it was a bad omen. 'Policeman' was neutral, so were 'golfer' and 'chief'. She had her own definitions for 'father' and she didn't share them with anybody. If you got 'bully' or 'bad man' it meant you were going to be in trouble.

Down the road Ben Gillies was trudging back to Daisy Irvine's cottage with a set of jump leads. He didn't see her at the wheel of her Suzuki, even though she had to slow down at the sharp bend – because as it happened, a lorry coming in the other direction obscured her completely. As he walked the last mile down the road, Ben rehearsed in his mind how he would greet her. Brotherly, he supposed. He'd always been a kind of a brother to her. It had been naïve of him to think she might feel the same way he did, just because he wanted to move on from there. She'd never given him any sign of it. Wishful thinking. Set it aside. Still, that wasn't going to be easy.

Round the final bend, he stopped. The cottage Daisy shared with Lizzie Little really was charming. A shepherd's cottage originally, he guessed. Behind the cottage lay fields, all the way to the hills, in front – the way he'd just walked – more countryside. Could he feel happy here? He thought of his cramped flat in London. There was no comparison.

He crossed the grassy patch in front of the cottage and knocked. There was a pause, then he heard a call from inside, 'Coming.' Not Daisy's voice. Lizzie's.

'Hi again.'

'Hi you.' The door swung open and she smiled at him. She had swept her hair up into some sort of twisted arrangement at the back. It fanned out in loose spikes behind her head. A couple of tendrils had escaped imprisonment and fell softly to the long, graceful arc of her neck. Jesus. He couldn't be the first man who'd wanted to touch the spot where it nestled against her skin.

'Daisy's not here. Sorry. Are you coming in?'

'Oh. Right.' He stood on the threshold, hesitating.

'It's cold with the door open.'

'Sorry.' A few minutes couldn't hurt. He stepped into the kitchen.

'What's that?' Lizzie indicated his carrier bag.

'Jump leads. My car wouldn't start last night. I was hoping I could connect them to Daisy's car and get some life back into the battery.'

'She's taken her car. She's gone off to her folks' for lunch. Reluctantly, I have to say.'

Lizzie was looking at him curiously. He became oddly

aware of her freshness. She was wearing what seemed to be a man's shirt, the sleeves rolled up to her elbows, the collar turned up so that it framed the curve of her neck. A pendant hung down to the valley between her breasts. He followed the shape of it. A small red stone, then a silver hoop. Some small red stones – garnets? – suspended by fragile chains. They dragged on her skin as she moved, then released and swung. It was hypnotic. He felt himself growing warm and drowsy, a slave to the gentle movement of the pendant.

'So you had to walk home last night?' She laughed, a rich, full, warm sound. 'Why didn't you come back in here? I'd have thought you two would be tucked up in bed anyway.'

Ben grunted. 'Didn't happen.'

She put her hands on her hips and studied him. 'None of my business, I know, but you're so right for Daisy, I was hoping you would get it together.'

'That makes two of us. But she's got another man in mind, it seems.'

Lizzie groaned. 'I know. She's still harking after Jack Hedderwick.'

'You don't think he's going to go back to her?'

Lizzie shook her head. 'Not a hope. If Daisy wasn't so obsessed she'd know that herself.'

Ben thought, *I've been a complete idiot.* For the last few weeks he'd thought of little else but Daisy Irvine. He'd gone to sleep seeing the storm-grey eyes with their flecks of gold, longing to feel the soft warmth of her body cradled next to his. What a bloody fool.

He thumped his fist on the doorpost in a sudden blast of anger. 'Is there something wrong with me?'

'What d'you mean?'

'I know my hair is verging on red. I know that's not everyone's cup of tea. But I'm pretty fit, I shower daily, I don't bite my nails, I'm kind to dogs and old ladies. And I'm not invisible. Am I?' He turned to her, his voice insistent. 'Am I? Because just recently, I've bloody well *felt* invisible.'

Lizzie laughed and laid a hand on his arm. 'No Ben,' she

said. 'I would have to say, you're very visible to me.'

Her eyes were the colour of sagebrush after rain, her lips looked soft and welcoming. He watched as they parted slightly. There was a glimpse of even, creamy teeth and she had moved so close to him that he could feel the warmth of her breath. She wasn't Daisy – but Daisy's indifference had hurt. And here, an inch from his grasp, was the sweetest balm to the sore. So then, somehow, he was kissing her, a gentle, inquiring, tentative kiss that nuzzled her top lip and moved on to the lower before settling somewhere in the middle. And she was in his arms and her hands were on his bum, pulling him close to her with an urgency that he had no will to resist. His hands were all over her, pulling aside the shirt, feeling the softness of the swelling of her breasts. Her back was against the kitchen wall, one leg was curled round his back, her groin was arcing towards his, and his kisses had moved from her mouth down her neck and were reaching greedily for her nipple.

'Wait! Ben.'

He eased away, his breath coming fast and ragged.

'We can get more comfortable.' She smiled at him, pulled her shirt back into place and reached for his hand. 'Come.'

At the door of her room, he stopped. 'I don't know about this.'

She didn't ask about his doubts. She didn't need to. Instead, she swung him round to look at her. 'Daisy is my best friend, Ben. I wouldn't hurt her. But she doesn't want you. At least,' she qualified her statement, 'not yet. I think she might, given time. She hooked her hands behind his waist and pulled him closer. 'But she has to make her own mistakes, decide what it is that she wants from life. If it's you ... well, perhaps she'll realise she's missing out on something if she sees you with someone else. Who knows? But until she gets herself sorted out, there's no reason you can't have a bit of fun, wouldn't you agree?

'And ...' she pulled his head down towards hers and cradled his face in her hands, 'let someone prove to you that you are ...' she kissed him on the mouth, '... very ...' kiss, '... very ...'

kiss, '… attractive.'

There didn't seem a lot to say. Ben lifted one finger and gently pushed aside the shirt. Underneath, she was naked. Abandoning all sense, he scooped her up in his arms and carried her in three easy strides across to the bed.

Afterwards, he propped himself on one elbow and studied her as she lay beside him, naked in the sunshine that streamed in through her window. He trailed his hand along the length of her body, enjoying the curves, loving the way she wriggled and inhaled when his hand touched her most intimate parts.

'You're amazing.'

'So I'm told.'

Her hair had come loose from its anchor at some point in their embracing. It lay round her shoulders, spread out across the pillow like dark straw in autumn.

She said, 'Ben.' One word that presaged a statement.

'Lizzie.'

'I don't do relationships. Not just now, at least.'

'Meaning?'

'I'm not into commitment. I like men. I like men who make love well and know when to be gentle, when to be rough. I like men who kiss nicely and don't start obsessing about me.'

'Is there a reason for that?'

Her mouth twitched into a smile. 'The usual. I was hurt. Jilted, actually. I had even made my wedding dress. Love's young dream … I cried for a year and told myself all men were bastards and I would never lose control of my feelings in that way again. I would see men, but on my terms. I wanted to be in control.'

'That's very sad, Lizzie.'

She shook her head. 'No. For a long time I was angry. I screwed men like they had to pay for Ritchie's faults. I like sex. I've always liked sex. I just don't like having to give up my independence to get it.'

'Surely no decent man would ask you to give up your independence? Even if you were in a relationship.'

'You'd be astonished. Anyway, I'm not angry any more. And I guess maybe one day I will find a man I'd like to spend a long time with. But not yet.' She laughed. Again, the rich, full laugh. 'I just thought I should tell you now. I don't want a partner. I don't want a husband. I'm very happy to find a friend I can enjoy great sex with. Until we're both ready to move on.' She studied him. 'Does that bother you?'

Ben rolled onto his back and stared at the ceiling. 'Will I see you again?'

'Do you want to?'

'Does the Pope speak in Latin?'

'No ties. No promises. No seeing other people while we see each other. And no tears when it's time to move on.'

'Suits me.'

And then she was straddling him, her long, thick hair falling round her face. 'Daisy's loss, Ben,' she whispered, 'is most definitely my gain.'

Chapter Nineteen

'Hello Daisy. You're late.' Her father, opening the front door to her, was characteristically critical.

Daisy took in his humour at a glance. She only needed the smallest signs to know if he was in one of his dark moods – the vein in his neck throbbing, his face a shade redder than usual. Whatever it was, she no longer let it get to her, consciously at least. After all, she had the option of walking out.

The greeting was curt but she spied his golf shoes under the hall stand. There were small blades of fresh grass visible from under the soles. He'd been out this morning, which was a good sign. Golfing usually lightened his mood – unless he'd had a really poor round.

'Good morning, Dad. Lovely to see you too.' She pecked him on the cheek cheerfully, determined not to be crushed. 'How was the golf?'

Eric, turning into the corridor that led along to the living room, grunted. 'Had a birdie at the third and the seventh, and three pars.'

Daisy knew enough about golf after years of listening to her father to understand that this was good. 'Great,' she smiled, 'Mum in the kitchen?'

There was another grunt. The atmosphere of the house settled round her now, muffling, stifling. Did she come here because of a sense of duty? Or did she still long for love? To please her mother or to try, despite everything, to win her father's approval for what she had achieved in life? Daisy stood at the threshold of the room, uncertain.

'Hello, Mum. Can I help?' Her voice wobbled a fraction.

Her mother wiped her hands on her apron, her face cracking

into a smile that put the light back into her eyes. 'Daisy, love,' she said.

Daisy need not have worried about being able to refuse pudding. She'd forgotten how her appetite dropped when she crossed the threshold of number five Laurel Lane. She escaped as soon as she could, fighting the feeling of disappointment she always had that things hadn't gone better with her father, and headed to the office. An hour's work would get her well ahead for the morning.

Christ. Ben. She'd been going to phone him. Something must have happened to him or why would he have left his car at the cottage? She pulled over and dialled his number. It rang out. She was just about to call off when a voice, light and melodious, said, 'Hello? Ben's phone?'

There was laughter, a shriek and a yelp, then Ben said, 'Hi. Who is this?'

'Ben? Was that Lizzie?' Daisy was puzzled.

'Oh Daisy. Hi. Hi.' Was he flustered? He sounded odd.

'Are you OK? Where are you? Are you with Lizzie?'

'Yeah. I'm at your cottage. I couldn't get my car started last night, so I came back with some jump leads. Lizzie's going to give me a hand in a minute. I should've called first, sorry, don't know why I assumed you'd be here.'

There was a whisper, a giggle, then another yelp. 'What's going on there?' Daisy smiled. 'You sound like you're having fun.'

'Fun? Yeah. I suppose. Lizzie's just horsing around. Listen Dais, were you phoning about something in particular?'

'What? Oh. No. I just wondered why your car was at the cottage. Now I know.'

'Fine. So I'll see you later then.'

'Tomorrow morning probably, at work.'

'Yeah. Great.'

'Right. I'm headed there now, for an hour. Tell Lizzie I'll be back by five.'

'Will do. Cheers.'

At the cottage, Lizzie and Ben stared at each other.

'We'll have to tell her. If we're going to carry on seeing each other.'

'No reason why not. She can hardly object.'

'No. No reason.' Ben, high on sex and laughter, didn't regret making love to Lizzie. Christ, she was one sexy lay. He pulled her close to him, closed his eyes, and showered her face with tiny kisses. But it was Daisy's eyes he was still seeing in his head. He hoped he hadn't closed that door for ever.

Daisy pulled up outside the offices of the *Herald* and turned off the engine. She felt oddly troubled. There was no reason Ben and Lizzie shouldn't be enjoying time together. After all, soon she would have Jack back. The more she saw of him at the gym, the more sure she was of that. She felt so comfortable with him again. It was just like they'd been in those first few years, before somehow – how? – their relationship had changed and begun to drift.

Even so…

'Right,' said Jay. 'What have we got for the front page this week?'

'Flooding in Yetholm,' said Murdoch. 'It's quite bad down there. There's a chance the old bridge might go.'

'Possible. Especially if it does go and we can't get Daisy down there in time.'

'There's the bullied soldier story,' ventured Dave.

'That's more tricky. No one's been able to produce any evidence yet.'

'I've got a story,' said Sharon.

'You've found Provost Porter with his hand in the till?'

'No, but he's having an affair.'

'You're kidding!'

'No way!'

'Who with, for heaven's sake?'

They all leaned forward, eager to hear the gossip.

'How do you know?'

The attention she was getting perked Sharon up. 'I've got a friend who works in The Black Horse down at Mains village. Couple of times a week there's a woman books in, name of Joyce Carlton. Comes around three o'clock, likes to work in her room, has dinner sent up. Quite often it's dinner for two.'

'Carlton?' Murdoch was pensive. 'Why do I know that name?'

'She runs a small company called Carlton Catering.' Sharon was well in her stride. She'd been doing her homework and had everyone's attention. The drawn look she'd had for the past couple of weeks had gone and the old animated Sharon was back. 'They have a unit down on the industrial estate?'

'Got it now.' Murdoch's bald head gleamed in the harsh light of the fluorescent tubes from above. 'Small place between the joinery works and the electrical supply shop.'

'Could be getting a lot bigger if Joyce Carlton's plan works,' said Sharon, the smugness back in her voice. 'There's a big catering contract up for grabs with the Council. Includes the local schools and all the Council properties.'

'Phew,' Murdoch whistled. 'And you reckon she's trying to influence the Provost?'

'She *is* influencing the Provost. Carlton Catering is on the short list for the final decision, which will be made later this week. And that's odd because you'd think they'd be too small to be in the running.'

'But surely that will go through procurement?'

Sharon nodded. 'Yes. But don't forget, the Provost's nephew is Head of Procurement.'

'Bloody hell,' Murdoch sat back, 'I had forgotten that. That's always been a tricky one, in my book. But Provost Porter has always insisted he's very hands-off.'

Sharon grinned broadly. 'Well he's having some very hands-on sessions with our Joyce. There's a back door into The Black Horse from the car park. The Provost's private car has been seen regularly in the car park, but no one's ever seen him in the hotel. He must sneak in and go straight up to her room.'

'Jeez.'

'That's a serious allegation to make, Sharon.' Jay was concentrating hard. Ever since he'd apologised to the team and pulled everyone together to try to improve sales and circulation, he'd been working overtime to try to turn things round. 'You'd have to have some hard evidence –' Dave sniggered in the background and Jay glared at him, '– some hard evidence of what you are alleging before we could publish anything. We can't land ourselves with a law suit.'

Sharon frowned. 'Yeah. I know. I'd like to get Daisy down there with me tomorrow. It's one of the days they often meet. For starters, we could get pictures of the cars, but you never know, we might get lucky and get something else.'

Daisy was dubious. 'I've never been one to stake people out, Sharon. Lurking behind bushes for the sleazy snap, that kind of thing.'

'Well maybe just this once that's what we'll have to do.' Sharon was short. She clearly felt she was onto a good story and wasn't about to let it go.

'A good scandal would send sales rocketing,' said Murdoch.

'Scandal certainly sells,' Jay said ruefully.

'The affair would be a good enough story on its own,' said Sharon determinedly. 'We could get the furious wronged wife angle too. But if we're careful, we can expose the affair and just mention that Carlton Catering is shortlisted for a contract without actually making any kind of allegation that there is a link.'

'Daisy?' Jay turned to her.

She sighed. 'OK. I'll give it a go.' It was a long way from an art-photograph exhibition, but it paid the bills.

'We need to try to get this story nailed this week if we can, before the contract decision is made. We could still expose it later, but there would be more impact right now.'

'Right. Thanks team.' Jay stood, signalling the end of the meeting. 'We'll get the flooding story in the bag for sure and use it on the front if this one's not a goer. OK?'

'OK.'

'Am I interrupting?' came a diffident voice as Sir Cosmo

Fleming poked his head round the door. 'Ruby said to go on in.'

'Not at all. You could be witnessing a great turning point. What do the stars say for us this week?'

Jay stood up and went over to shake his hand. He'd decided not only that they should retain the horoscopes, but also that Sir Cosmo was an influential local contact. And charm was something Jay Bond did very well when he chose to. Daisy smiled inwardly. Cosmo was such a sweetie, she'd have hated to see him given the chop.

Cosmo, who had been stealing covert glances in Sharon's direction, focused on Jay.

'You're Aquarius, aren't you? For you, the aspects are exceptionally good. You like to solve problems, rise to a challenge, bring fresh approaches but always have to seek balance.'

'Hey Cosmo, tell me mine.' Sharon, who was attending a business lunch later in the morning, was dressed to kill in a smart suit and high heels. Cosmo looked at her with such longing that Daisy almost laughed, but Sharon seemed blissfully unaware of his feelings.

'With Mars high in the sky, you are in fighting mood,' said Cosmo gravely, 'but Venus is rising. You only have to look in the right place and you will find the love you seek.'

'Oo-er,' Dave whistled. 'Hey Shar, go on, look at me!'

'Piss off,' said Sharon.

Chapter Twenty

The car park at the Black Horse was quite full, but Daisy and Sharon had two pieces of luck. First, having checked Joyce Carlton's car registration with Sharon's friend on Reception, they discovered that on this occasion it was parked adjacent to the Lexus they knew belonged to Provost Archie Porter. And second, they managed to park Daisy's Suzuki, its bumper still dented from the nose dive into the ditch near Kelso, facing square on to the back façade of the building – and to the room that Joyce Carlton was in that night.

It was the only luck they'd had, thought Daisy miserably as she huddled down into her fleece, her camera on her knees at the ready. They'd been here two hours already and to her mind, there didn't seem any point in waiting any longer.

'We're never going to get anything,' she said to Sharon for at least the fourth time. 'I mean, Christ, the curtains are drawn. What could we possibly get, for heaven's sake?' Even if a miracle happened, she would have to shoot without a flash if she could, to avoid being caught.

'Dunno,' said Sharon curtly. 'We just have to hope for something.'

'Just seems a waste of time.'

Sharon sighed. 'Just shut it, Daisy, will you?'

Daisy's hand went to her pocket before she remembered that there was no Tiny Ted to stroke for comfort. It was so automatic a gesture that she still did it a dozen times a day and still had the same feeling of loss when she remembered he'd gone for ever.

'Well I just …'

'Shut … it.'

She clamped her mouth shut resignedly. A stake-out. She was sitting here doing a *stake-out* when she could have been at the gym or making plans for how to get Jack back. Then there was Ben and Lizzie. Last night, when she'd got home from work, Lizzie had poured her a large glass of wine and sat her down in the kitchen to tell her what she had already guessed – that she had started seeing Ben Gillies.

'You don't mind, do you, Dais?' Lizzie had the look of a woman who had recently enjoyed very exciting sex. A glow had settled around her. Her skin was looking peachy and her eyes sparked with life. 'Do you mind?' Lizzie asked again, 'because if you do I'll stop seeing him right now. But Ben said you'd made it clear you weren't interested.'

''Course I'm not interested. It's never occurred to me to date Ben. He's just a friend.' It was how she'd always thought of him – until she knew he'd fallen into bed with her best friend. Now she understood that it was possible to view Ben Gillies in a different light.

Sharon sat up straight. 'What's that?'

'What's what?'

'I thought I saw something at their window.'

'How? Nothing to see, Shar. Curtains.'

'They moved, I'm sure they did.'

'Perhaps fat Archie farted and she tried to open the window.'

Sharon laughed. 'You can be quite funny, Daisy. Anyway, whatever it was, it seems to have stopped. I can't see anything now.'

She couldn't see anything either. Curtains had closed in front of her and she couldn't see past them. Of *course* she still wanted to win Jack back. Whatever it took.

But she felt indefinably uneasy about Ben and Lizzie.

Sod it. She was chilly. 'Got any of that tea left?'

'Yeah. A bit.'

'Any chance of another cuppa?'

'Nope.'

'No? Why not? Don't be mean.'

'Sorry Daisy, it's too early. We could be here for hours. I

can't have you running off for a pee at the crucial moment and missing the money shot.'

Bugger. Daisy lapsed into a grumpy silence and moved her mind on to Jack – never a difficult thing to do. How was she going to move things on? He was really friendly now, but somehow she had to precipitate a crisis with Iris – surely that wouldn't take much doing? Or at the very least, she had to find a way to have a real conversation with him, the kind you couldn't have in the gym. A thought occurred to her. Thursday was the day of the cookery evening class. Jack had stopped going ages ago, he'd told her so, but Iris still went every week. Ideal. She'd buy a really good bottle of wine and go and knock on his door. Perfect.

'There!'

'Where? What?'

'Look! Get your fucking camera ready Daisy, for God's sake.'

Daisy fumbled on her lap, lifted her camera to her eye, watched as the curtain flipped back and a hand pushed the window open. A hand, followed by a naked arm.

'Told you. He farted.'

'Shhh. Just snap.'

She snapped. And snapped, and then snapped again as two very naked bodies very closely entwined came briefly into view before another arm flipped the curtain shut again.

'Did you get it? Jeez, Daisy, *did you get it?*'

Daisy's hands were shaking as she flipped the camera to Review and looked back at what she'd got. The hand and arm. The window position changing. And then, for four extremely clear frames, the heads, shoulders, two naked breasts and one bare and rather large belly. All with Provost Archie Porter's and Mrs Joyce Carlton's faces clearly visible. She stared at them numbly. Sharon whooped.

'You did it, Daisy. You fucking did it! Have we got a story! Hallelujah! Come on, let's get it to bed.' She switched on the ignition and slid the car out of the parking space. 'Way to go, Daisy. This could save the paper.'

139

'Provost in sleazy sex romp.'

The banner headline on the front page, accompanied by an image showing a hand, an arm and the two heads, ensured that *The Hailesbank Herald* sold out its first edition within a couple of hours of hitting the newsagents. Daisy had had to spend some time with Photoshop to dim and blur the naked bodies, as Jay – and the paper's lawyers – had deemed them too explicit to print on the front. They had the originals though, along with the ones of the two cars as further ammunition, stored on the office computer and on a CD lodged with the lawyer.

Sharon's story had been checked and rechecked and then checked again. It was cleared for publication. The sex scandal in itself was enough to sell the paper in thousands, but add it to the mention of 'Cookiegate' as they dubbed it, and a whole series of wheels were set in motion that ensured they could keep the pot bubbling for weeks to come. Jay had ordered a large run for the second edition before ten in the morning and, uniquely so far as anyone – even Ma Ruby – could remember, they printed a third edition before the end of the day.

The elated *Herald* staff regrouped in The Duke of Atholl at six.

'Here's tae us,' Murdoch lifted his glass.

'Wha's like us?' said Dave.

Daisy said, 'Cheers Angus MacMorrow, may your paper live for ever.'

They all clinked glasses.

'To us.'

The following Monday, Ruby was seen ushering in a distinguished looking visitor to Jay's office. Tall, grey-haired, and handsome in the kind of way that Jay was handsome, though much older. Smart navy coat. Good suit underneath it, with the whitest of cuffs just visible, secured by gleaming gold cuff links. Sharon lifted a questioning eyebrow at Murdoch, who shrugged. Daisy shook her head. She'd never seen him before.

'Who's that, Ruby?' Sharon hissed when the door closed

behind the man.

'Sir Oliver Wyndham, he said his name was. Posh, isn't he?'

'Why do I know that name?' Sharon wrinkled her nose.

'Because he's only the fucking Chairman of the Board of the Havering Group of Newspapers,' said Murdoch.

They all stared at each other. What did it mean? A visit from the Chairman? Could be good news or bad.

'*You will be only too aware of the falling circulation of* The Hailesbank Herald ... *concern* ... *unless the circulation and advertising figures are back to their previous levels* ... *forced to close* ... *obvious consequences* ...' There probably wasn't a person in the room who didn't have the words imprinted on their brain.

'He's Jay Bond's uncle,' Daisy said into the silence.

'Jeez.'

'Fucking hell, he isn't, is he?'

'How do you ...?'

'*Shhhh.*'

Jay's door was opening. The two men were emerging. Pretending to be busy at their computers, everyone was straining to gauge the expression on their faces. Daisy was the first to catch Jay's eye. Behind his uncle he looked at her and winked. Definitely winked. Was that a good sign or a bad one?

'Team,' he started, 'Gather round, will you?'

They mustered in the only place in the office that was big enough, round the water cooler.

'I'd like to introduce Sir Oliver Wyndham, Chairman of the Board of the Havering Group. It's the first time he's visited the paper, and I hope you'll all make him feel welcome. Sir Oliver – would you like to say a few words?'

Had Jay known he was coming today? He'd put a suit on. The two men not only looked alike, they were also dressed alike. Dark suits. White shirts. Striped ties – red on navy in Jay's case, gold on petrol for Sir Oliver. The old boy network, or nepotism? The world of business, anyway. That's what it all came down to. Not freedom of speech or upholding democracy or fighting for justice, which is how Daisy liked to think of

141

newspapers – simply making money. If you made it, you were a good proposition. If you lost money, you were history. A hundred and forty years the *Herald* had been in print, even keeping a skeleton paper running during two world wars – but could they survive now, in the digital age? Daisy could feel the office, collectively, holding its breath.

'... difficult times ... credit crunch ... inflation ... rise of the internet ... tablets ... standards ... competition ...' He'd been speaking for ten minutes and so far Sir Oliver hadn't said a single thing that had sounded remotely encouraging. '... and so at the beginning of the year we gave your dear editor, Mr MacMorrow, due notice.'

God, it sounded dire. Was this it then? It hadn't been anything like six months yet. It was early May. Angus got the letter in February. Surely the Board wouldn't let the axe fall already, just as they were beginning to pick up?

'Naturally, we've been monitoring the paper very closely ever since then. We put Jay here –' he indicated Jay, who was leaning elegantly on the table behind him, legs crossed at the ankles, arms folded, '– in charge. I admit to it being somewhat of an experiment and I have to be honest,' he turned and looked at Jay, 'we had our doubts in the first month or so about how things might go. But I'm pleased to say that we feel the paper has improved on three counts.' He held his hands out in front of him and counted on his fingers, 'One, the appearance of the newspaper. The design and layout have improved considerably.' Daisy glanced at Ben, who avoided her gaze. That was all down to him, she thought. 'Two, the quality of the reporting and the photography generally. Well done.' That was her! 'And three, there has been a noticeable upturn in the circulation – with last week, of course being quite exceptional.' He dropped his hands and smiled. 'I can't give any definitive judgement yet, of course. We said six months and it's unlikely we'll make a decision before that. But I can say we're pleased. Very pleased.'

The gaze that swept across them all had definitely warmed

as he concluded, 'It's looking promising. Keep up the good work.'

She wanted to celebrate with Lizzie, just as she would have done a few weeks ago. They'd have cracked open a bottle of bubbly, thrown some spaghetti in a pan, and tossed together a quick salad. All the makings of a great evening. They would have gossiped and chewed it all over, had a good go at Jay for being a posh git before affectionately allowing him some credit for turning the paper around. They'd have tried to match make for Ma Ruby and speculated about Dishy Dave's latest lay, but none of that would happen now, because tonight Ben was taking Lizzie to the cinema.

They would probably ask her to join them. 'Keep Daisy happy.' 'Don't upset Diz.' 'Friendship …' … blah, blah blah … But the last thing Daisy wanted to do was play gooseberry to Lizzie Little and Ben Gillies. They were still friends, but the fact was that she felt she could confide in neither of them and was less close to either than she ever had been. She felt – if she was being completely honest – rather lonely.

Chapter Twenty-one

'So I'm feeling a bit more cheerful,' Daisy said bravely to Jack on Wednesday.

It was only the teeniest lie. In many ways she was feeling rather good. For starters, even though she'd washed her jeans at the weekend (which usually made them a bit tighter for a day or two) she'd noticed that they were almost too loose. She was near having to drop a whole size. Physically, she felt very fit. She was sleeping well, eating well, and, even though she was feeling oddly unsettled about Ben and Lizzie, she had managed to avoid slipping backwards in terms of her healthy diet. Then there was the paper. Sir Oliver's slightly patronising pep talk had, in the circumstances, been encouraging. Though they couldn't be sure about things yet, there appeared to be light at the end of the tunnel. If they kept the figures up, surely – *surely* – they'd keep the *Herald* going. All she needed was to get Jack back and a rosy glow would be restored to her world.

'That's great, Daisy. Tell me, is there more to run on the Provost story? The whole town is agog.'

'There is,' she said, privately proud of her role in their achievements. They'd been working hard on it all week. She'd managed to get a great picture of Archie Porter, his head hidden under a coat, running to his car with a savage-looking Doris scowling three paces behind him, brandishing her umbrella at Daisy and her camera. Genius. Joyce Carlton's husband had approached the paper and said he was demanding a divorce and that he'd always found Archie Porter sleazy. Bald Jimmy Johnston – who was thrilled with the whole business – had been ferreting around in the depths of Procurement in the Council and had come up with a number of irregularities he was trying to lay at the door of the relationship between Porter and his nephew. He was effectively doing Sharon's work for her and removing the possible threat of a libel suit at the same time. 'But I can't say,' she said mysteriously to Jack. 'We haven't finished our legal checks yet and anyway, I don't want to spoil the excitement.'

'Spoilsport,' Jack grinned.

Daisy's heart pumped a little faster as she basked in the warmth of his smile. She loved the intimacy of these moments, just her and Jack and a cup of coffee. Talking, laughing, smiling, relaxed, just like it used to be.

'You still going to that cookery class?' she asked, knowing the answer. But she did want to double check whether Iris was still going.

He shook his head. He was sitting directly under a downlighter and his hair, fresh from the shower, fluffed up around his head like the fuzz on Easter chicks. Daisy longed to reach out and stroke it. Instead, she sat resolutely on her hands. *Not yet.*

'I stopped ages ago. I thought I'd told you?' One fair eyebrow arched neatly towards the fluff. 'Iris is still going though. Every Thursday, seven till nine and then usually a quick trip to the pub with a few of the others in the class.'

'Don't you mind?'

'Why should I mind? She always comes home with something tasty. Anyway, Iris and I have a pretty easygoing relationship. She likes to do her thing, I like to do mine.'

There. She was right. They didn't have much time for each other. The novelty had worn off, definitely. All she had to do was find a time and a place to get Jack on his own and show him how much she still loved him. The glint in his eyes as he looked at her now was enough to tell her he still cared.

He stood up, leaned forward for his bag, and kissed her cheek. 'Bye, kitten. Glad things are going well. You're looking terrific, by the way.'

'Bye, Jack.'

Terrific. He thought she looked terrific. She watched as he

146

crossed the room, his fluffy head like a beacon in the night, drawing her to his flame as inexorably as a moth is drawn to a candle. She touched her cheek where he had kissed her. The spot felt as though it was burning. She was quite literally glowing with pleasure at his compliment.

Ben, his arms cradling Lizzie, closed his eyes and thought about how much his life had changed in the last few weeks. He'd spent so much time dreaming about Daisy Irvine, and all for nothing because she hadn't been in the least bit interested. Then Lizzie Little had fallen right in his lap like a ripe peach, soft, strokeable, and utterly delicious.

It was too soon after Martina to start a new serious relationship. Anyway, independence was so much better. No rows. No lectures about underpants dropped on the bedroom floor or damp towels on the bathroom tiles. No nagging to wipe the kitchen surfaces. No need to justify himself about coming home late after a night out with the lads. With Lizzie, he had the best of all worlds.

And yet … Daisy Irvine … dear Diz …

In the kitchen, not ten yards from where Ben and Lizzie lay, Daisy was foraging in the fridge for supper. Fresh from the gym and Jack's compliments, she hummed happily as she rooted in the depths of the cluttered and rather disorganised, badly-lit space. The fridge light had blown weeks ago and neither she nor Lizzie ever remembered to get a new bulb.

There was a bowl with some baked beans in it, thickly crusted at the top. They looked inedible so she shoved them back inside. She took the lid off a small container and peered inside before recoiling hastily. Whatever that was had gone completely mouldy. Another container looked more promising. Tomato sauce? She sniffed it cautiously, then ventured a finger and a lick. It tasted good, rich and garlicky. Daisy hazarded a guess that it was only three or four days old. She set it on the table and continued her search. There was cheese – cheddar, and some parmesan in a small tub, ready grated. They were put

147

on the table too, along with the makings of a salad, which looked as though they'd be fine so long as she picked the brown bits off the lettuce. The cupboard yielded a tin of mince and spaghetti. She stood back and surveyed her findings. It all looked quite manageable. She'd do a quick ready, steady, cook and have it ready for Lizzie when she came in.

Then she remembered that Lizzie's car had been outside when she'd got back from the gym fifteen minutes ago. She'd just check that she wanted to eat tonight. Crossing to the door of Lizzie's bedroom, she knocked lightly and poked her head round the door.

'Hi Lizzie, you hungry yet ... oh!' Daisy leapt back in embarrassment. 'Sorry!' Hastily, she backed out, closing the door rapidly. In the dim light of a dozen candles, she'd seen the broad shoulders and slim, very naked, backside of a man curled up on the bed. Presumably round Lizzie. Presumably Ben. Her face aflame, she hurried back to the kitchen table and started peeling the dry flaky skin of the onion into the sink. Bugger, bugger, bugger. Ben Gillies. Her Ben.

No Daisy. Not your Ben, she reminded herself. She'd probably never enjoy lying on Ben's floor listening to Cream again. That was Lizzie's job now. Cream listener of choice. For a fleeting second, Daisy remembered how it had felt when Ben had kissed her under the railway bridge, then she reminded herself that that had been twelve years ago. What was going on in her head, for goodness sake? She couldn't be jealous of Lizzie, could she? That would be ridiculous. Lizzie was doing what she did best. She just happened to be doing it with someone Daisy was finding, to her great astonishment, she was rather fond of.

She started chopping her onions with great vigour. Chop, chop, chop. Her thick dark hair fell in front of her eyes and she used the back of her hand to scrape it back, with the sole effect of getting the juice from the onions in her eyes, which promptly started to stream with tears. She was not upset though. Why should she be upset? Ben wasn't the man for her, Jack was.

'Hi.'

A voice behind her made her jump. Ben had emerged from the bedroom and was standing just two feet away.

'Oh. Hi.' She kept her head down. She didn't want him to see the tears. He would think she was crying and she was not, she was *not*. It was just the onions.

'Can I help?'

She shook her head vigorously and kept chopping.

'Sure? I'm a good cook.'

'No. Thanks. Listen, it'll be ready in ten minutes.'

'Diz?' Ben's voice was very gentle, full of concern.

'Maybe nine minutes.'

'Are you OK?'

'Close to eight now. Just go and get ready, will you?' Her voice, to her own ears, sounded childishly petulant.

'Right.'

She heard him move and at last she was free to reach out her hand and grab a piece of kitchen roll so that she could blow her nose. She had a horrible feeling that the tears, which had definitely been started by the onion, were now all too real.

Chapter Twenty-two

The Provost Porter story ran for four whole weeks. Every week, the circulation of the paper rose. Daisy focused almost wholly on her job. Her visits to the gym were disappointingly intermittent – or at least, she didn't manage to keep up the routine that saw her workouts coincide with Jack's. She didn't stop going though. In fact, because Ben seemed to be spending more and more time at the cottage, she found the gym a convenient excuse for going out.

'That's a good picture, Dais.' Murdoch stopped behind her chair on his way to the kettle.

Daisy scanned the image on her monitor. She was just in from photographing two teenagers who had struggled with drugs, become interested in hip hop dancing thanks to the inspired efforts of a local youth worker, and had been picked to perform at the Edinburgh Fringe Festival in August.

'Front cover?' she suggested hopefully. The picture showed both boys high in the air, one performing a back flip. It was dynamic, full of motion and fun.

'Unless you get Porter mooning at your camera or Joyce Carlton with her tits out, I'd say it's got a chance.'

Daisy grinned. There was little hope of that. Even though both marriages appeared to have failed amid great acrimony, the adulterous couple appeared to have parted. As a serious positive outcome, furthermore, Carlton Catering had been ruled out of the Council contract, which had now been awarded to another company.

Sharon, talking into her phone with her spare hand over her ear to blot out their conversation, started flapping the spare hand in the air excitedly. Dropping the phone back onto the receiver, she swept a small pile of papers onto the floor, jumped onto her desk, and started dancing. The sight of her legs kicking and hopping on the desk made Murdoch reach for a shorthand notebook to fan himself.

'Ya beauty!' she shouted, a smile splitting her face.

'What?' Daisy demanded.

'Hey Shar, what are you on?' called Dave.

She pumped her fist in the air and crowed, 'Yesss! He's resigned!'

'Fucking hell.'

'Christ!'

'Porter? Really?'

Jay, emerging from his office at the commotion, was as delighted as the rest of them. 'Well done, team. Great result!' He shook hands, caught Sharon as she jumped down from her desk, hugged her, hugged Daisy, and even hugged Ma Ruby, who had abandoned her position in Reception and come in to see what all the noise was about. Then he disappeared and came back ten minutes later with half a dozen bottles of Cava and Sir Cosmo.

'Spot on, Cossers,' Murdoch thumped him on the back. 'You said Taurus's week would be "tumultuous and full of change".'

'Is Provost Porter a Taurean then?' Sir Cosmo, looking as rumpled as ever, his tousled hair windblown and a twig hanging from the sleeve of his rough tweed jacket, was shyly pleased.

'Sure is. The tosser even had the nerve to throw himself a little birthday party last week, though for the first time in living memory he had it at The George and not in the Town Hall like he usually does. Even he wouldn't have dared wangle that one on taxpayers' money, not this year.'

'Did the missus turn up?'

'Nope. Nor La Carlton.'

Sharon giggled. 'Someone sent him a strippogram though. The girl leapt out of a cake, appropriately, wearing a brassiere designed to look like cup cakes, with cherry nipples. He claimed he knew nothing about it.'

'Wish you'd been there to record the happy scene, Dais,' Murdoch chuckled. 'Whoever thought up that wheeze deserves a medal.'

Cosmo tucked himself into a corner and joined the celebrations from the edge of the room, happily surveying everyone and beaming. After his third glass, Daisy noticed, he seemed to find some Dutch courage because he moved over to Sharon and started talking to her. And she, clearly in a benign mood, didn't ignore him as usual.

Everyone, thought Daisy slightly dismally despite the general air of euphoria, had someone special. Except her. But she would soon. Jack just needed a bit of a nudge.

Jay raised his glass in a toast. 'To *The Hailesbank Herald*!'

'*The Herald*,' said Sharon.

'*The Herald*,' they all chorused.

The door into the office swung to with a crash that made heads turn. Chantelle Richardson, the *Herald*'s head of advertising, came in looking decidedly uncelebratory. Her long, thin face was normally dour but there was something about her expression now that made them lapse into an uneasy silence. She took two steps into the room and said, 'I don't know what everyone's so happy about.'

Dave, irrepressible as usual, broke the silence. 'Haven't you heard, Chantelle? Provost Porter has resigned.'

'Haven't *you* heard?' She turned on him, her voice brittle. Dave's smile faded and he took a step backwards. Chantelle reached into her bag and slapped a paper down on the table. They all stared at it, puzzled. 'We've got competition starting up.'

Her words fell into a silence so profound that it was almost tangible. Then Jay took two long strides across the room, picked up the paper, and asked curiously, 'What is this?' He unfolded the paper and stared at it. From where she was standing, Daisy could see the masthead. *The Hailesbank Messenger*. Her mouth dropped slightly open and her eyes widened. *The Hailesbank Messenger?*

Chantelle's face, always angular and usually rather sour,

153

looked positively funereal. 'I got it from Valerie Patterson. You remember? She used to work here till she went on maternity leave and decided not to come back. Well, she's taken another job. This is a mock up. A sample. As you see, it's a newspaper. A freesheet, in fact. And it's being launched in a fortnight.'

A freesheet. Daisy chewed anxiously at her bottom lip. *A freesheet.* My God. They'd lose all the advantage they'd managed to build up over recent weeks. How would a freesheet work? Would they have their own journalists? Their own photographer? Maybe the quality wouldn't be so good, she thought hopefully. But at the end of the day, Daisy realised, that wasn't what would dictate the future of *The Herald*. That would be decided by whether they could sell enough advertising to keep the Board of the Havering Group happy. Looking at Chantelle's face, she had a horrible feeling that doom was in the air.

'Right.' Jay said decisively, snapping into leadership mode, 'back to work, everyone. We're not going to be browbeaten by an upstart freesheet. I'm proud of you all and what we've achieved here in the last few weeks. Really proud. So get back to your jobs and let me worry about this. Chantelle –' he nodded towards his office, '– would you mind? A few minutes?'

As Chantelle followed him into his office and the door swung to behind them, there was dead silence in the office. Daisy became conscious of the peeling paintwork above the row of filing cabinets on the far wall. How had the Havering Group allowed the place to become so shabby? They'd been starving the *Herald* of investment for years. How had they not seen it? How had Angus MacMorrow not seen it? Why hadn't he done anything about it? The computers were antiquated and they struggled to meet deadlines with the dodgy technology. Even her camera equipment was well out of date and she'd been too stupid to insist on having it regularly updated. The camera Hammy MacBride had been carrying at the rugby match had been one of the latest models.

Pay rise? She thought back to the modest sum she'd been

planning to ask Angus for when he'd dropped dead. She could kiss that goodbye. Was her job safe? The anxiety she'd felt way back when they'd first discovered the threat to *The Herald* resurfaced. She wanted to chew everything over with Lizzie. She longed to ask Ben what he thought. He had more experience than the lot of them.

Jack. She needed Jack. She *really* needed Jack. Daisy's hand stole into her pocket and she felt the absence of Tiny Ted like an ache. Her fingers, so long accustomed to the comfort of his fur, his tiny nose, his soft contours, twitched and itched and curled round empty space. She felt adrift, alone. Worry had gripped them all. Even Murdoch looked sober as they drained their glasses, leaving the last two bottles standing unopened and forlorn on the draining board next to the sink.

'What're your predictions this week, Cosmo?' he muttered moodily as he slumped back in his chair and clicked his mouse.

Cosmo looked as shattered as the rest of them. He fiddled with a loose thread hanging from the cuffs of his worn checked shirt, just visible under the thick brown tweed of his jacket.

'Here.' Sharon fished a pair of scissors out from her drawer and handed them to him. Then, as he held them clumsily in his left hand and attempted ineffectually to cut the thread on the right cuff she said, more tolerantly than Daisy would have expected, 'Oh, give them here,' and cut the thread for him.

'Let me guess,' she said. 'Astral fucking chaos. Right Cosmo?' she laid a hand briefly on his arm and looked up at him.

Daisy had never seen their two heads so close together, Sharon's bright blonde and Cosmo's autumn-brown mop. She watched as the colour rose from Cosmo's neck up to his face. It suffused his cheeks and spread to his ears and finally migrated to his hairline. He looked, thought Daisy, rather sweet, like a small boy.

'C-c-chaos?' he stuttered. 'I don't know, I'm sure.'

Daisy sneaked a look at Ben. He'd said nothing since Chantelle had slapped the paper down on the desk. Not a word. In fact, she thought, he seemed to be with them more in body than in spirit. Since he'd started seeing Lizzie he'd become more distant. He didn't josh and laugh with everyone as much. He didn't join them for drinks in The Duke of Atholl. It was as though he was withdrawing. Worst of all, it seemed to her that she really had lost a friend.

Together with the constant ache of anxiety about her future and the future of the *Herald*, thoughts of how she could win Jack back now dominated Daisy's every waking moment.

Life went on, of course. Saturday was filled with football matches that needed to be covered and, in the evening, a Council reception that would normally have seen Provost Archie Porter and his dumpy wife smugly lording it over everyone. That, at least, was a welcome change, thought Daisy as she photographed his deputy. The mood all round seemed to have lightened in the Town Hall. Even members of the former Provost's own party looked cheerful. Afterwards, she went to the office to download all the images of the day. Normally, she would have watched the clock impatiently as the files moved across to the computer. Tonight, instead, she spent some time filing and sorting, checking the images and deleting the least satisfactory. She did everything she could, in other words, to put off going back to the cottage, in the knowledge that Ben and Lizzie would be there. Even if they were closeted in Lizzie's room, she'd be conscious of their presence.

She felt like a gooseberry.

Sod it. On Thursday, she'd make her move. Iris would be at her cookery class. She'd have two whole hours. Maybe three. Jack didn't go to the gym on Thursdays. He liked having the house to himself. 'It's great just to be able to chill.' She pictured his face as he'd said it. The corner of his mouth had twitched in amusement at his confession and his blue eyes had never looked bluer. 'Slob out for a couple of hours. Watch inane car chase programmes on Sky. Iris really hates them.' He'd grinned at her conspiratorially.

It would be her ideal opportunity. On Monday, her day off, she'd catch the train into Edinburgh and buy herself some new clothes. Jack-catching clothes. Bugger the budget. She'd just use her credit card and splurge for once.

She glanced at the clock on the wall. It was after midnight. Sighing, Daisy switched off her computer and grabbed her bag.

She couldn't put off going home much longer.

Chapter Twenty-three

Sunday morning. Slob day. Her bed was cosy, she could sense that outside the curtains the day was dull. Daisy would have happily pulled the duvet over her head and slept for longer, except that at half past nine her mobile rang. Bother. Why hadn't she turned it off last night? She could be excused not answering it. She had Sundays and Mondays off. It was almost certainly her mother, asking her round for lunch. She tried to ignore it for a minute, then gave in and reached out her hand for the phone.

'Dais?' It wasn't her mother, it was Sharon.

'What's up?' Normally Daisy would have been resentful, anticipating a call-out to some incident eating into her precious time off. But today, she would welcome any diversion.

'You'll never guess.'

'You're right, I won't.'

'Go on.'

'What?'

'Guess.'

'Erm ...' What was this? Twenty Questions? Sharon's voice was filled with repressed excitement. 'You caught Porter shagging La Carlton on top of Tarbert Knoll and snapped it on the mobile?'

Sharon giggled. 'Nope. Try again.'

'Your numbers came up on the lottery?'

'I wish.'

'You ... no, I can't think of anything else.'

'Well ...' her voice sank conspiratorially. 'Promise you won't tell?'

Christ, she hadn't got her hooks into Jay Bond, had she?

Despite everything he'd said?

'Guess who I went out with last night?'

She *had* gone out with Jay. 'Not ... not Jay?' she ventured hesitantly.

'Silly. I put him out of my mind when you told me he was still stuck on his wife.'

'Who then?' Daisy asked, relieved.

Sharon started humming. 'Starry, starry nights ... Got it?' she asked.

'Sorry, no,' said Daisy, wriggling herself into a sitting position.

Sharon tried again. 'When you wish upon a star ...' she hummed.

'Erm ... am I being dense? I never was much good at pub quizzes.'

'Really Daisy, you are being dozy! *Stars*.' She paused.

'Stars?'

'Horoscopes.'

Horoscopes! 'Cosmo asked you out?'

'Finally got there. Well done.'

'Wow!' Daisy, well and truly awake now, shuffled her feet into her slippers and padded across to the window. It *was* raining. A grey mist had rolled in and she could hardly see the trees at the far side of the garden. 'At long last.'

'What d'you mean "at long last"?'

'Well Shar, he's fancied you for donkey's years.'

'Really? How d'you know?'

Daisy sighed. 'Sharon, *everyone* knows.'

'Well, couldn't someone bloody well have told me?'

'That was up to Cosmo, surely?'

'Hmm.' Sharon appeared to consider this before abandoning the effort and skipping from past to present in one excited sentence. 'He's so shy, Dais, that's why I never noticed, but he's really terribly sweet.'

'Where did you go?'

'He took me down to North Berwick for dinner. I never thought I'd enjoy it so much. When he asked me I was, like, yawn, but I wasn't doing anything so what the hell? But he was so easy to be with, Dais, you would never have guessed he could be like that. We talked for *hours.*'

'Great.' When was the last time someone had taken her out for dinner? Daisy tried to remember, but failed. Unless you counted the meal in Kelso with Jay the night they'd been snowed in.

'Hey, that was why I was ringing you. D'you fancy a trip to Edinburgh this afternoon? Or tomorrow? I kind of feel my wardrobe isn't quite right, you know? I need something a bit more ... I dunno ... more *country* I suppose.'

She sounded a little shy herself now, thought Daisy. Where was the Sharon Eddy she'd known all these years? 'Fµnny you should say that,' she said. 'I was thinking of getting some new things myself. Not country, though. A bit more kind of ...' she hesitated. '... sexy?' she ventured. *Jack-catching* was what she really meant, but however much she'd warmed to Sharon she wasn't about to tell her about her plans.

Sharon laughed. 'Oho. Man ahoy?'

'Maybe.'

'What about it then?'

Daisy looked out again at the rain. No time like the present. 'You're on. Station at eleven?' That would give her time to shower, dress, and have breakfast.

'See you there.'

Ben still felt uncomfortable about encountering Daisy in the kitchen of the cottage. It felt like an intrusion into her space and she clearly felt the same. She'd hardly shown her face over the last few weeks and if ever she did materialise when he was there, she made herself a quick coffee and a sandwich and disappeared back into her room. He felt guilty.

Lizzie was sitting on the window seat in her bedroom, dressed only in a luxurious velour dressing gown. She'd just come out of the bath and her hair was wound into a towel and piled high on her head. She was supping the coffee Ben had just made, checking the kitchen surreptitiously for signs of Daisy

161

before he'd ventured forth. When he'd heard her chatting on her mobile in her room, he reckoned he'd have enough time to do the necessary and get back into Lizzie's room before being seen.

'She's there now,' said Lizzie. 'I can smell toast.'

'Could we ...?' He stopped. Could they what? Persuade her to sit down at the kitchen table with us and eat some breakfast? Join them for a walk? Over the weeks, they'd tried everything, but Daisy had sidestepped every invitation. Politely, sweetly, but declined nevertheless.

'It's just a shame she hasn't got someone right now,' said Lizzie. 'Poor Dais. I wish I could find someone for her. She's not really dated anyone since she stopped seeing Jack. It's not good for her.'

She unwound the towel from her head with easy, flowing movements and ran her fingers through the thick damp hair, then leaned forwards to reach to her dressing table for a brush. The robe fell away from her body slightly and Ben could see the valley between her breasts, shadowy and inviting. It didn't stir him though. Oddly, he was beginning to realise that a few weeks of Lizzie Little was enough to satisfy his sexual appetites for quite a while. Fully dressed now, he lay back on the bed and propped himself up on his pillows, cradling his coffee in his hands and watching her as she dried her hair. Her head was hanging forward, the long hair falling towards the floor as she brushed it in front of her drier. Now he could see the bones of her spine, delicate as a cat's. What was not to like?

Lizzie finished off her hair, sitting up straight and tossing her head backwards so that the gleaming mane caught the light. It settled back round her shoulders, easily, like a gorgeous soft cape. She caught his gaze and smiled, laying her brush down and rising to her feet in one easy movement. 'I'll go and see if we can persuade her to have breakfast with us.'

'Good idea.'

She moved across the room, her stride long, her hips moving easily. Ben watched her thoughtfully. Her walk, like all her other movements, was languorous, lazy, and very sexy. He still loved making love to Lizzie but, he realised with the beginnings of a self-awareness that surprised him, that was it. That was the basis of their relationship and the full extent of it. Sexual adventure. There was no emotional engagement. Lizzie, true to the rules she had laid down at their first encounter, didn't encourage that. And a relationship that went beyond sex was not what he wanted – or so he had told himself, over and over and over again.

Daisy, with the puddle-grey eyes to drown in. Daisy, dear ditsy Daisy, who had phoned him in the midst of her mini dramas so that he could rescue her from whatever fix she had got herself into. She didn't do that any more, not since the day she'd discovered that he'd started seeing Lizzie. He missed that. He missed the way she had sweetly trusted him not to reveal to the others how the silly, simple things of life sometimes defeated her.

He put his cup on the small table by Lizzie's bed, swung his feet to the floor, padded across to the window. Lizzie's room was at the side of the cottage. It faced onto a patch of rough grass, which might once have been a lawn, and across into the protective shelter of a small stand of trees. It looked as though rain had been falling steadily all night. The delicate blooms were saturated, the branches hanging low and heavy. On the grass, hundreds of petals had fallen to their death and lay forlorn and hopeless, early victims to the holocaust that would follow if the winds rose or the rain continued.

Sex without love. It was just a function. He'd never thought of it that way. For him, always, there had been the thrill of the chase, followed by sweet surrender, a meeting of minds, the frisson of a look exchanged that touched the soul. It had been like that with Martina, early on. Later, it felt as though he'd held their relationship together more through a determination not to fail, but at least there had been a connection. Challenging, frustrating, but real.

This … *thing* … he had with Lizzie … was empty at the core.

Ben watched as another small flurry of petals drifted softly to the earth. Perhaps he would finish things with Lizzie. Perhaps Daisy had been wrong about Jack Hedderwick. Maybe she was deluding herself. And if that was the case, there might, just possibly, be a chance for him.

Chapter Twenty-four

Jack's front door was green. Not a lovely, rich forest green, nor even a spring-fresh bright green, but a kind of light sage. Daisy didn't like it. It was the shade she called 'old people's green', the colour that seemed to be universally favoured by decorators of public lavatories.

She was standing in front of the door, dressed in her finest Jack-catching outfit (chosen so carefully with Sharon's advice) and plucking up the courage to ring the bell. It was eight o'clock on Thursday evening and she hadn't seen Jack for nearly two weeks. She'd been working so hard on the Provost Porter story that her schedules had been seriously disrupted. But now was the time to go for it. Her confidence was high, thanks to her new slimline figure and the success of her work at the *Herald*. She needed to capitalise on that before the Ben/Lizzie situation began to get her down, because there was a real risk of that.

It was nothing to do with jealousy, she told herself. She didn't mind Ben and Lizzie being together. She was pleased for them. Rather, it was the difficulty of the situation – sharing the cottage with Lizzie, being there when she brought Ben home with her, knowing they were together in the next room, feeling … feeling so isolated in the face of their obvious happiness. It wasn't *jealousy*, because it was Jack she ached for, not Ben.

Jack Hedderwick. Jack of the baby blue eyes and the feather-soft golden hair. Jack, who she was going to offer herself to *right now*. Dressed in the micro-length black satin dress, with its plunging back and deep cleavage, the pieces held together only by the slim halter looped round the back of her neck, her luminous purple heels so high she was seriously nervous about falling off them, she was the absolute image of sexiness. She knew that because Sharon had assured her it was so, despite her slight doubts about looking tarty rather than sensual.

'You wanted a man-catching outfit, and that's exactly what this is, Dais,' she'd said, admiring Daisy in the harsh light of the changing room of the high street store. 'Team it with purple accessories and a bit of bling and you can't fail.'

'Really?' Daisy had been dubious.

'No doubt about it. You've lost so much weight recently, you're looking breathtaking.'

'Promise?'

'Cross my heart and hope to die.'

So she'd gone for it. But after Sharon had gone upmarket and bought a slim, calf-length skirt, twin set teamed with Mallorca pearls, immaculately cut wool slacks, and a pair of flat brown leather loafers, she'd voiced her reservations again.

'Are you *sure* that dress isn't tarty, Shar? I want to be sexy, not trollopy. Perhaps I should get something a bit less flashy.'

'Trust me, babe. You look hot.'

She looked different, that was for sure. In all her life Daisy had never worn a dress made of so little fabric. Closing her eyes to blot out the ghastly green of the door, Daisy drew a deep breath, raised her hand, and pressed the doorbell. Nothing. She couldn't even tell if the bell had rung and she was just lifting her hand to push it again when the door was pulled open. There was Jack, looking divine in a sky blue shirt that exactly matched his eyes, and with a flush on his cheeks that gave him a healthy glow.

'Hello, Daisy!'

He was surprised to see her, naturally. She'd never called round before and she hadn't told him she was coming. 'Hello Jack.' She gave him her sweetest smile and waited.

'You're looking … you're looking …' Jack didn't seem to be able to find the words to describe how she was looking.

'Delicious?' she supplied hopefully.

'… different. What are you doing here? Did Iris invite you?'

'Iris? Invite me?' For the first time, Daisy was dimly aware of the hum of noise from behind a door in the hallway. Like voices. A lot of voices. Jack wasn't on his own. The realisation dawned on her in the same instant as the living room door flew open and Iris appeared, wearing something long and floaty and floral, her hair swept up in a loose coil, her face flushed with excitement, looking prettier than Daisy had ever seen her look.

'Who is it, darling? Oh, hello Daisy. Are you coming in?'

She'd picked the wrong night. It *was* Thursday. It was cookery class night, She'd checked and double checked that, but for some reason, Iris hadn't gone to the class. They were having a party instead. Pink with embarrassment, Daisy hovered uncertainly. Her every instinct told her to run. Swivelling on one very high purple heel, she started to turn. Then her ankle, wobbling with nerves, twisted over to one side and she crashed to the ground, arms akimbo, legs splayed, her micro skirt riding up the last inches of her thighs to reveal the flimsy purple silk knickers she'd selected so carefully to match the bag and shoes.

'Careful! Daisy! Are you all right?'

Her head had banged backwards onto the border at the edge of the neat lawn. Rain earlier in the day had dampened the earth and she could feel small lumps clinging to her hair. Hastily rearranging her legs and trying to tug her skirt down, she rolled onto her knees.

'Here. Let me help you.'

Jack was standing above her, looking alarmed. Behind him she could see Iris, her face concerned. One of her shoes had gone flying. She took Jack's arms and hauled herself up slowly. Her right leg was some four inches shorter than her left and she felt as though she was lurching at an alarming angle. 'I'm fine. Sorry. Listen, I was just … I thought … I'll head off. Sorry …' she mumbled, her embarrassment now excruciating.

'Here's your shoe. Are you sure you're all right?' Iris had found the shoe that had gone flying and had laid it neatly in front of her foot so that she could slip it back on.

'Thanks. Yes. Thanks. I'd better … Ouch!' Her ankle

seemed to be swelling rapidly. 'Damn!'

'Listen, come in. Bring her in Jack, she's hurt, poor thing. And looking so nice for our party, too. What a shame. We'll get you cleaned up, Daisy, don't worry. One of my friends is a nurse, I'll get her to look at that ankle for you.'

Iris was chattering on, being solicitous. Being nice. Daisy didn't want her to be nice. She couldn't bear it. She liked to think of Iris as a cow, the woman who'd stolen her Jack. If she was nice it would make it much more difficult – in so many ways – to win him back again.

'And it was so sweet of you to come to our engagement party, wasn't it Jack? I'm so glad you asked her.'

Engagement party. The noise from inside the house was loud now. Someone had put on music and people were spilling out of the living room to see what the excitement was outside. Jack, still supporting her weight on his arm, was looking down at her with the oddest of expressions. He hadn't asked her – and now he knew that Iris hadn't asked her either. She'd got it all wrong. Realisation flooded into her numbed consciousness with a sudden clarity, like walking out of a patch of damp fog into an icy landscape where the air was pure and bright and shiver-makingly cold. *Jack Hedderwick didn't love her at all.* At least, not in the wanting-her-back, still-really-loving-her kind of way that she'd imagined.

He was getting married.

To Iris Swithinbank.

She had lost him.

For ever.

'Sit down, Daisy.' Jack's touch was as gentle as his voice. But she knew now that it wasn't love she was hearing, it was pity. All the time, at the gym, he'd just been being nice to her. Fucking, fucking *nice.* Nice because of what they'd had in the past. Nice because he was sorry for what he'd become at the end of their relationship. Maybe even nice because he was *sorry* for her. The full horror of her misjudgement seemed to hit her behind the knees because she collapsed onto a chair in the dining room, where he'd brought her, blinking away the tears. She would not cry. She absolutely *would not cry*. Instinctively, her hand went to her pocket in search of Tiny Ted.

Only she didn't have a pocket.

And she didn't have Tiny Ted.

She didn't have Lizzie.

She didn't have Ben.

She didn't have Jack.

And very probably, she wouldn't even have a job in the very near future.

Now she was shivering for real. The stark reality of her situation had moved somehow from her knees to her solar plexus and she started to feel very sick. She had nothing. *She was not going to cry.*

'Here. Put your ankle up on this.' He pulled across another chair and eased her leg onto it. 'That's not looking too great. Let's get it cleaned up.'

'No really … it's OK … sorry … I need to get home …'

'You can't drive. Not yet anyway.' He looked at her again. 'You're shivering.'

'I'll get her a wrap.' Iris's voice.

'No really … I'm …' But her teeth were chattering.

She looked down at her leg. There seemed to be a great deal of it. She wasn't used to short skirts. Her knee was covered by a large greeny-brown smudge. Pushing back her hair, Daisy glanced down at her hand. It was smeared with earth too. What a sight she must be. At least he hadn't taken her into the room where all the action seemed to be.

'Can I help? Oh, it's you, Daisy dear.' Hell. It was Jack's mother. She hadn't seen Mrs Hedderwick since the night, a whole year ago, that she'd raced round to her in floods of tears, hysterical, begging for her help to get Jack back.

'Arthur?' Mrs Hedderwick called to Jack's father, who appeared at her shoulder. 'Look who's here.'

'Daisy. How nice.'

Daisy tried to smile, without success. Of course. It was an engagement party. It would be just her luck if the whole

169

Hedderwick tribe appeared soon. She was right. Within minutes, Jack's two sisters and their respective partners, four cousins, and assorted nieces and nephews had all crowded into the dining room and were milling around, their greetings surprisingly friendly and concerned. She couldn't bear it. She simply couldn't bear it. She'd known them all so long, they felt like *her* family. They had been more of a family to her than her parents had ever been. But the truth was they weren't her family. And now they never would be. With each greeting, Daisy felt her mouth growing more and more numb, her words more and more asinine, her head more and more dizzy. And when, finally, Jack's favourite little niece Emily, five years old now and the spitting image of her uncle, put her chubby arms up for a hug and lisped, 'Love you, Auntie Daithy,' her mind imploded completely and she felt the world grow dark.

When she came to, she was on the carpet. Someone had covered her with a blanket and put a cushion under her head. The room had been cleared of people. Mercifully, it was perfectly quiet. A small table lamp had been left on in the corner of the room. Daisy lifted her head a fraction and looked around. The dining room door had been closed. From behind it, she was dimly aware of the hum of conversation. So the party was still going on.

She sat up, carefully. What *was* she wearing? In the semi darkness, she felt her cheeks grow hot with embarrassment as she remembered. The tarty dress. She'd kill Sharon. Why had she ever trusted her? When Jack's parents had come in she'd felt like a whore – or at least, what she imagined a whore must feel like. In comparison with Iris, so tastefully covered from head to toe in a pretty floral silk, she felt cheap and shabby. She had to get out of here, now. Tentatively, she rolled onto her knees and tested her ankle, then yelped with pain. Fuck. She really had twisted it.

'Here. Let me help.'

A woman's voice, one she didn't recognise. She looked up.

'I'm Carol. I'm a nurse. Here.' The girl who was speaking

was young, petite, auburn-haired and she positively radiated calm authority. Her mind still in complete turmoil, Daisy relaxed gratefully into her care and allowed herself to be helped onto a chair.

Carol inspected the injured leg. 'It's quite swollen. Can you waggle it?' Daisy waggled. Carol tested the area gently, feeling with her fingers. 'That's good. I don't think it's broken. Let me clean it up a bit, then I can put a bandage on it. Iris had one in her first aid kit. How are you feeling?'

'Fine,' Daisy lied, allowing Carol to sponge the dirt away. Of course Iris had a bandage in her first aid kit. Of course she *had* a first aid kit. Iris would be organised, efficient, ready for every eventuality, the kind of girl that Jack really wanted, not a shambolic, forgetful, indecisive worrier like Daisy Irvine.

'Dizziness gone?'

'Yes,' said Daisy, more truthfully this time. 'Listen, you're very kind, but I have to get home.'

'Can you stand?'

'Not very well,' Daisy admitted, trying.

'Can someone come for you?'

Daisy sat back down on the chair and looked around for her purple handbag. It looked ridiculous to her now, cheap and plastic. She found her mobile and reluctantly dialled her parents' number. No answer. She tried her mother's mobile, but without much hope. Janet Irvine hardly ever had her phone switched on. Damn. What was she going to do? She absolutely had to get out of here. Lizzie. She'd have to phone Lizzie. She dialled the number but the cottage phone rang out and she remembered that Lizzie had talked about staying with some friends over Melrose way. Sharon. She'd got her into this mess, she could bloody well get her out of it. Sharon's mobile switched instantly to voice message. She finished the call without bothering to leave a message.

'I'd take you myself but I've had too much to drink,' said Carol sympathetically. 'What about a taxi?'

Daisy tried two local taxi firms, but one had three drivers off sick and the rest all out and the second firm had a block booking and no spare cars.

Ben. Ben Gillies was the only person she could think of to call. She wasn't too keen on the idea, but better calling Ben than staying here. His number was still on short dial. She pressed the button and was connected at once.

'Hi, Daisy. You all right?'

Relief flooded into her as she heard the familiar timbre of his voice. Then finally, unable to hold back any more, she burst into tears.

Chapter Twenty-five

'Circulation's dropped.'

Sharon was perched on her desk, her legs swinging rhythmically, her fingers drumming on the desk top.

'Oh for fuck's sake, Shar, stop that noise will you?' Murdoch, trying to file a story, was irritated.

'What?' She looked pained, but the drumming stopped.

'Who says?' Daisy asked from her corner. She'd had to take a week off after her disastrous attempt to win Jack back. Her job was more or less impossible if she couldn't drive. *The Stoneyford Echo* had lent their trainee, who had succeeded in achieving quite a presentable portfolio over the week, much to Daisy's chagrin. Since then she'd been subdued, depressed. Her world had imploded. She'd spent the week at her parents' house, unable to bear the idea of Lizzie tending to her or, worse still, Ben. Even with the ankle mending, she was finding the sheer effort of getting through day by day a daunting one. The fight had gone out of her. She felt deflated and defeated. There was no point in anything any more. No point in going to the gym. Why, if she couldn't use it as an excuse to be with Jack? No fun in sharing meals with Lizzie – to say that their relationship had become strained was an understatement. As for work, she felt defeated there too. Everyone could see the writing on the wall. Sharon's bleak statement was no surprise.

'Figures are just in.' Sharon picked up a piece of paper and waved it disconsolately. 'Chantelle says advertising's down too.'

Dave was angry. 'But *why*?' he exploded. '*The Messenger*'s crap. Their journos can't write, their photos are practically non existent –'

'– they get all the celeb gossip from the mothership with half the pages laid out for them and their overheads are really low,' Murdoch broke in.

'You and I know the writing's rubbish, Dave,' Sharon said gloomily, 'but half the neighbourhood doesn't seem to care. It's free. It's not great, but it's not bad for free.'

Silence fell. Daisy packed her camera and limped out. She had a school class to photograph over at Main village. Planting trees. It would be no surprise to find one of the freelancers flogging their photos to *The Messenger* there, trying to out-think her, grab a cuter image. *The Echo* she could handle. That, in a way, seemed like a fair fight. This was grim, because she was not alone in feeling they had lost the battle already. Hungry freelance or no, she was pleased she had a shoot. Going anywhere was better than being in the office.

The Hailesbank Herald survived for exactly eight weeks after the *Messenger* was launched.

Of course they all knew the end was coming. Chantelle and the advertising team did their best, but in a small town there simply wasn't enough money to go around. Curiosity drove the locals to pick up the freesheet, which had been supported by a massive promotional programme, including give-aways of chocolate bars and DVDs. Their competitions had great prizes, making the *Herald*'s look inferior. The dejected staff of the *Herald* had to admit that the content, design, and photography of the *Messenger* were actually not bad. *The Hailesbank Herald* simply did not manage to sustain its advertising revenue and circulation figures in the face of competition from the new freesheet. A last-ditch attempt at salvaging the ailing paper was made in the form of an appeal to the locals. The staff took their places outside the offices holding sad-looking placards reading 'Save our Paper' and 'Don't let *The Herald* Fold', but they were unable to stir up enough feeling to get a full-on campaign going.

At the end of June, Jay called everyone into a meeting. They could tell, from his body language, that the blow they'd all fought to stave off was about to fall.

'When I arrived in this office, just a few months ago,' Jay said, speaking into absolute silence, 'I was a conceited git who thought he knew it all.' There were a few murmurs of dissent. 'There's no need to be kind. I look back at the person I was then and shudder.' He paused and looked around. 'But you've changed that. All of you. You've changed me. I used to think the only place worth being was London, the great metropolis. I thought that by taking a job in Hailesbank I was really scraping the barrel. And heaven knows why, but I thought that after television news reporting and presenting, running a small local newspaper would be a piece of cake.' He ran his hand through his hair and looked around. There was no sharp suit today. No striped tie. He was wearing denim jeans with fashionable soft brown leather trainers and a washed-blue polo shirt. He looked oddly young. 'I was wrong on all counts. Running the *Herald* was the biggest challenge I ever faced. I found that actually, I began to value the things that Hailesbank offered me. Fresh air. A sense of community. People who care about people. The biggest regret of my life is that I have let you down. This week we will be printing the last edition of *The Hailesbank Herald*.'

The silence continued. It was hardly a shock, but there was a terrible finality about hearing the words they'd all dreaded. No one seemed to know what to say, so no one said anything. Jay pursed his lips, spread his hands in a gesture of helplessness, and continued, 'There will be a process to go through, of course. A few of you will be given the opportunity to work for *The Stoneyford Echo*…'

'Bugger that,' said Ma Ruby stoutly. 'What would Angus MacMorrow say?'

Daisy, remembering how news of the threat of closure had felled Big Angus outright, had no doubt about what he'd say. And it wouldn't be polite.

'… others will be offered a redundancy package. I'm sorry, guys. I thought we'd done enough to turn the paper round, but the *Messenger* has knocked our future firmly on the head.'

He was a changed figure from the rather bored-looking,

egotistical man who had walked through the door back in February. Was the failure of the paper his fault? Daisy's view was that it had been the competitive market that had finished them off, not Jay's leadership. But one thing was certain in her mind – he was a much more likeable person than he had been five months ago.

'What will you do, Jay?' Daisy asked afterwards, as they milled around aimlessly, discussing what had happened, each worrying about the future.

His smile was rueful. 'Oddly, this closure has come at rather a good time for me. It seems crass to admit it, when everyone is so down, but I'd say – rather cautiously – that I've started mending relations with my wife again.'

'That's great.' *Everyone has someone to love. Except me ...*

'Yes.' He smiled, briefly, apologetically. 'I thought I was doing so well, going clean, starting to turn the paper around, feeling I had even made a few friends here –'

'You were, Jay.' Impulsively, Daisy laid a hand on his arm. She'd warmed to Jay considerably since the Kelso incident.

'Thank you, Daisy. Ironically, it wasn't until Amelia realised that things were starting to go wrong that we began to get close again.' He gave a short laugh. 'Ironic, because she'd kicked me out saying that unless I made a success of my life she never wanted to speak to me again. And now, job-wise, I don't know what I'll be doing. A five-month stint as the editor of a failed newspaper is hardly the recommendation for a high flying post, but if I've got Amelia by my side again ...' He straightened up and an air of resolution returned to his body language, '... I feel that things will be all right.'

'I'm sure they will.' Daisy smiled. Jay would be all right. But as for what would happen to her ... her mouth twitched and the small movement changed her expression from sadness into anxiety. She'd been right, the night of Jack's engagement party, when she finally realised what an arse she'd made of herself. She had lost everything. Every single thing she cared about. Even her camera kit belonged to the newspaper.

'What will you do, Daisy?'

'Oh, I'll find something,' she said airily. 'Don't worry about me.'

Ben, laying out the last ever pages of the paper on the other side of the room, *was* worrying about Daisy. He'd spent a great deal of time worrying about Daisy ever since he'd gone to pick her up from Jack Hedderwick's house the night she had twisted her ankle.

'Take care of her, will you?' Jack had said to him when he arrived, drawing him aside to explain what had happened.

'She's hardly mine to look after,' Ben said stiffly.

'No? She always speaks very highly of you.'

'Even so.' He could hardly accuse Jack of anything. It would be easy to lay blame at his door, to accuse him of misleading Daisy, but actually, she had propelled herself along that particular cul-de-sac. 'Where is she?'

Daisy, sitting forlornly in the dining room, looked whiter than paper. She was wearing the skimpiest of dresses, a little black affair held together by hope and prayer. Her feet were bare. One ankle had been neatly bandaged. A pair of very high-heeled purple shoes sat on the floor beside her. There seemed to be earth in her hair and there were grimy streaks down her face where she appeared to have wiped tears off with grubby hands. Ben longed to scoop her up in his arms and protect her, banish the miserable delusions that had haunted her, set her back on her feet. He wanted to watch her beauty blossom in the sunshine of his love, but her face was guarded, defensive.

'Hello, Diz.'

'Hello, Ben. Thanks for coming. I'm sorry to bother you but there really wasn't anyone else.'

Last on the list. That was how low she rated him. 'No bother. Glad to help.'

Helping her to her feet, he realised that it was the first time he had touched her since she'd snuggled up to him on the sofa after the concert. That night he'd thought, for a few sublime minutes, that they were going to get it together. Wrong. She'd never thought of him in that way. She'd had eyes only for Jack.

Ben's heart melted with the pity of it. But Daisy didn't want his pity and she didn't want his love. Her body felt stiff and resistant and it seemed to him that she leaned as far away from him as the need for his support would allow.

They drove all the way back to the cottage in silence.

'I don't think I can manage going to the cottage,' she said in a small voice when he turned off the engine.

'Wait there, I'll come round.'

She took his hand, needing help to get out of the car, and she put her arm round his waist, leaning on him heavily as she hopped to the front door.

'I'll manage now. Thanks, Ben.'

'Sure? Lizzie's away, there's no one to help you get to –'

'I'll *manage.*'

'OK, fine, if you're sure.'

There was no option but to leave. His car, ever temperamental, started first time, just when he might have used it as an excuse to stay – at least then he would have been able to keep a watchful eye on Daisy, make sure she was managing. Sometimes she seemed to need him, then she seemed so damned determined to manage on her own.

He reversed into the road and turned the nose towards home. It all felt horribly final.

A Human Resources team from the central office of the Havering Group was dispatched to Hailesbank to sort everything out at the paper. Ma was over retirement age and got her pension. Murdoch was only a year away from retiring and was happy to go early. Dave was offered, and accepted, a job with *The Stoneyford Echo*. Sharon was also offered a job, but at a more junior level than her current position. She decided to turn it down.

Daisy, much to her surprise, was offered a post too. She decided not to accept it, which was even more surprising because she hated insecurity, so the decision was completely out of character and certainly well out of her comfort zone.

'Surely it's a good offer?' was her father's comment when

she told them.

She'd anticipated his disapproval but she no longer cared what he thought. 'It's not bad,' she conceded.

'Then what will you do, Daisy?' her mother put in. 'Why not accept?'

Why not indeed? She'd had three days to think about the situation. It had been the oddest of years. Angus's death. Ben coming back. Her naïve delusions about Jack. Fighting to save the paper. Failing.

Feeling that ... feeling that there must be more to life than this, that maybe, after nearly ten years as a newspaper photographer, there might be something else waiting for her and that now was the time to find it.

Feeling that she'd missed out on something really special, a chance of building the kind of sweetly loving, strong, mutually caring relationship that maybe only came once in a lifetime.

Wondering whether Ben Gillies had ever felt anything for her, in the way that she was beginning to think that she felt for him.

Realising that her stupid, blind refusal to accept that Jack Hedderwick really did not love her any more might just have driven Ben into Lizzie's arms.

She'd been looking in the wrong direction all the time. And now there was only one course of action. She had to get out of Hailesbank, out of Scotland, out of her comfort zone, away from anywhere Ben and Lizzie might be.

'I need a break. That's all. Sharon's asked me to go on holiday with her, just for a couple of weeks. We're going to France. She's found a great deal in Nice and we can fly direct from Edinburgh. I'm getting some redundancy money, enough to keep me going for a while. After that, we'll see. I'll find something. I can always freelance for a while.'

Her mother looked dubious. 'Well, no one would grudge you a break, Daisy. I just hope you'll find something when you get back.'

'Don't expect us to support you,' her father grunted.

As if, thought Daisy. 'It'll all be fine. It's just a holiday.'

179

Two weeks in the sun. Two weeks to relax and empty her mind. Two weeks to consider the future.

What could be better?

PART 2

Chapter One

Edinburgh airport was busy. Where was everyone going? Would she find the right check-in? Daisy, entering the airport through the automatic sliding doors, was fretting.

Tickets – yes. Passport – safe. Euros – yup. Credit card – check. Certain she had everything she needed, she arrived early at the airport, was third in the queue and checked through in record quick time. Sharon was right – there was nothing to it. Hovering uncertainly at the bookshop upstairs, she decided to go through Security before shopping. That way she could relax. She'd agreed to meet Sharon in the departure lounge rather than at the check-in, because Sir Cosmo Fleming had insisted that he would deliver his new paramour to the airport himself.

'He'd take you too, Dais, but he's going on to the architectural salvage yard in Leith to flog an old door and some ironmongery that's been lying around in his stables, so the back of the Volvo'll be full. Sorry.' She pulled a face – apologetic, but still, a kind of you've-got-to-understand-I'm-in-his-life-now face. 'I'll be there in plenty of time, don't worry. But you'll be more comfortable air-side. You can just relax.'

'Wouldn't it be better if we …'

'Don't *worry*, Daisy.'

She had worried, but she didn't want Sharon to think of her as completely hopeless. She was determined that this was going to be the start of her new life. The old, disorganised Daisy would be banished.

In the departure lounge there was an air of expectancy. Everyone was on the move, going somewhere different. Excited by the atmosphere, she wandered around, observing. There were businessmen and women, easily spotted with their smart dark suits, briefcases, and mobile phones, holidaymakers like herself, and a rowdy group of girls, headed off to the sun for a hen weekend, judging by the outrageous accessories they were sporting. She pressed her face up against one of the huge glass windows that overlooked the runways. The sky was heavily overcast and it was raining lightly. Small rivulets of rainwater trickled down the window and splashed onto the tarmac below. She could see them forming puddles that reflected the grey skies above. A plane outside the window started pushing back, ready to join the queue for take off. Soon she'd be on one too, heading off to the sun. She shivered in excited anticipation and checked the departure boards for the tenth time. Still an hour and a half to go. Too early to worry about Sharon, but she couldn't quite quell her anxiety all the same.

Calm down Daisy. Just enjoy yourself.

She queued for a newspaper and a coffee, settled comfortably, unfolded her *Guardian*, and scanned the jobs pages. Did she want to carry on working for a paper or do something else? She glanced at her watch. There was only an hour to go now. Where was Sharon? Maybe she should call her to check. She pulled her mobile out of her bag and switched it on. It rang at once. Please dial 121. She accessed her voice mail.

'Daisy? Hi, it's Sharon at seven thirty. Thought I'd call really early to give you some notice. Listen, something's come up and I'm not going to be able to come with you. Sorry. Call me back and I'll explain.'

Not able to come with you. Stunned, Daisy replayed the message to be sure she had heard Sharon correctly. *Not able to come with you ... not able ... come ... not...* The words boomeranged around her skull until she could feel the beginnings of a migraine.

What could have happened? Had she had an accident? Come down with food poisoning? Had someone died? If she'd picked up Sharon's message first thing she'd at least have been able to make a decision about going, but now she was checked through, more or less committed.

Not able to come with you. Her hands trembling, she dialled Sharon's number.

'Hi, Sharon here.'

'Sharon. Are you all right?'

'Oh hi, Daisy. Listen, I'm really sorry to let you down. Honestly. But you'll never guess what's happened.'

'What?'

'He's proposed.' Sharon's voice was ecstatic. 'Cosmo has proposed to me! I was so stunned, honest, I never saw that coming. But he took me out for dinner last night, really romantic, he took me to Tom Kitchen's in Edinburgh, and we walked down to the sea afterwards, under the stars, it was so beautiful, you just can't imagine. Well what could I say? I know it's been a bit of a whirlwind but of course I had to accept. He's such a dear. I'm so lucky, aren't I? And just think, Daisy,' she prattled on, oblivious to Daisy's astonished silence, 'I'll be Lady Sharon Fleming. What about that? Huh?' She paused at last.

Daisy couldn't speak. She was too stunned.

'Daisy? You still there?'

She gulped. 'Yes. Sure. I'm … congratulations. But …'

'Of course Cosmo said I should just come away with you anyway, he's so unselfish, the sweetheart. But how could I? I mean, at a time like this. There's so much to think about, so many plans to be made, the announcements, telling my family, an engagement party, wedding plans … I mean, you can see it would be impossible, can't you?'

'Couldn't it have waited a couple of weeks?' Daisy asked timidly.

'Well no, not really Dais. How could it? I mean, you can see … impossible … need to get on … must talk to Lady Fleming … so exciting … can't wait … Daisy? Are you there?'

'Oh, sorry. I was just –' Just shattered at being abandoned like this? Just pissed off with Sharon? Just depressed that no one, *but no one*, seemed to want to spend time with her? '– just thinking. I'm at the airport. In the departure lounge. I've only just checked my phone.'

185

'Really? Well, go, girl, go. You'll love it. Great little hotel. Lovely place. You can't go wrong.' Sharon's excitement was still evident. 'I'm really sorry I won't be there, Dais. Honest. I was looking forward to a bit of sunshine, French grub, and vin du table, lots of it. But hey, to be honest, I got a better offer.' She laughed. 'Listen, have a great time. Send me a postcard. And when you get back, I'll tell you all about the wedding plans.'

'Right.' Daisy's head was spinning. She should have known better than to have trusted Sharon, however nice she'd seemed recently. Sharon had thrown Tiny Ted in the river. She should never have relied on Sharon for anything.

'Bye, Dais. Sorry again. Honest.'

She rang off.

Honest? That was hardly a word Daisy would use to describe Sharon Eddy. She didn't blame Sharon for accepting Cosmo's offer – but couldn't she have put off the arrangements just for one week, instead of abandoning her here?

'Sorry!'

A passer-by knocked over her coffee and dashed off to his gate with a glance of apology and a shrug of the shoulders. Daisy watched the stain spread over her *Guardian*. If there were any media jobs in the pages, they'd be obliterated now. Maybe it was a sign. It didn't matter. What did? She picked up the dripping pages and crumpled them into a ball, walked slowly to the waste bin and tossed the paper in. Her hands felt sticky and dirty.

She couldn't go back to the cottage, not with Ben and Lizzie there, and there was nowhere else she could go. She stared at the bin sightlessly. Around her, people were moving to a gate, boarding. What was she to do? Go on her own? The thought was terrifying. Automatically, her hand went to her pocket for the comforting snout of Tiny Ted before halting at the seam as she remembered. Tiny Ted was long gone, cast into the fast-flowing waters of the Hailes by Sharon Eddy, her one-time colleague and so-called friend.

The options went round and round in her mind. She could simply wait here, miss her flight, go and explain, get her bags back. But then what? Slink back to the cottage? Spend the time suffering her parents' censure? Go to a bed and breakfast in some retro seaside town? She'd still be on her own and she'd still be miserable.

She straightened up. What was she so worried about? She had a hotel room booked. It was only two weeks, for heaven's sake. She could sit on the beach, enjoy the sun, read books, chill out. No one would know her. What did it matter? She might even enjoy it. And did she need a toy bear for comfort? Even one she'd treasured since childhood? She checked the departure board. The flight to Nice was delayed and she had another hour to wait. Picking up her bag, she stood up. She didn't have a plan. She'd just have a look at the shops, maybe see if the newsagent had a guide book to the south of France or take a look at the duty free. It would all be fine.

Cameras. There they were. Rows of them. Neatly lined on shelves behind glass windows. Little cameras, pocket cameras, video cameras, cameras to sneer at, and cameras to die for. Black ones, silver ones, pink ones. Cameras with tiny built in zoom lenses and cameras with sophisticated interchangeable professional gear. Automatic cameras. Cameras with the capacity for infinite manual control.

Daisy, forgetting her situation, was transported with delight. Peering at the array of equipment on offer, she realised that she couldn't even remember the last time she had been in a camera shop. For the best part of a decade, she'd been supplied with all her photographic needs. The equipment she'd used at the paper had hardly been state of the art, but it had been adequate. Now it occurred to her that the digital camera she had in her pocket was probably more suited to taking the odd snap on a drunken night out than anything affording the slightest bit of professional self respect.

'Can I help you?'

The young assistant had come up on her shoulder as she

peered at a fantastic-looking piece of high technology. Riveted by the camera, it took her a few seconds to focus on the youth's face. Youth? Heavens, he looked as though he was barely out of school. His skin had the kind of spottiness she associated with teenagers struggling with the emergence of adult hormones. His lank hair looked unwashed and greasy. Didn't they vet their staff?

'Can you tell me about this one?' She indicated the most expensive camera she'd seen on display.

'Yeah, sure, that's more aimed at the professional,' he started. 'It's a bit complicated. Perhaps I could start by showing you this ...'

Something in Daisy's head exploded. She had lost the love of her life. She had become estranged from her best friend. She had completely messed up a relationship that might have become really special. She had lost her job. She'd been abandoned at the airport on her way to a country where she knew no one and could hardly speak the language. And to cap it all, she was being *patronised* by this spotty twit.

'And that's precisely why I'm interested in it,' she said, holding back her anger and focusing perversely on the camera, which was way more expensive than she'd been considering. 'So if you'd kindly allow me to look at it.'

It should never have happened. If he'd been just a little more respectful it never would have happened, but somehow, half an hour later, Daisy walked out of the shop the proud owner of an extremely expensive bit of kit and with a credit card that was taking the strain of the heavier side of three thousand pounds. She'd been in a daze when she'd gone in. When she came out, she was excited to the point of euphoria and by the time she looked at the departures board, she realised with a shock that she had just a few minutes to get to her gate. She rushed onto the plane in a complete funk. What had she done? She was totally without means of support and she'd blown a goodly part of her redundancy money on a camera. Was that a mature, grown-up thing to do?

She gazed distractedly out of the window as they soared

heavenwards through the cloud. The land below them disappeared and they emerged into a space filled with bright sunshine. It was the first time Daisy had seen the sun for some days. It was an uplifting moment. All at once she was in another world, a world full of hope and light, and who knows, maybe joy. Miraculously, the sunshine transformed her mood. It was just plastic. It wasn't real money. She could justify it – after all, she was a photographer and what kind of a photographer didn't have a decent camera?

'Would you like a drink, madam?'

She glanced at her watch. It was just past midday. 'It's a bit early,' she said dubiously, thinking desperately that a glass of wine would actually slip down rather nicely.

'I will if you will.' The voice came from the man in the aisle seat.

Daisy looked at him across the empty seat between them. He looked like a businessman. He was probably around sixty, was dressed in a lightweight business suit, with a crisp white shirt and an extremely bright silk tie. His hair was grey but abundant and his eyes, behind silver-rimmed glasses, were amused and friendly. He was smiling at her.

'I've just lost my job,' Daisy said, apropos of nothing at all. She hadn't meant to. It just came out.

'Then it's on me.'

'Oh, I didn't mean … I can buy my own … I wasn't asking –' she blurted out, embarrassed.

He laughed. 'Shall we have champagne?'

'Oh I …'

'Don't you like champagne?

'I love it, but –'

'No buts. I insist. Now,' he went on when the bottles were in front of them and the cabin crew had moved on, 'are you going to tell me about it?'

So Daisy Irvine found herself telling her story to a complete stranger and discovering that the experience was oddly comforting.

190

Chapter Two

The hotel, near the station, seemed to be fine. It was comparatively new and nicely decorated, the room was clean and she had a nice view of the street, with all its comings and goings. The sea was just ten minutes' walk away, the station ten in the other direction, and Nice's picturesque old town was a brief walk to the east – but there were snags. The walls were paper thin, the rubbish collection took place every night at one, the street cleaners followed along at two, and at six in the morning the hotel took its deliveries for the day. To compound all this, the bedroom doors were heavier than the walls and were self closing, which resulted not only in constant banging, but also an alarming kind of juddering and shaking of what seemed to be the whole fabric of the building. Two days later Daisy was at screaming point and after three she was ready to murder someone.

'Please, have you got another room? A quieter one?'

The girl on Reception was polite, but unmoved. She shrugged and spread her hands helplessly. 'Sorry. Ze hotel, he ees very busy. Ze rooms zey are all full.'

'At the back? Do you have a room at the back?' If she was insistent enough, perhaps the girl would find something. 'Could you look again please?'

A shake of the head. 'Sorry, madame. *Complet.*'

Daisy was close to tears. She couldn't stay here another night. She didn't know what to do. She had to get out, do something, go somewhere. Turning, she pushed open the door and felt the full heat of the sun blasting into her face. She'd walk around, go into other hotels, find somewhere, anywhere.

The business card was in her pocket. She felt it while she

was trying to pull out a tissue to blow her nose. Not that she was crying, of course, her eyes must be watering because she was so tired.

Daniel Bryce, Art Dealer.

The man on the plane. She'd slipped his card in her pocket while they were chatting. 'Give me a call. I'll be in Nice for a week or two,' he'd said. In her nervousness and her excitement at exploring the town, she'd forgotten about it. He'd been nice. Genuinely sympathetic. He didn't have to give her his card. It would have been easy to say *au revoir* when they left the plane. On an impulse, she found her mobile and dialled the number.

'Hi Daniel. It's Daisy Irvine here. From the plane? I hope you don't mind me calling.'

'Daisy! Hello. You still in town? Enjoying yourself?'

'Yes. No.' That sounded confused. 'I mean, yes, I'm here.'

'But you're not enjoying yourself.'

'Not really,' she confessed. 'The hotel's very noisy and I'm not getting much sleep –' Her voice tailed away. For goodness' sake, Daisy, she chided herself, don't be such a drip. Why would anyone want to talk to such a misery? 'I love Nice, though,' she added hastily, trying to sound more cheerful, 'and I've seen lots of things. Anyway, I thought I'd say hi.'

'Hi. Got time for breakfast?'

'Sure. Lovely. Thanks.'

They met at a small café near the sea front. He wasn't alone. He was with a small, shiny-eyed, balding man dressed very stylishly in the palest of grey suits. Daniel said, 'Daisy,' and kissed her three times on the cheeks, before introducing him. 'This is Monsieur Lefèvre.'

This time, it was her hand that was taken and kissed, in a charming gesture of old-world courtesy. '*Enchanté*'.

'So, you're not enjoying Nice?'

'It's lovely.' She hesitated. 'I'd love to get to know it better. But,' she shrugged. She'd told Daniel about her job, she didn't need to explain again.

'Work? I've been thinking about that. In fact, I was talking to M. Lefèvre when you called.'

The little man beamed at her. 'I was sayeeng to M. Bryce zat I do a lot of work for ze new Musée Jaune near the Matisse Museum. Eet ees a collection of objéts – objects – not paintings. Vessels, céramiques, glass, jewellery, paper, metalwork. Fantastique.' He spread his hands expressively, his dark eyes darting from Daniel to Daisy and back. 'Beautiful objéts. A private collection. The objéts, they are owned by a wealthy woman, an Américaine.' He leaned forward, his arms in front of him on the table, his head just a foot from Daisy's. 'Zey need a *photographe*. A photographer, you say. Just to record ze objects, you understand. Eet ees not glamourous work. Set up ze object, *cleek*,' he held an imaginary camera in front of his eyes and pressed the shutter, 'put eet away, zen out with ze next one, *cleek*. Of course, ze light, eet must be *parfait* and zat ees not so easy, I sink? But you can do zat, yes?'

He looked at her expectantly. Daisy, seeing the fabulous objects in her mind's eye, set pristine and beautiful in a room of perfect white, took a moment to catch up. 'Me? But I ...'

Daniel said, 'Why not? What's to stop you?'

'But I ... I don't have anywhere to stay. I don't have many clothes with me.' Excuses tumbled out. It was so unexpected, so sudden, so terribly outside her comfort zone. Her French was poor. She had a return ticket for Saturday. She should go home because ...

Why? Why go home? The sun was blissfully warm. Just yards away was the Mediterranean, its vivid blue the exact colour of the tour operator's propaganda. What was there to draw her home?

'The contract would be for the summer, Daisy. It's a matter of recording the collection and once that's done, the job may be complete. Of course, you'd need to see the Director, Madame Prenier, for an interview, but I imagine if my friend here recommends you, it's a formality.'

She opened her mouth. Closed it again. Her lips moved as she thought about it all, screwing up first to one side, then the other. She looked at Daniel. Then at Monsieur Lefèvre. It was unreal. If Sharon had been here, this would never have happened. But what did she have to lose? She smiled. Her mouth relaxed, she felt alive in an excited, nervous, ridiculous kind of way. Her world had just opened up and she had no idea what lay in front of her.

'Wow,' she said. 'Just ... wow.'

Chapter Three

Dear Lizzie,

Nice is very nice. Yeah, yeah, I know it's an old joke but still, it's true.

Did you hear about Shagger? She got engaged to Sir Cosmo Fleming! Guess it was something he'd been trying to predict for ages. Which meant she didn't come here with me. Unexpected, huh? But I decided to come anyway and boy, am I glad I did because guess what? I've been offered a job already!

Yup. Photographer-general at a new museum of objects. Don't know how long I'll stay – the summer, at least. So I'm afraid I'll have to give you notice on the room in the cottage because I can't afford to keep it and pay the rent here too. Sorry. Truly. But time to move on anyway, wouldn't you say? I've asked Mum if she can drop by for my things sometime in the next few days – she'll give you a ring first to make sure you'll be in.

Hope life's a dream. Take care of Ben, have fun,

Lots of love,
Daisy xxx

Daisy sealed the letter to Lizzie after three drafts. Achieving a natural tone had been the big challenge and she had to take care with the words.

The last week had been a whirl of activity – meeting *la directrice* at the museum and, apparently passing some sort of interview; delightedly checking out of the hotel and into L'Hirondelle, a small *pension*; buying a whole new set of clothes on her wilting credit card; starting work.

It was a big step. She was more alone than she had ever been, but she had surprised herself in a hundred ways. For a start, her French was better than she could possibly have anticipated. Five years of schooling had not been completely wasted. She found the local accent difficult and her efforts weren't helped by everyone wanting to speak English with her, but hearing the language all around her, watching television, reading the local newspapers all helped to bring the lessons back.

She started her job. The work could not have been more different from life at *The Herald*. Instead of days filled by rushing from shoot to shoot or snatching quick people shots, she had all the time in the world to set up an object, light it, get the image precisely and absolutely right. Perfection was what was needed and the change of pace, far from being tedious, was balm to her bruised soul.

She settled into her new accommodation. The room was small, but bright and self-contained, having its own tiny kitchen, a small en suite bathroom, and – delight of delights – a balcony, from which she could just see the sea above the rooftops of old Nice. Three floors below was the narrow street, not on the tourist radar but full of small shops where locals bought their bread, fruit, and wine and all the makings of the delicious meals that were the hallmark of French life. From the street below, Daisy could already smell the delicious aroma of garlic frying. Soon it would be time to make her own supper.

She smiled. First she had to complete her break with the past. The next letter was easy.

Dear Jay,

I was so pleased to hear about the new job. Back on the telly again, huh? That's where you belong and I'm sure the fashion-for-men show will be the first of many great contracts to follow.

I'm so glad you and Amelia are back together. It was very kind of you to invite me to stay at your riverside warehouse conversion if I'm in London – it sounds fab! In the meantime, though, I have taken a job in the south of France,

*photographing wonderful objects for a new museum in Nice.
Quite a change from dashing around East Lothian!*

*I just wanted to thank you for everything. You did a great job
at* The Herald, *don't think you didn't. The closure just reflects
the whole newspaper industry at the moment.*

Just wanted to say thanks for everything – and good luck.

*All best,
Daisy*

Now for Sharon. Sharon, who had bossed her around for years.
Sharon, who'd thrown Tiny Ted in the river. Sharon, who'd let
her down by abandoning her at the airport.

Sharon who had been lonely and who had found love.

Dear Sharon,

*Congrats on your engagement. Cosmo must be seeing stars!
(ha ha). But he's the right man for you, I'm sure of it.*

*You really missed yourself here – Nice is just the best. The
sea is a blue to die for, the sun never fails, and the food and
wine are tops. So good, in fact, I've decided to stay.*

Look after Cosmo, won't you, he's such a dear.

*All best,
Daisy*
Photographe-general, La Musée Jaune, Nice

She liked that one. Short and simple. Adding her new job title
as a sign-off was a great touch. What would Sharon make of
that? She'd love to see her face when she read it. But Sharon
would be very good at Fleming House. She was energetic and
organised. She'd find a way of managing Lady Fleming – years
of practice as a journalist meant that she knew how to get what
she wanted out of people. As for Cosmo, he'd blossom under
Sharon's touch.

She laid down her pen and wandered inside for some water.
The bottle in the fridge was delightfully cold. She sipped from

it greedily.

Should she write to Jack? She still felt a dark hole inside her whenever she thought of him, but the feelings that had dominated her emotional life for the past eighteen months were changing. They were less raw. A scab was growing over the wound. From time to time she still felt compelled to scratch it, but like all healthy scabs, the crust round the edge was beginning to drop away and the remnant was getting smaller. Thoughtfully, Daisy picked up her pen. She was closing doors. She needed to close this one as well.

Dear Jack and Iris,

Not sure when I'll see you both again but hope the wedding goes well. I'm planning on staying in France for a bit – got a new job. Say thanks to your friend Carol, Iris, and sorry about squashing your bedding plants.

Daisy

No kisses this time.

Jack and Iris. He'd swapped one flower for another, she realised suddenly, and laughed out loud. That was funny. On the balcony next door, a dark head turned at the sound and she was aware of a face of great beauty, of olive-brown skin and dark eyes and a smile of infectious brilliance. She smiled in return. The sense of emerging from a dark place into sunshine intensified. Jack and Iris. So be it.

One final card and she was done. It was the hardest of all to write. But it was another door that had to be closed.

Hi Ben,

I liked it so much in Nice I decided to stay! Have been offered a job too good to resist. And anyway, the vino is better and cheaper than anything in Hailesbank. What can I say? Hope you find a job soon – sure you will.

Be happy.

Daisy x

Like the letter to Lizzie, this one took her three drafts. She had to get the tone and the message right. She had to wrap things up, she couldn't just disappear.

Be happy.

Daisy

She pondered for a long time on the question of whether to add the final kiss. Her pen hovered over the space for a long time, then she laid it down again. Finally, she snatched it up, added the 'x' impetuously, sealed it in the envelope, stuck a stamp on, and put the letter with the others to post, before she could change her mind. He could read into it what he wanted. Nothing probably. What did it matter? She'd blown it with Ben and that was that. Now she was half a continent away and that part of her life was well and truly over. A new existence was opening up in front of her.

Chapter Four

Ben got Daisy's card three days later.

Hi Ben,
*   I liked it so much in Nice I decided to stay! ... been offered a job ... Be happy.*

Daisy x

He studied the final kiss for some time.
    Daisy x
Daisy kiss. Kiss Daisy. If only he could. If only he had. Maybe *if* he had, his life would be very different now. He should have been bolder, seized the opportunity when he'd had it, told her how he felt, even if it risked being rebuffed. But then, she'd been stuck on Jack Hedderwick.

'Did I fuck it up completely, Nefertiti?' he asked the dummy. For some reason she was wearing a feather arrangement on the back of her head. 'A fascinator' his mother called it. Road kill, thought Ben. Nef was beginning to get on his nerves – and besides, it was time he left. He hadn't been gainfully employed since *The Hailesbank Herald* had been closed, nearly a month ago now. What's more, since Daisy had left for Nice, his relationship with Lizzie had seemed increasingly meaningless.

Nefertiti's blue eyes stared at him accusingly.

'Really?' Ben asked. 'You think I should have said something that night I picked her up from Jack Hedderwick's?'

Boy, Daisy had been in a state. She looked as though she'd been fighting with the prize pansies. What the hell had happened? He unclasped his hands from behind his head, uncrossed his legs, stood up, and stretched. Then he walked across to the bay window where Nefertiti Gillies stood, picked her up, and waltzed across the room with her.

'Are you dancing?'

'Are you asking?'

'I'm asking.'

'Then I'm dancing.'

Fuck it Daisy x.

She had no idea what she had done to him.

The drive to Lizzie's cottage from Ben's parents' house necessitated stopping at three sets of traffic lights, negotiating one roundabout, and navigating a short one-way system. As luck would have it, Ben was held up at every point along the route, so Nefertiti had her day in the sun.

'Nice one!' A man in a luminous vest and hard hat stuck his thumbs up and grinned.

'Phwoar!' 'Grab an eyeful of that!' and 'Shagtastic!' were the only comments he could pick out from a gaggle of lads clustered round the crossing at the end of town. Two women pushing prams did a double take, then laughed. And a whole crocodile of schoolchildren, spotting Nef in the front seat, giggled, pointed, and squealed. Ben grinned. That was the great thing about Nef – she'd always been an attention grabber. She was a burden too, though. You couldn't stick Nef in a cupboard, it would be insulting. You had to dress her and talk to her. It was like having a wife, though the good thing was, she never answered back. She deserved to be loved. And he knew just who would give her the love she needed now.

'Hello, Ben,' Lizzie answered the door, her arms full of some fancy printed fabric. Her hair was scooped up at the back and her black cardigan, buttoned with tiny gleaming pearls to just above her cleavage, seemed to have a dozen or more dressmaking pins criss-crossed near the shoulder, put there, he supposed, for ease of access and safe keeping rather than as a barrier to an embrace. 'I wasn't expecting to see you this morning.'

'I wasn't planning on coming.' He bent and kissed not the lips that were offered, but her cheek.

'Are you coming in?'

'I brought you a gift.'

'Yeah?' Lizzie glanced at his hands, which were empty.

'She's in the car.'

'She?'

Ben turned and went back to where the car was parked. Behind him, he was aware of Lizzie, standing puzzled in the doorway. He hadn't rehearsed this. He hadn't even thought about it until this morning, when the course of action he had to take had suddenly become clear. He stood for a second in the warmth of the summer sunshine. From the trees above the cottage, he could hear the melodic calls of a dozen small birds and out of the corner of his eye, he sensed their flittering movement. The wild roses by the gate were in full bloom and the warmth was bringing out their scent. It was sweet and richly perfumed, heady. The slightest of breezes ruffled his hair. He liked it here. He'd always liked this place. For a second he wavered. Was he doing the right thing?

'Need any help?' Lizzie's voice reached him, breaking the spell.

'No, no, I'll be there in a sec.' He wrenched open the car door and began to manoeuvre Nefertiti out into the garden.

Lizzie was laughing. 'What the heck have you got there, Ben?'

The last trailing leg was released by the sill and she was out. He'd relieved her of the fascinator, dressed her in his old joggers and sweatshirt, and topped her off with a baseball cap. His present to Lizzie. A memento. *A farewell gift.*

'May I introduce Nefertiti Gillies?' He made the dummy bow. 'Or, perhaps I should say, Nefertiti Little. Of course, you may want to rename her completely and if so, please feel free.' He frogmarched Nef back to the cottage and held her out to Lizzie.

'For me?' Lizzie was laughing. 'Is this the dummy Daisy

told me about? The one you brought all the way from London?'

'Can I put her in your room? I thought you might like her for your fabrics. Or to hang your scarves on. Or to model your hats. I dunno, Lizzie, she just seems exactly *you* somehow.' He turned to her, his face serious. 'Thing is, Lizzie, I'm moving on. I hoped you'd take care of her for me.'

Lizzie, reaching up to embrace him, froze in shock. Her arms dropped, her mouth slackened, her eyes opened wide. 'Right,' she said, her tone expressionless. She stood back a step and crossed her arms in one of the swiftest changes from loving to defensive he'd ever seen. 'Just like that.'

'No ties. No promises. No seeing other people while we see each other. And no tears when it's time to move on.' He quoted back at her the agreement she had insisted on when they had started out.

'Yes,' she acknowledged, swinging away from him, her face unreadable.

'Come on, Lizzie. You were the one who laid down the rules.'

'Yeah. I know. It's funny though,' she turned back and paused, reaching up to let her hair down. For a minute there was silence as her words hung in the air and she twirled it round her fingers, let it hang loose again, then twirled it up and stuck the pin back in with a savage movement, 'funny because for the first time ever, I don't want to let a lover go.'

He hadn't anticipated that. For him, Lizzie had always been an interlude. A delightful one, it had to be admitted, but no more than that. And he'd expected that she would feel the same way.

'I'm sorry,' he said.

He could see her small breasts moving up and down as her breath quickened. Poetry in motion. Her body was a kind of poetry, perfectly symmetrical, beautifully shaped, with its own rhythms and form. Beautiful – but for him, in the end, empty verse, lines without resonance.

'Is it because of Daisy?' she asked.

He couldn't look at her. He turned away and pressed his face to the window. You couldn't describe the space outside as a garden. It was more of a wilderness on which some small semblance of order had been imposed. There was grass you could walk on, but it was more like a meadow than a lawn. There was a border, of sorts, with bushes that someone, in the cottage's past, had planted with care, but they had grown unkempt and ragged. In the corner a large clump of a pretty, wispy red flower with long, thick leaves like iris leaves, dominated the space. It looked as if it had colonised a large part of the rest of the garden too. Some things had to be controlled.

Is it because of Daisy?

If he changed the focal length of his vision, Ben could see his own reflection in the window. The sun, streaming into the kitchen, was catching the reddish brown of his hair. It looked rough. Maybe he'd forgotten to brush it this morning. Once it had come to him what he had to do, he'd acted on it with all speed.

Is it because of Daisy?

'I don't know, Lizzie, that's the honest truth. I think I've lost her.'

He heard the sound of a nose being blown, then Lizzie's voice came again, more controlled now. 'You could try again, Ben. She's over Jack now.'

He turned quickly. 'You don't know that,' he said, his voice rough. 'She's run away, hasn't she?'

'Maybe she's angry. Maybe she's confused. Maybe she's hurt. But I do know that it's finally got into her sweet, obstinate brain that Jack is no longer available.' She drew a deep breath. 'And I would put money on it that you could find a way to reach her.'

Ben glanced at her. She was standing very tall and erect, her shoulders square, her head tilted back, her chin up, as though she was fighting her own inner battle. But her voice, when it came, was very gentle. 'Reach her heart, I mean, Ben.'

The generosity of it nearly broke him.

206

Chapter Five

The smell drifting out to her table from inside the small restaurant was delectable, meat cooking with herbs of some kind, fragrant and mouth-watering. For some reason, the memory of Lizzie's fridge in the cottage came back to Daisy. They'd been so poor at managing things, she and Lizzie. Neither of them ever remembered to cover half-eaten dishes of food, or throw things out, and as a result they were for ever stumbling across yoghurt that was green with mould or baked beans welded into a sculptural whole by a thick crust. Already it seemed another world away. Perhaps now that she was out of the way, Ben would have moved in. She wondered idly if that thought upset her, but before she could work out the answer, a man stopped at her table.

'May I sit here?'

For a minute, Daisy forgot to breathe. This was the most beautiful man she had ever seen. Teeth whiter than the waves, eyes as brown as conkers and shinier. Fingers long and graceful. Tight white jeans slipping down over the slimmest of hips, and a stomach flatter and more muscular than any pale imitation at the Fitness Centre – and she'd seen him before. On Sunday, when she'd been writing her letters. He'd smiled at her from the other balcony when she'd laughed.

'No, do sit down.'

'Thank you. I am Majik.' He held out a hand. She took it. It was dry and cool and soft. Majik was here, spraying magic in the air.

He put down an instrument case – his guitar? – and studied the menu. 'Thank you. It's so busy tonight, and this is my favourite restaurant.'

'Mine too.'

They were sitting in the street just below L'Hirondelle. Now that the pay checks were coming in, Daisy allowed herself to eat out sometimes and the food in these back streets was not tourist Nice prices.

Majik was entrancing. By the time the food arrived, steaming and fragrant and delicious, Daisy was captivated. His voice lilted and swayed and rose and fell with every heavily accented word, to the accompaniment of a gentle tinkling chink chink of his silver bracelets. Daisy watched them, mesmerised. They slipped up his arm as he raised it in some expressive gesture, then plummeted to his wrist again with a jangle as he reached for his glass or his fork or spread his hands to make a point. He wore his hair pulled back tight, in a pony tail, which flicked gently from left to right as he moved his head.

At ten, he drained the last of his wine, stood up, and bowed with comic formality. 'I must go. I must work. We shall meet again soon, Daysee?'

'I hope so.' *I do hope so.*

She watched him as he picked up his guitar and wove his way down the crowded pavement – young, lithe, casual, colourful, and completely bewitching.

Daisy never supposed for one second that she would see Majik again so soon, but later that evening, unable to sleep because of the heat, she slid open the door to her balcony and stepped out into the cool of the night air.

Three o'clock. The sounds of the night were beginning to recede. Even the traffic had dwindled to a trickle. Across the rooftops she could just see the dark expanse where the sea rolled in to the long beach by the Promenade des Anglais. She felt oddly at peace. She padded across the small balcony, her feet bare. The tiles were still warm from the day's sun. She leant on the rails and stared into the blackness.

'Pssst. Daysee!'

She jumped back.

'Here Daysee. 'Allo.'

She turned her face to the sound. Majik was standing on the balcony next door, his dark hair catching the soft light of the moon, the sculptured profile of his cheekbones dark against the white wall of the *pension*.

'Hello Majik. You startled me.'

'Sorry. Why are you not asleep?'

'Too hot. You?'

He shrugged. 'I 'ave been working.'

'Oh.'

'Can I come across?' He gestured towards her balcony. There was a gap of about two feet between the railings, below that a drop of three storeys. Before she could reply he had climbed onto the short stretch of stone wall just before his own railings started and stood, perched like a bird, but perilously.

Daisy's heart jumped violently in her chest and started hammering. 'Christ, Majik, be careful!' she said in alarm, but he had already leapt, safely, across the gap, throwing himself into her arms in the process. She staggered back with the force of it before bracing her feet and bringing his flight to a halt.

'Dear God, Majik, why did you do that? You're mad! Quite, quite mad.' She was angry with him, scared at what might have happened. If he had fallen …

He laughed softly. 'Mad per'aps. Mad for you, pretty Daysee. Mad to get at you so I flew …' he opened his arms wide and flapped them, birdlike, the bracelets tinkling softly, '… phttt, and here I am.'

'You could have been killed! Haven't you heard of doors? All you had to do was …'

Majik lowered his head, tilted her face up towards him by cupping one slender dark hand under her chin, and turned his full attention to kissing her. It was gentle at first, like the touch of velvet on her lips, soft and warm. Then he became more insistent. Daisy's heart, which had been beating at triple pace for the last five minutes, quickened still more. If he had swept her up in his arms and carried her in to her bed and made love to her, she would have been powerless to resist him. He didn't. Instead he stepped back, smiled sweetly, and said, 'And now,

Daysee, I will leave you to sleep. Until next time.'

He turned, as if ready to jump back across the treacherous gap.

'Stop! Majik, for heaven's sake.' She grabbed his shirt and swung him round to face her.

'Daysee, sweetest Daysee, eet ees late and I must sleep. You too.' His fingers trailed softly down her cheek.

'Yes. You're right. But there is a door through there,' she pointed inside her room, 'and it leads to the corridor. And you know what? There's another door just along that corridor and it goes into your room. You do have the key?'

He laughed. 'I 'ave the key, but zat ees boring. You are not romantic.'

'Damn romance. I don't want to die tonight of a heart attack. Now go,' and she steered him firmly through her room, opened the door, and pushed him gently into the corridor. 'Good night.'

'Good night, sweet Daysee.' He brushed her lips once more with his own, and then he was gone. She closed her door and leant against it, her knees buckling. She had just been kissed by the most handsome man in the world – and she couldn't wait for it to happen again.

Chapter Six

'So you don't know where you'll be staying? You're just going to set off?'

Ben grinned at his mother affectionately. 'I'm going to be moving around, sure. I need to do my research.'

'The guide book?'

'French rustic food and wine. What could be better?'

Kath Gillies gave a rueful smile and the laughter lines at the corner of her eyes crinkled. 'Anyone would think I haven't been feeding you properly here.'

'You've fed me too well,' Ben tucked his arm round her fondly and he planted a kiss on the top of her head, 'you know you have. But this time I'm going to be paid for eating.'

'Only my son could land on his feet like that.'

Martin, finishing his breakfast tea, looked up from his newspaper. 'Give the boy some credit, Kath. He went out and got the work. It didn't just happen by itself.'

Ben might be footloose but he was not fancy free. He had a destination in mind and a goal. His savings wouldn't last for ever. It had taken him a couple of weeks of phoning around, but he eventually managed to make contact with a publisher who had commissioned a new series of guide books.

'Fancy France?' The editor sounded friendly and he had a gap to fill. 'One of my writers has gone and broken his leg, so there's the chapter on food and wine going begging. Think you could cope with that?'

'I reckon I could force myself.'

They'd agreed the brief, the regions he would cover, the fee, and the deadline. He had two months to finish the job. Ten thousand words. Expenses. Travel, hotels, meals up to a certain budget.

Lizzie had pinched the extra flab on his waist and laughed. 'Go easy, big man. Portion control.'

He'd prodded her back, playfully. Since agreeing to part, their relationship had settled into relaxed harmony. She had found someone to take on Daisy's room – a fascinating bear of a man called Dave Grafton, a marine scientist who was studying some abstruse aspect of temperature change in the world's oceans at a field base on the coast not far from Hailesbank. So far as Ben was aware, Lizzie's relationship with him was still simply that of housemate, but he was comfortable in predicting that it would move on from that and maybe this time, Lizzie would settle for something more durable and lasting. He hoped so. Dave would be the perfect match for Lizzie, maybe offering her the kind of independence and respect she needed, but within the structure of a loving and monogamous relationship. Despite her assertions that she wanted to be in complete control of her relationships, he'd seen enough to know that underneath the protestations, she longed for more.

His mother moved gently out of his embrace. 'Are you going to see Daisy?' she asked.

He shrugged. Time for goodbyes. 'I don't know, mother,' he answered as he turned and walked into the hall to pick up his bags.

'Give her our love.'

Ben grinned and squeezed her in a bear hug until she squealed for release. If anyone in this world understood him, it was his mother, but he hadn't been lying. He had no idea whether he would see Daisy Irvine – but he did know he wanted to.

The day was a glorious one, France lay ahead, and a new adventure was starting. Ben was on the ferry from Portsmouth to Cherbourg. His rucksack was safely stowed down below, his only encumbrance was a canvas satchel with his laptop and valuables – passport, wallet, cards, mobile. Sitting on the top deck in the bright sunshine, he threw back his head and closed his eyes, feeling the warmth on his face. He had two months to wrap it all up – do the research for the book, write the ten thousand words – and then head for Nice, where Daisy x was. What would happen then, he didn't dare imagine.

Crossroads. It seemed to be something of a theme. Again he was at a crossroads in his life. Was this the third time in less than a year? First, leaving Martina and heading back up to Scotland. Second, starting an affair with Lizzie Little. And now, heading off once more into the unknown, no long-term plans, no ties, no commitments, only a goal of sorts to keep him headed in the right direction.

But was it the right direction? And had he taken wrong turns earlier? Splitting with Martina, that had hardly been a decision, more an inevitability. Lizzie? Lizzie had been a scenic route, a diversion from the main way, delightful, hugely pleasurable, but the kind of journey that wastes a lot of time and might cause you to miss the connection when you rejoin the road.

At crossroads you make choices. This time, his choice felt clear to him. Whether the outcome would be what he hoped for, only time would tell, but he had to try. Daisy Irvine. Little Daisy x, with the mist-blue, smoke-blue eyes and the mouth that twisted and turned and worried at things until he longed to still it with a kiss. This time he would tell her how he felt. He had to. He was prepared for rejection, but his fault last time had been that he hadn't even tried. He'd read little signs and accepted them for their surface value, but Daisy's reaction after he'd started seeing Lizzie had told another story. Or had it?

She'd tried to shut everyone out of her life, start over in France. Lizzie had shown him the note Daisy had sent her. *Hope life's a dream. Take care of Ben, have fun.* No contact address. Her mobile was dead. Nothing.

Sharon had called. 'You heard from Dais, Ben?'

'Yup. Short note.'

'She give you any contacts?'

'Nope. Nothing. You?'

'Only in a kind of a way. She's got a new job.'

'So I heard.'

213

'Somewhere called La Musée Jaune in Nice.'

He gathered the information and stored it in his memory. It was all he had to go on. He was reluctant to let Sharon know how little Daisy had told him, so he took a blind guess. 'As a photographer, yeah?'

'*Photographe-general* is how she signs it, so yes, I guess. I'm going to write to her there. I hope it'll find her.'

Photographer at a museum? That was different. Objects, not people. How would she deal with it? Ben envisaged a small store room somewhere with Daisy immured in the dark, communing with pots. She was hiding, wasn't she? He sighed. Women. How the hell did you learn to read them?

A sudden breeze off the sea ruffled his brown hair. He opened his eyes and ran his fingers through it to smooth it down. At Lindisfarne, life had seemed full of possibilities. On the beach near Aberlady, he'd felt exhilarated by what lay ahead. Now, once more, he felt the same, only this time he was prepared to make a fool of himself, to test things to the limit. Wherever Daisy was at in her head right now, he was determined to be there for her.

'You can reach her heart, Ben.'

Right.

Chapter Seven

Daisy was learning independence and patience and French. *Le Figaro*, a French dictionary and a chilled and quite passable bottle of Chablis made pleasant companions. Released from her duties at the Museum, she had spread everything out on the table on her balcony and was brushing up on her language skills.

'*Putain*, I know that word,' she muttered to herself as she found it in the dictionary and sucked her breath in. So *that* was what that story was about.

Music floated softly in the air. She became aware of it gradually. It slid into her senses as easily as a knife into hot butter, meeting no resistance, offering no difficulty. It was sweet, melodic, French in some ways, in others unlike any kind of music she had ever heard. She put down the paper, closed her eyes and listened. A guitar, accompanying a voice. Complicated, rhythmic harmonies. Very polished, very difficult. The voice had an amazing range. It was very special. Who was it? She had to find out, buy a CD.

Half way through a phrase, the music stopped. The phrase was repeated. Then again. Daisy opened her eyes. This was no CD, this was live music. And now she recognised the voice. It was Majik's and it was coming from next door. She stood and went to the corner of her balcony. His doors were open just a fraction, but she couldn't see him. The song ended. Softly, Daisy started to clap.

'You like eet?'

Here he was. Majik Jamelsky, maker of music, maker of magic, leaper of balconies, kisser extraordinary. 'I like it.' She smiled shyly. He looked even more beautiful than she remembered, with a T-shirt the colour of a flaming sunset and a floaty shirt of the finest and whitest cambric, rolled up to the elbows to reveal the jingling silver bracelets. 'Are you practising, or would you like a drink?' She waved at the bottle on the table. 'But only,' she added hurriedly and in her firmest voice, 'if you use the door.'

He came across to the edge of his balcony, leaned against the low railings and peered down. 'Ouch,' he said, and grinned disarmingly at her. 'Een ze daylight eet looks more dangerous, huh?'

'If you do it again, I'll die,' said Daisy, her expression stern.

He laughed. 'Eet ees more likely I would die, *non*? Sweet Daysee, shall I visit you, *hein*?'

She had a glass for him in her hand by the time she opened the door, but as he pushed it closed behind him, he reached for the wine and laid it back on the dresser, circling her waist with his arm and pulling her close all in one single, fluid movement.

'So pretty, so sweet, such eyes.'

Her eyes were level with his neck. She could see the vein near his throat pulsing under the golden skin. He smelt like damp earth and fresh cut grass and honeysuckle. He was too beautiful to be real, he was too beautiful to desire her and yet here he was. There was no time for wine. They needed no stimulus. Majik's fingers ran down her neck and he turned his wrist so that the back of his hand trailed down in the valley between her breasts. She caught his wrist. Looked down. His arm was deep brown against the white of her skin.

'You want zees, my pretty Daysee?' His voice was the faintest of whispers.

She didn't answer him. With infinite slowness, she lifted his hand to her mouth and started to lick his hand, her tongue moistening the pale spaces between his fingers, her eyes holding his gaze.

'Day–,' he gave a soft moan, '–see.'

For the first time in her life, Daisy felt a quiver of power. She was holding this man in her thrall, building his desire, making him wait, though her own desire was threatening to overwhelm her. Smiling, she turned his hand back to her body and slid it under her shirt. Released from her hold, his hand found her nipple and she cried out softly, closing her eyes as the sensation intensified.

'Day-see,' he whispered again.

Then they were on the bed and their clothes were on the floor and Majik's slim legs were twined round hers and Daisy knew that she had never wanted to make love to anyone so much in her whole life, not even Jack. Just as well, she thought, that she'd not stopped taking the pill.

Afterwards, as they lay next to each other, panting, she was embarrassed.

'I'm not … I don't usually … please don't think I –'

He rolled onto one elbow. The band had come off his hair and the dark locks hung loosely round his shoulders. He looked strangely sexless, neither man nor woman, just unarguably the most beautiful being she had ever seen in her life.

'You don't what, sweet Daysee? Make love with strange men? But why not? Eet ees so lovely, don't you theenk? And I am not so strange, *hein*?' His hand smoothed its way down the length of her, across the swell of her breast and the roundness of her belly with all the sensuousness of a sculptor feeling the finish of his marble. 'Ees thees not nice? *Hein*? You like? I like. Eet ees good. Never apologise, Daysee, for being a beautiful woman.'

Then, astonishingly, he found renewed energy and Daisy, who almost had a heart attack at Majik's reckless balcony-jumping last week, thought she must have died and had floated to heaven.

Later, studying him as he lay, sated, she asked, 'Do you really think I'm beautiful?' It had been a long time since anyone had called her that. Jack, sure, when she'd been eighteen. Later, they'd fallen into the way of each other and the endearments had lessened. And in the last couple of years, her confidence and self esteem had fallen to such a low that she no longer believed she was attractive at all.

'You need me to tell you thees?' Majik's eyes opened in puzzlement.

Daisy's mouth was working from side to side, She caught her lower lip with her teeth, stilling it. Her insecurities, she realised, had not disappeared with her retreat to France, merely been submerged.

'You are ...' he kissed her forehead, 'the most lovely ...' he kissed her nose, 'most delicious ...' he kissed her lips, 'most ravishing ...' his mouth moved down her throat and between her breasts, 'tastiest ...' his lips were fluttering across her belly, 'most ...' and his words were finally lost as his mouth found the sweetest and most delicate part of her entire body.

Daisy was transported. Was this what Lizzie liked? Had she found this kind of bliss with all her lovers? Had she found it with Ben?

Ben –

But even the thought of Ben Gillies couldn't divert her from the sweet sensation she was experiencing. Majik Jamelsky. Musician *extraordinaire*. Magician *extraordinaire*. Mythical, beautiful, fabulous creature. He said he found her beautiful. And – astonishingly – he managed to make her believe it.

She asked if she could photograph him.

He seemed pleased.

'In bed? 'Ere? '

Daisy studied him. 'To start with.' She drew aside the filmy muslin that was draped across the window and the light sharpened. She had been having problems with some lamps at the museum and had brought them home to practise with. Now she set them up and turned them on, watching carefully as the beam lit the dark smoothness of his arms. She adjusted the levels and played with them until he was in part backlit, the light throwing rich areas of contrast across his body, emphasising the strong, fluid contours of his chest. Majik's hair was still loose, flowing round his shoulders. It gleamed and shone in the light. His face, shadowed, was enigmatic, the eyes bright but the lashes dark, the teeth brilliant, the lips rich and velvety.

She played with her camera for an hour, while he co-operated gracefully. She used the sheets like Greek robes, draped loosely round his body so that the folds led the eye to his nakedness, teasingly. She took some nude photographs, as he lay curled on the bed. He was comfortable with his own body and that came through in the images she captured. He loved the attention and was patient with her demands.

Finally, she fetched his guitar, dressed him in jeans and his loose shirt, open to reveal his gleaming chest, and captured the best images of all as he played for her, oblivious to her work as he lost himself in his music.

'Enough.' A sense of satisfaction and achievement swept aside her exhaustion.

'You are content?'

'I am content. Would you be happy for me to show these, Majik? If I ever got the chance of an exhibition?'

He laid down his guitar and stood, taking her face between his hands. At her ears, the bangles jingled. '*Bien sûr*. Of course. On one condition.'

'Which is?'

'That I can use zese ones also for my music, my album, when I am famous.'

'I'd be honoured.'

They sealed the agreement in the best of all possible ways; with a kiss.

Chapter Eight

Ben's journey was nearing an end. By bus, by train, and by bicycle he had traversed France, meeting with farmers and chefs, bakers and fishermen, local stallholders and rural shopkeepers, restaurateurs and housewives known for their cooking. The problem was not finding information, it was containing his research and making judgements about how he could pare it down into the ten thousand words he had been allocated.

What he lacked, he realised, was great images. His pocket digital camera had stood him in good stead, but Daisy ... Daisy could have taken stunning images of everything he'd seen. In the lands around Paris there had been the fruits and vegetables that supplied the capital's tables. Leafy spinach, baby leeks, onions, celery, tender young peas and mange-touts, carrots brighter than fresh oranges. In the Loire, earthy mushrooms from the caves and wetlands, their colours in the spectrum from a hundred different browns through reds to the sunniest of yellows. Fish, silver and gleaming, oysters from the offshore beds. Lambs and hams and beef, pig's trotters and ears and unmentionables. The cheeses – Camembert, Brie and local cheeses in the north, the fantastically salty and addictive Roquefort in the Dordogne. And now, as he approached the south, hot red peppers and cherries, tomatoes and garlic and grapes by the vat load, for eating and for winemaking.

He had met amazing people. Farmers whose French was so strongly accented it was incomprehensible but whose love of their work shone through. Chefs whose fire and passion translated into dishes ranging from simple but delicious to subtle, complex and technically expert. Bakers, ruddy from the heat of their ovens. Fishermen, weather-beaten and sun-kissed.

Daisy would have loved it. And the more Ben thought about it, the more he wanted to have her by his side, to retrace his steps and to write a complete book on the subject, lavishly illustrated by Daisy's skilful images. And after France – who knows? Spanish food? Portuguese food? Or maybe Thai, Chinese, Malaysian, Indian, Russian? The world had got smaller and people's appetites for global cuisine had become insatiable.

One night, he sat outside a small café near the harbour in a small town called Collioure near the Spanish border thinking, inevitably, of Daisy.

'You two love birds ... Love birds. That's funny.' She hadn't felt the same. How could he forget those words? She'd slipped away from him, wriggling out of his grasp. *'I'd've hated to lose you as a friend and if we'd got it together, I probably would have.'* Had she been right?

No. Emphatically no. Surely? Their friendship was real and it was strong. On the other hand – Ben weighed the words again in his head and tried to be realistic. If they'd got it together as teenagers, could it have lasted? He had to be honest and admit that it was doubtful at best. Reluctantly, Ben had to acknowledge that Daisy had been right. For once, the words she'd spoken had been wise ones. But surely they'd both changed over the years? He should have persuaded her of that, snogged her stupid, made her realise that everything had changed.

'You can reach her, Ben.' Lizzie, so brave and so generous. *'Reach her heart, I mean.'* He could cry when he thought of that moment. Lizzie didn't deserve to lose Daisy's trust and friendship – that was one fence he had to mend.

'Monsieur? Désirez vous autre chose? Un café, peut être? Un cognac?' Would you like a coffee, a brandy?' The waiter was hovering, smiling, unhurried. Above him, the night sky was lit by a million stars, their light beaming to Earth across a trillion light years. Timeless. Beautiful.

'Merci, rien. No thanks. Nothing.'

What was she doing now, Daisy Irvine? Was she happy or sad? Content in her new life or hiding from rejection and failure? As his journey reached its end, excitement and anxiety rose in Ben in equal measure. He needed to find her, tell her how he felt, persuade her that what he offered was real and lasting and built on rock, not sand. He needed to put himself on the line and pray that his honesty triggered the response he longed for. And if it didn't, he needed to come to terms with it and move on.

He paid his bill and stood. Twenty paces away, the harbour wall stretched out, guarding the land from the lapping waves. For some reason he felt he needed to walk as far as he could into the darkness, to lose himself in the anonymous blanket of the night. Only the low yellow light of a few sparse street lamps were there to guide him but he stumbled out to the furthest-most point and found a comfortable part of the wall on which to perch.

'Hello?'

Ben had called Lizzie pretty much every week since he'd left Hailesbank. He'd nipped their relationship in the bud just in time for them to be able to pull it back to a real friendship. Any longer and Lizzie would have tipped too far into emotion, despite her firm ground rules.

'Hello? Dave?'

'Hi Ben.' Dave's deep voice boomed out of the phone. 'Are you looking for Lizzie? She's having a shower. I'll give her a call.'

There was a muffling of the tone and a distant sound of voices, then Dave came back. 'She'll be right here. How's things?'

'Brilliant. I'm sitting on a low wall by the harbour in a small town called Collioure.'

'South-west France? I know it. Pretty little place. Bit of an artists' colony.'

'That's the one. How's things with you?'

'Cool. Very cool, thanks. Listen, here's Lizzie.'

Was that a grin in Dave's voice? The man sounded as

though he was purring, like a lion in the sunshine, sated and hot and luxuriously sleepy. Ben knew that feeling. He'd felt the same way with Lizzie after ... and she'd been having a shower. He grinned too. Well, well. He'd been right.

'Hi.'

'Hello, Lizzie Little.' He laughed. 'No need to ask how you are, I think I'm getting the picture, right?'

'What d'you mean?' Lizzie asked, her tone innocent.

'Come on, Lizzie. Dave. You. It's not difficult to figure.'

Her laughter was rich and warm. 'You'd never have guessed, would you? Him with his baggy cords and his tweed jackets and his beard. Not my type at all, hey?'

It wasn't jealousy that surged through Ben, he was delighted for Lizzie. What he was feeling was probably self-pity. Lizzie had found something special at last, while he was still waiting, uncertain about whether his own dream could ever be realised. 'I'm so happy for you,' he said gamely.

'Bless you. How are you, anyway?'

'Good. It's blissful here. Lizzie, have you heard from Diz yet?' He asked every time and every time he got the same answer.

'Sorry. No. But I went round to see her folks yesterday and refused to leave until Janet gave me her contacts. Address and moby. Want them?'

'No.'

'No?' Lizzie sounded stunned.

He laughed. 'Just kidding.' He was already hooking his notebook and pen out of his pocket. 'Give.'

'Ha ha. Hang on –'

He noted the details carefully and read them back.

'When will you get to Nice, Ben?'

'I still have to work my way along the coast and into Provence. Two weeks? Early September, perhaps.'

'Will you call her?'

'I'd rather try to see her if I can.'

'I'm going to write to her this week. D'you want me to tell her you're on the way?'

'No,' Ben said hurriedly. He needed to play this his own way. 'No thanks, Lizzie.'

'OK. Must go. I'm still dripping here and Dave's cooking.'

He pictured Lizzie in her dressing gown, long and lithe and sensual and had a frisson of regret, but it was his body responding, not his heart. 'He's a lucky man.'

'Thanks, Ben. Bye for now. Let me know how you get on, won't you?'

'Of course.'

He cut the call and slipped the phone back in his pocket. The breeze had dropped and the sea was still, its vast blackness highlighted from horizon to shore by a streak of silver – the shimmering, reflected light of the moon. It lit his path as he stood and strolled back along the front to his hotel.

His way was clear.

Chapter Nine

'Madame?'

Daisy's heart was in her mouth as she stopped in front of Madame Prenier's office and tapped lightly on the door, which was open. The Director was standing gazing out of the window. At the sound of Daisy's timid knock, she swung round.

'Mademoiselle Irvine! *Bonjour*. Good morning. Come in, please.' She crossed the room quickly, her bouncy, energetic stride carrying her over the space in four quick movements. 'What can I do for you today, *hein*? Is everything fine for you? You are not needing more equipment? Sit, please. *Du café*?'

She swung one of the large, comfortable leather chairs round so that Daisy could sit and instead of retreating behind her desk, took the other guest chair. The office, like every other room in the museum, was floored in white Carrera marble, its cement walls also whitewashed. In this building, light streamed in everywhere from floor to ceiling glass windows, except, of course, in the many rooms where protection from sunlight was vital for the conservation of the objects, or where carefully designed lighting was necessary to bring out the best in the valuable pieces of the collection. It was calming and at the same time uplifting. Daisy thought back to the offices of *The Herald* and how she'd seen them, as if for the first time, on the day that Jay Bond had walked through the door and started criticising everything. It seemed like a lifetime away. She'd been a different person then. Now here she was, in Nice, in a world-class museum, in the Director's office, and about to pitch an ambitious idea that she had thought up and developed all by herself. *Go for it, Daisy*.

'Madame la Directrice, I have an idea. *Vous permettez*? May

I explain?'

'Of course. At La Musée Jaune we welcome innovation and creativity.'

Daisy took a deep breath. 'The reception area. You have a space we are not really using,' she started. The foyer of the museum was, like the rest of the building, generous in size, floored in the same white marble and with the same white walls, but all it housed was a desk for the payment of entry fees and for inquiries, along with a couple of stands for leaflets and brochures and three huge ferns. Daisy had always felt that it was wasted space. 'I was thinking, we could have an exhibition there. Not of our objects, but on the walls. Photographs.'

'Photographs of the objects from the Collection?'

'Maybe. Maybe sometimes. But maybe other things too. We could invite guest photographers from around the world and ask them to interpret the space in their own way. Maybe sell prints too, in the shop.'

Madame Prenier looked thoughtful. 'Why not? *Bon.* And you have an idea of how we should start, yes?'

Here came the self-promotion bit. Daisy lifted her portfolio and unzipped the case.

'Yes. Forgive me. I have some photographs. People and places. A statement, I hope, about my own work.' Carefully, Daisy laid them out, one by one. Over the last few weeks she had spent a great deal of time on this project, working late at the museum, in her own time, to hand print the images to the standard she wanted.

An old image – Lizzie Little, her hair pulled back and twisted behind her head, secured by a clasp so that the ends stuck out, framing her face like a halo. She was draped in silks and velvets from her workroom and she was looking up at something outside her window, a rapt expression on her face. The light was soft and the acute angle highlighted the structure of her face perfectly. It was an old photo, but one that Daisy had always loved. It had been taken spontaneously one day when she'd been fooling around with the *Herald* camera and she'd downloaded it and stored it carefully.

An even older photograph – older by almost ten years. A picture Daisy had taken when she had still been at school. The day she'd seen Jack Hedderwick for the very first time. It was a naïve photograph, she could appreciate that now, but it was part of her personal journey and she still loved it. She'd caught Jack asleep by the river, his perfect body framed by the leaves and the branches of a tree, his soft blond hair slightly ruffled by the breeze. A youthful Adonis.

Snow outside Kelso. The day she'd had to stay over with Jay Bond. The fields stretching into the distance, vast and white, a few sheep staring puzzled at the camera and in the distance, her car, nose buried deep in the snowdrift. A powerful story in a single image.

The butcher with his sausages. 'The last link in the chain.' For some reason, of all the pictures Daisy had taken at *The Herald*, this one had pleased her the most. Somehow it captured so many emotions in one image – the character of the man, his sadness, the context in which he operated. And besides, it was a great composition and it appealed to her aesthetic senses.

A more recent image – a potter she had visited in a small village outside of Eze, his hands thick with clay as he spun his wheel, his face inches from the pot as he checked its thickness. She loved this image for its rich textural quality.

The olive grove in front of Renoir's Villa des Collettes, just along the coast. The vines, gnarled and twisted, the ground between them stony and arid. A sense of heat and stillness and utter peacefulness.

Majik Jamelsky, photographed lying in her bed, a soft white sheet draped only across his privates, the rest of his nut-brown body gleaming and gently curved and of startling beauty. It was her favourite of all the images she had taken. Laughing and giggling, she had perched a chair on top of her small table and clambered up so that she had a vantage point high above him and could photograph the whole length of him, spread-eagled on her bed with total abandonment. The result had been a picture of astonishing sensuality and powerful beauty.

Lastly, for good measure, Majik playing his guitar, caressing the instrument like a naked woman, his raw sexuality leaping from the image with a force that was almost tangible.

Twenty images in total. Scotland and France. Man and woman. Place and object. And a way of looking at things that was all her own, printed only in a rich, deep black on white, all colour removed. The effect was intense.

'Phewww.' She could hear Madame Prenier's breath whistling out from between her teeth. 'Can I buy tickets?'

She was staring at Majik. Who wouldn't? Daisy, who had seen him only a handful of times since taking the photographs, had understood that Majik was not her man, would never be her man. He was just as her first impressions of him had been – an exotic hummingbird, flitting from fragrant flower to honeyed calyx and back again, elusive and utterly beautiful. She had been privileged to know him and to experience his generous and bountiful love. He had gifted her these images. Whatever happened to them both in the years to come, Majik Jamelsky would remain forever young in her memory.

'Do you like them?' she asked, her nerves wound taut.

Slowly, Madame Prenier sifted back through the images. 'They would need to be bigger – and framed.'

Daisy's heart stopped for a fraction, then restarted. She *did* like them. 'I can get that done.'

'*Non.*'

She *didn't* like them. Again Daisy's heart seemed to stop beating.

'We will get them framed in the workshop. They must be done just so. What date is it, let me see …' she consulted an ingenious hand-carved wooden calendar on her desk, '… we could start the exhibition in two weeks' time, yes? The beginning of September? We must do it while the season is still strong, but of course, the promotion will be only minimal. A poster – this one I think.' She lifted the image of Majik on the bed. 'The usual distribution. It will be enough because all who come here will see the exhibition. And of course,' she smiled at Daisy, 'you must talk to the programme team about your ideas for other *photographes*, yes?'

'Thank you,' Daisy said breathlessly, as the Director's words sank in. 'Thank you so much!'

She seized the Director's hand and pumped it up and down excitedly, repeating over and over again, 'Thank you, oh thank you, thank you,' as the smile on *la directrice*'s face widened and became a laugh.

So it was that the first thing that Ben Gillies saw when he walked into the Musée Jaune on the third of September, was an entrancing image of Lizzie Little in the room with which he was so familiar and a young Jack Hedderwick, looking like the shepherd who'd lost his sheep and didn't know where to find them – and didn't care either. And a spectacular photograph of a striking young man with whom the photographer clearly had a rather intimate relationship.

He stopped dead in his tracks. Daisy was here. Nothing could be more certain. If she'd scrawled the words in scarlet letters six feet high it couldn't have been clearer. Reluctantly, Ben worked his way round the foyer, examining each image. They were good photographs. Not great – excellent. The more recent ones showed real promise. Even Lizzie's photo was good. It had captured the essence of the woman and at the same time, fixed her firmly in the context of her work and her vision. Because that was what Lizzie was all about – touch and feel and the senses, just as the soft folds of the velvets and silks showed.

When he came to the final two images – 'Majik sleeping' and 'Air of Majik', it was hard not to see the pictures in the same way. This was a man who was all about grace and beauty and self-absorption, though there was nothing arrogant in the cast of his features. 'Majik sleeping' was an essay in loveliness, there was poetry in the folds of the sheet, in the lines of the body and in 'Air of Majik' she had utterly captured what made the man tick – his music. It made Ben long to be able to hear the kind of sound this Majik played, because it made you understand that it would touch your soul.

Fuck it.

The Daisy Irvine that had taken that picture was not the

Daisy Irvine he knew. He was used to her comfortableness behind her camera, but this displayed a self-confidence that was not familiar to Ben. She'd moved on. She wasn't hiding, here in Nice, as he'd thought. She had grown up. There would be no room for him in this photographer's life.

'Monsieur? You are entering the museum? There is a special display today of contemporary American ceramics, very beautiful.' The girl at the desk was smiling at him.

Ben shook his head.

'No. Thank you. Not today.'

He swung round on his heel and left the building, unpadlocked the bike he had hired for the week, and freewheeled off down the hill. Not today. Would he go back again? That, thought Ben as he entered the narrow streets of the old town, was something he would have to consider very carefully.

The exhibition's first review, in the local newspaper, was hugely congratulatory. *'Magnifique'. 'Images extraordinaire.' 'Jeune photograph écossaise.'* Daisy, walking home that evening, felt as though she was still on cloud nine. It was more than she had expected, much more. At the museum, everyone had been kind. Madame Prenier was delighted because the exhibition had drawn in more visitors. At last, Daisy thought, she had achieved something all by herself. She didn't have the prospect of her father's negative reaction to face – a thought that lifted her spirits even further. She was beginning to realise, after all these long years, just how his influence had dragged her down.

She turned across the square near the sea and into the narrow streets of the old town. She loved the hustle and bustle, the lively atmosphere. In the warmth, people lingered, mingled, smiled. In Hailesbank, in September, people would be donning their sweaters, pulling on an extra layer, hurrying out of the wind to the comfort of their homes.

At the end of the street, a van squeezed through a small gap between a badly parked car and a shop window and accelerated. A bicycle was moving towards it on the wrong side of the road.

Seconds later, Daisy was watching in horror as the van hit the cyclist, throwing his body up in the air and onto the tarmac with a sickening thud.

'*Jesu!*'

'*Merde!*'

'*Mon Dieu!*'

Around her, she was aware of cries of alarm, of people hurrying to the spot. For some reason, though, she couldn't move. Something in the shape of the body, the merest glimpse of the colour of the hair was familiar. As the van driver emerged and the crowds encircled the cyclist, she knew, with awful certainty, that the man who had just been thrown from the bicycle at the end of the street was Ben Gillies.

She stumbled forward. The cyclist was lumbering unsteadily to his feet. Her heart was hammering. The strangeness of him being in Nice had not even struck her. All she knew was that Ben was here – and he was hurt.

'Ben?' A voice came from somewhere and she realised that it was hers. 'Are you all right?' Someone had picked the bike up off the road and was attempting to straighten the wheel. Amazingly, Ben located her face in the crowd. The smile was shaky, but real. 'Remind me to revise the Highway Code next time I try to cycle in France, will you? Listen, can you tell this guy I'm OK? And that it was my fault and I'm sorry?' Ben was looking at the van driver, who was still clearly shaken.

Her French came confidently, fluently, she didn't know quite how. The crowds retreated, the van driver, satisfied that his vehicle and his victim were unmarked, moved on, and Daisy was alone with Ben Gillies, in Nice, on a balmy September evening.

'Hello,' she said, her whole expression a question.

'Hi Diz.'

Chapter Ten

The bicycle squeaked and bumped as they worked their way through the streets.

'I'll take it back in the morning and complain they should make them with round wheels, not square,' said Ben, turning to humour in his awkwardness.

'The fall hasn't injected sense into you, then.'

There was so much he wanted to say. Above all, he needed to explain why he was here – but could he do that? After seeing the exhibition? Now that she was with him, he felt like a shy schoolboy. His arrival had hardly been cool.

The image of 'Majik sleeping' was burned onto his retina. The Majik of the photograph was unarguably exquisite. By comparison he felt sturdy, plain, and very, very Scottish. How could he compete with the attractiveness of the long, elegant limbs, the fine lines of the face, the beguiling seductiveness of the dark, dark eyes?

'You didn't warn me you were coming.'

'I was worried you wouldn't want to see me.'

'Why wouldn't I?'

Ben studiously watched the traffic, but he was conscious of her gaze on him. Directness. That was what was needed. 'You've hardly been communicative since you disappeared.'

'I've been busy.'

'So I saw when I was at the museum.'

There was no break in her stride. 'You've been there?'

'It wasn't what I was expecting, but there was no mistaking the photographer. I told you that you should show that snow scene, didn't I? I'm pleased you chose the butcher, too. Quite took me back to the old days.'

'Do you love Lizzie?'

She wasn't skirting round the topic. The wheel wobbled away from the pavement alarmingly as it hit a small obstruction in the road and he had to divert his attention to wrestle with it. 'No. I don't. I never did.'

'We're here.' Daisy, ignoring him, looked in her handbag for a key and unlocked the front door to her apartment block. 'You can leave the wreck at the bottom of the stairs.' She glanced at her watch. 'I was going to go to my French class tonight but I'm late now anyway – so how about supper?'

Ben propped the bicycle up against the wall beneath the stairs, out of the way. 'I don't want to be a nuisance.'

'Are you hungry or not?'

In truth, not. He was still feeling rather shaken, but he lied. 'Starving.'

She led the way back outside. 'Then let's go.'

Had she heard his answer? About Lizzie? He was sure she had. Maybe she didn't want to talk about it now, in the street. Maybe she just didn't want to talk about it, full stop.

On the way to the restaurant she was talkative – about the museum, about the change of pace, about how her French had improved, how she loved Nice and, especially, the area round about the town. She didn't mention the Majik of her photographs and she didn't ask about home. Significant omissions, thought Ben, half a step behind her, watching her thick dark hair bouncing on her shoulders and realising he was here with Daisy, just as he'd wanted to be. Deeper down, there was unutterable sadness that it wasn't in the slightest how he'd hoped it would be.

Daisy ordered for both of them. Ben just wanted to get drunk, but he allowed her to go ahead. When the food came, he toyed with it, but the bottle emptied fast and he called for another. It didn't seem to be having any effect on him.

What's he doing here?

She was trying to keep cool and appear indifferent. He'd said something about Lizzie, about not loving her, about never having loved her, and she'd ignored it. How can you talk about things like that in the middle of the street? Where, in the framework of the life she had built for herself, did that comment fit? Ben's dramatic appearance confused her. Everything had happened so fast – he'd almost literally landed at her feet from nowhere.

They talked inconsequentially. Ben described his travels through France, his food research for the book, the fact that he'd almost finished writing it all up.

'Have you enjoyed it?' she asked, spearing a piece of squid on her fork and admiring the pattern it made round the tines.

'Enormously. It's given me the urge to do more travelling. More food writing.'

'That's good.' *Crossroads.* She had met him at an intersection, that was all. There was to be no travelling along the same road. 'Any news from home? Have you seen Shar?'

'What, the soon-to-be-Lady Fleming?'

'That one.'

'There's to be a big wedding just before Christmas. Six bridesmaids and two pageboys, so I'm told.'

Daisy laughed. 'Well, good on her. Is Cosmo still happy?'

'As happy as one of his Labradors with a bone, I believe.'

'Great.' She wanted to ask more about Lizzie, but was reluctant to scratch at that scab.

Ben, perhaps reading her mind in that moment of hesitation, said, 'Lizzie's got a new man, by the way. After your mother took your stuff away, she advertised for a new lodger and along came this man called Dave, a bearded academic.'

'No!'

Ben raised one eyebrow. 'Yes. Unlikely as it might seem, it turns out that marine life is not our Dave's only area of expertise. He's good at netting mermaids too.'

Daisy giggled. 'It's serious?'

'Seems to be.'

'Wow.'

Ben laid down his fork and said quietly, 'She'd love to hear from you, Diz.'

She glanced at him briefly, but couldn't hold his gaze. 'I'll call her. Soon.'

Neither of them ate much. Ben was downing quantities of wine. She switched to mineral water. 'So Lizzie's found love and you're playing the wandering muse. What really brings you here, Ben?'

'It's a long story.'

'So, shoot. I've got all evening.' She pushed her plate away, folded her serviette and laid it on the table, sat back, crossed her legs, and tried to appear calm, friendly, interested but not agog.

He told her about the travel book, about his journey through France, the adventures he'd had, the people he'd met, and the food he'd eaten. 'I tried to keep the weight off by doing a bit of cycling here and there.' He patted his stomach. Food or no food, he was looking fit, thought Daisy. 'I never had an accident before though. Not till tonight.'

'What happened? It looked as though you were on the wrong side of the road.' Ben's gaze held hers. His eyes, burnt almond, had an intensity she didn't remember. *What's he doing here?*

'I was thinking of other things,' he admitted.

Stop, she told her heart. She could feel the pulse of it right through her body. *Stop. You made a fool of yourself over Jack. It's not going to happen again.* 'Not a good idea when you're in a strange place,' she teased.

'Nope – and certainly not when you've just seen something that turns your world upside down.'

'What do you mean?' Now she was puzzled.

Ben emptied his glass again, refilled it, turned himself square to the table, and leaned forward, closer to her. 'It's like this,' he said. 'Once a young boy knew a young girl and she was sweet and skinny and liked to do all the things he liked to do. Her eyes were light grey and her hair was dark brown and she loved dancing and picking mushrooms in the woods and damming the streams in Highland glens.'

Daisy forgot to breathe.

'She was funny and innocent, but her heart was held prisoner by her father, who wouldn't let her think for herself, or make her own mistakes, or do what she wanted to do. It seemed to the boy that the father squashed the life out of her and although he longed to help, he knew in his heart that the only person who could really change things was the girl herself.'

Daisy closed her eyes. The story was painful.

'Once he kissed this girl,' Ben went on. 'For a few minutes he thought he could turn her from a sleeping beauty into a real princess, but he overestimated his powers. For a few years he went away, and after a time he heard that another prince had stolen her heart from the fortress. He was pleased for her because he never really thought he could win her anyway, but a long time later he discovered that the prince had abandoned her and that she was now a very sad girl. He longed to become her prince, but it wasn't as easy as that because the first prince had cast a spell on her and she thought that he still loved her.'

He paused to draw breath. 'Do you like my story, Daisy?'

Daisy pursed her lips and shook her head. Her eyes were still closed. She couldn't have spoken even if she'd wanted to because there was a lump in her throat the size of a grapefruit.

Ben's voice was very soft as he went on. 'Just when he was feeling very sad himself, a beautiful village girl came by and offered him a gift. He thought it was the gift of friendship, but when he unwrapped it he found that it also contained the gift of self-esteem. The village girl made him feel good about himself, in a way that he hadn't felt good for a long time. He didn't love her, but she was fun, and kind, and carefree. She told him that maybe when the girl with the grey eyes and the brown hair saw the boy with someone else, she might notice him at last.'

At these words Daisy's eyes opened wide. She stared at Ben as he went on, 'She was wrong. The girl just ran away.'

'No.' Daisy shook her head. 'It wasn't like that.'

'The boy decided to follow the girl to find where she had hidden. His plan was to tell her, at last, how he felt. He didn't find the girl, but he saw something she had done, something that told him she had changed – she had found a new man and made a new life for herself and he decided that probably she didn't need him after all –' he paused, then finished, '– and that was what turned his world upside down.'

Daisy gave a soft moan. Ben picked up the bottle and poured the last of the wine into his glass. 'OK, tale over.' His voice had returned to normal from the soft, mesmerising tones of the storyteller. 'It's a corny yarn anyway. But now you know why I was on the wrong side of the road.' He drained his glass in one long, gulping draught and sat back. His expression was thoughtful as he watched her, maybe gauging her reaction to his confession.

For a full two minutes there was silence. Daisy's mind was racing, turning over so many thoughts, so many possibilities, scenarios, and options; looking into a shadowy future, reviewing a murky past. She couldn't find her voice and was finding it impossible to decide where her turbulent emotions were leading her.

At last he said, 'Bugger it, Daisy, you're a photographer. What do you call it when you hold the camera shutter open for a long time, letting the light in to reveal the tiniest specks of dust in the very darkest corners? Maximum exposure. That's how I feel right now. I've opened the core of my being to maximum exposure and let you see the dust. Please tell me it's been worth it.'

The sound, Daisy realised, was the noise of her chair scraping on the floor as she stood up.

'I can't do this Ben,' she said. 'I'm so sorry.'

'I can't do this Ben,' she said. *'I'm so sorry.'*

It wasn't what Ben had wanted to hear. *'You can reach her heart, Ben,'* Lizzie had said – and he'd been stupid enough to believe her. Lizzie, however, didn't know about Majik and she hadn't seen Daisy in this setting.

His mouth had gone very dry and his lips seemed to be numb. He wanted to speak, plead, beg, say something – anything – to keep her here, to change her mind. He'd come a long way for this and his instinct was to fight his corner. 'Is it Majik?' he asked.

'Majik?' She looked at him as if he was stupid. 'Majik?'

'The man in the photographs.'

'Oh. That Majik.'

'Are there a lot of them? Daisy?'

She was standing above him, looking down at him in a vague, unfocused way. He reached up a hand and touched her, gently, on her arm. She didn't move, but looked down at his hand as if it was alien. He withdrew it and stood, moving round the table to get closer to her. She was rejecting him, but he didn't know why. What did his pride matter? Fuck his pride. He had to get her to talk. Hesitantly, he reached out both his hands and took hold of hers. He felt them twitch in his grasp, as though she wanted to withdraw them, then they went still, passive. 'Daisy? Look at me. Please sit, talk to me, tell me – has he hurt you? It's all right. Just tell me.'

Around them, he was conscious of a brief lull in conversation. There must be an air of drama around them because he sensed that they were attracting attention. At least she hadn't pushed him away. 'Please sit, Diz. Here.' He guided her back to her chair, then moved his own chair round the table, carefully, still maintaining contact. If he broke that delicate thread, even for an instant, he would lose her for ever. That was how it seemed to him. He could feel her pulse under his hand. It was very slow.

'Talk to me, Daisy.'

From a nearby table there was a shout of laughter. The noise seemed to break Daisy's trance and at last she looked at him.

'I'm so sorry, Ben. Your story was –' she hesitated, '– very moving. It's making me feel more selfish than I can say, but for the first time in my life, I have to be honest, and true to myself.'

'Of course. That's good. Very good.' The words were right but despite the warm evening, he had begun to feel chilled.

'You've seen my pictures, Ben. You've guessed at some of what lies behind them, but you're not quite correct. You see, when I came here, to Nice, I was about as low as it's possible to be. I'd lost my job, I'd finally learned in the most public and humiliating way that there was no chance of ever getting Jack back in my life. My best friend was having an affair with my best mate, which left me pretty much out in the cold –' Ben shook his head and started to say something, but she went on seamlessly, '– and to cap it all, Sharon had decided that staying at home to arrange her wedding was more of a priority than spending time with a friend who needed her.'

She snorted and pulled her hands away from Ben's. He felt their absence like a pain. Her hands now reclaimed, she picked up her serviette and started twisting it into odd, screwed up shapes.

'I was adrift and alone – but then some good things started to happen. I met a guy on the plane and, miraculously, he fixed me with a job. I revived my French. I found I could manage rather well on my own. The work I was producing was high quality. I even managed to re-engage with the real, creative me, the side of me that somehow I was never quite confident enough to believe in. I was free, at last, of my father's constant carping. I didn't need Jack to look after me.' She glanced sideways at Ben. 'Here there was only me. I had to do it all myself – and do you know what? I rather enjoy it. I *like* having to rely on myself. I'm proud of myself for the first time in my life. It's a great feeling.'

The chill had spread from Ben's hands to his very bones. What he was feeling was the bitter, arctic coldness of rejection. 'And Majik?' he managed to ask.

She smiled. He watched, helplessly, as her mouth curled softly, sensuously, upwards. He longed, more than ever, to feel the touch of those lips on his, but that move, he understood, was barred to him.

'Majik Jamelsky, Ben, was my "village boy", to use your metaphor. He offered friendship, and self-esteem, and laughter, and liberation. I adored him, but only because he was a creature of great beauty and a gift-wrapped parcel, if you like, with no strings. I knew I could never possess Majik. He wasn't that kind of man. One day, perhaps, he'll settle lightly somewhere but not yet, and certainly not with me. He's gone.'

'Gone?'

She nodded. 'Last week. Right after the opening of the

exhibition. He only stayed for me. That was his final present.'

Her eyes were bright. Ben guessed that Majik's departure had not been completely painless for her and a tiny, reprehensible part of him was jealous of the power to affect her in that way. Staunchly, he put the feeling aside.

'So now?'

'Don't you see, Ben? I loved your story. I was so touched by it, honestly, but I've just found what I need to be, what I *can* be. I can't give that up now. I care for you in a really serious way, I hated it when you were with Lizzie but I don't know whether it was because I'd lost my closeness with her or whether I missed your attention.'

He sat, helplessly silent.

'I have to stay here, Ben. For a while at least. I like Nice. I'm supporting myself, I'm even making a bit of a name for myself. I was dependent on Jack for years and I was getting dependent on you too, till you chose Lizzie. I can't let myself be that girl again, I *have* to stand on my own two feet until I'm sure I can, and I'm sure I know what I want. And if that means not being in a relationship, well so be it.'

She smiled again, but it wasn't the uncertain, mouth-twisting smile of old. It was new and assured.

His heart seemed to swell like a balloon so that it filled his chest cavity and pressed into his lungs, making breathing difficult.

In her smile he read his dismissal.

'I'm sorry Ben. Truly.'

The phone call came at six the next morning, when the sun was still cushioned in its own dark duvet. Hazy with sleep, Daisy hauled at a frail thread of consciousness and emerged blinking. So far as she knew, only four people had her new mobile number. Her mother. Madame Prenier. Daniel. And Majik.

Of the four, it was the connection she least wanted to make – her mother – and as soon as she heard the timbre of her voice, she knew that her dream of making a life for herself in Nice was over.

PART THREE

Chapter One

Flying back into Edinburgh in late October, Daisy had no shield against the shock of her arrival in the capital. She put her nose to the small window in the aircraft as they circled out over the Forth and saw the steel-cold grey of water far below. Pale sun filtered through a meagre crack in the dark clouds, blinding her for a second before the plane banked. Now she could see the city, spread out against the sky – the distinctive skyline, dominated by the bulky lump of Arthur's Seat and the crumbly rocks of Salisbury Crags, the new Parliament building, the Castle. They were past it all in an instant and then all she could see was the tarmac, coming up fast to meet them and the rain streaming down the window as the plane juddered and screeched and came to a halt.

The drop in temperature was noticeable as soon as the doors were opened. It must be fifteen degrees colder than it had been in Nice.

'You all right, hen?'

'Fine. Thanks.' A youth with a bad case of acne and greasy hair was gazing at her familiarly.

'Need a hand wi' yer bag?'

'It's fine, thank you.'

'Hope ye've got on a simmet,' he laughed, indicating her inadequate clothing.

She smiled. She couldn't remember the last time she'd worn a vest, but in the low early winter temperature it seemed a sensible idea. On the other hand, it wasn't just the cold she needed shielding from, she thought as she stood waiting to descend the steps into the night air. No vest – not even a bullet-proof one – would offer any buffer against the scene that awaited her at home.

Janet was waiting for her in the Arrivals Hall. Daisy caught sight of her a moment or two before she was spotted herself. Her mother looked older. Lines of worry were etched deep down her face from the sides of her nose to below her mouth and her cheekbones stood out starkly below eyes that appeared sunken and hollow.

'Darling!'

'Hello, Mum. Good to see you.'

The hug she received was possibly brief, but it was the longest she could ever remember. Daisy could feel urgency in it, and an edge of desperation.

'How's Dad?' She drew back, smiling, to ask the question.

Janet's face stiffened and the worry returned to her eyes. 'He's fine. Better than he was. Still in the wheelchair, of course.'

As they walked to the car park, Daisy ran her mind back over what she knew. Her father had had a stroke. If her mother had found him earlier, apparently, the doctors might have been able to treat him, with positive results. As it was, she'd been out at her book group the evening it had happened, and hadn't found him until some hours later. By the time the ambulance had arrived and got him to hospital, it was too late for any corrective drugs.

Unsurprisingly, Janet Irvine shouldered the burden of blame for this. Daisy had gathered that from the bombardment of anguished phone calls over the past weeks – calls that pulled her inexorably back to Scotland. How could she refuse? Duty, doing the right thing, not failing others – they'd all been drilled into her as a child. *'Stop whingeing, girl, and step up to the mark.'* She could hear her father's voice ringing in her ears, even now. She had never known where 'the mark' was or how she could step up to it, but the implications were clear enough. Grow up. Stand taller. Put yourself forward to do what's right. And always she'd felt she'd failed. So how could she fail her mother now?

Close to, the taut lines of Janet's face were more obvious.

248

Dark tracks incised into her grey, tired skin. She'd aged a decade in a matter of weeks. Daisy was furious with her father for inflicting this situation on them, and the fury was followed by shame that she could think anything so unworthy. The stroke had hardly been Eric's fault.

'The doctors say that he can probably think reasonably clearly, but he can't link his mind to his mouth or to words,' Janet told her as they watched the carousel begin to move and the first cases were spat out through the gaps in the rubber curtain. 'Is that your bag, darling?'

Daisy halted one of the cases and took a quick glance at the label, then let it go. 'No, not mine. Go on.' She had to brace herself for what she would face at home.

'When he can't make himself understood, he gets deeply frustrated. Then he gets angry. Once or twice he's actually thrown things at me – anything he can reach with his good arm. It's not his fault,' she said hastily, as Daisy opened her mouth. 'Really it isn't. When it doesn't end in anger, it usually ends in tears. His usually, sometimes mine, quite often both.' She faced Daisy wearily. 'It's not good, Daisy, and the worst of it is I don't know if it will get any better. I can't see any end to it. I'm so glad you're home.'

Daisy, spotting her case and hauling it off the carousel onto her trolley, had to turn away from her mother so that her face could not be read. 'So am I,' she lied. What else could she say? The thought of having to stay at Laurel Lane, even for a few nights, was wretched. Obligation, like an iron weight, pressed on her shoulders.

She was thankful that her mother took the wheel. She was able to sit and stare out of the window, reorientating and thinking morosely about the trap she was walking into. When the call had come from her mother, very early on the morning after she had boldly made her declaration of independence to Ben, she'd at first been distressed, then appalled, then concerned for her mother, and finally furious, as the knock-on effects of the incident began to sink in. Independence? Even now, six weeks later, Daisy's mouth started to twist as she thought about just how hollow that declaration had turned out to be.

'I need help, darling,' Janet had said, her voice so sadly pathetic that Daisy was unable to ignore the plea. 'I need you to come home. I don't know how I'll be able to cope.'

By the time Ben came back for his bike, the anger had started. She couldn't let him see it, though. She was ashamed of her reaction and despised her own selfishness.

'Your father? I'm sorry to hear that, Diz. What will you do?'

'I'll have to go back, for a bit at least, when he's out of hospital.'

His look drilled into her. 'You don't need to give up your life here, Diz. I know how important it is to you, your parents don't.'

The irony of the situation was not lost on her. Had it been only yesterday that she had turned down what Ben had offered her so that she could battle along her own path? Her hubris had been swiftly punished. Freedom of choice had been withdrawn from her. She was being kept in detention for ever for daring to harbour such ludicrous ambitions.

'Yes. You're right,' she acknowledged. But she knew – and she guessed that he knew too – that she would go back to Hailesbank.

'Hello Dad.' Daisy stooped and kissed her father's forehead.

She thought she'd been prepared for this moment, but she wasn't.

Eric Irvine was sitting in an armchair in the living room. His body, still strong and muscular, was hunched over to one side and his head lolled loosely to the right. His eyes had moved towards her as she entered the room, but his expression hadn't changed. One side of his face was sagging, all muscle control gone. His good looks had been savaged by the stroke.

'Duh ... uh.' The sound that emerged was little more than a stuttering grunt. 'Duh ... uh.'

Was he trying to say her name? 'Yes, it's me. I'm back.' *Back to step up to the mark. Back to fortress Laurel Lane.* 'How are you feeling?'

'Ba … aa.' His lips contorted and he was clearly trying to express himself. Daisy saw something flare in his eyes, then die.

She pulled a chair next to him and took his hands in her own. They felt warm and dry, papery almost. 'Bad?' she inquired, trying to interpret. 'You don't look bad, you look OK. Same old smile.'

The mouth twisted again.

'Naugoo … naugoo.'

She strained to catch his intent, but failed and sat smiling encouragingly.

His left fist slammed onto the arm of the chair. Daisy, alarmed by the sudden speed and force of the movement, jolted back. '*Naugoo!*'

'I think he means "not good",' said Janet, coming into the room. 'It's one of his words. You'll get used to them.' She turned to her husband. 'You're coming on, with the help of the speech therapist, aren't you, dear?'

'*Baa ...*'

The fist slammed down again. Daisy released his other hand and stood. For the last few weeks she'd felt her impending return to Hailesbank like a sentence of imprisonment. Now it felt as though the door of the cell had slammed shut behind her.

Ben's walk had taken him down to the coast. He'd reverted to the old hiking habit on his return from France. It was one of the few activities that gave him any pleasure at the moment, apart from his new life as a freelance writer, which had taken off with surprisingly little effort on his part. A recommendation from the publisher of the travel book had led to other commissions, he sold a series of anecdotes about his travels to *The Scotsman,* and other papers seemed to like his writing style because he had as much work as he could manage.

He felt the first flecks of rain just as he reached the beach. He didn't care about the weather. Actually, the rain felt cleansing. He needed renewal. Though he'd made an effort not to betray how bruised his feelings were, Daisy's rejection had hit him hard.

'You can reach her heart, Ben.'

Funny. Lizzie wasn't usually wrong. But she'd been wrong this time.

When the shower came, he didn't bother lifting his hood, he simply threw back his head and let the rain course down his face. Daisy's eyes still haunted him. Above him, the sky was exactly their colour. At his feet, golden lichen on the rocks picked up the shade of the bronze flecks in the stormy grey of her irises. Everywhere he looked all he could see were echoes of Daisy. Sod it. He bent and picked up a flat pebble off the beach and sent it skimming far out over the rolling waves, the sheer force of feeling behind the throw giving it the power it needed to move on the water.

'You looked as if you meant that.'

Ben spun round at the sound of the voice behind him.

A figure stood behind him, hooded and hunched against the rain and wind. Ben recognised the beard and the voice immediately.

'Hi Dave. Good to see you.'

'I'd heard you were back. Lizzie told me things didn't work the way you'd hoped.'

Ben grunted.

'I'm sorry, Ben. So's Lizzie.'

'Yeah, well. There are other fish.'

'Fancy a pint? Get out of this piss?'

Ben grinned. He liked Dave Grafton.

'Yeah sure,' he said. 'Why not?'

Chapter Two

Every avenue of retreat, it seemed to Daisy, had been cut off. She'd given up her room in Lizzie's cottage. She'd lost not one job, but two. She'd been so discouraging to her friends that she no longer had any. She'd been so incompetent in managing relationships that she'd allowed first Jack and then Ben to slip out of her life and by way of a final reminder of how useless she was, she no longer had the slightest semblance of an independent life. In fact, her life had turned a full circle since the day she'd walked out of the house, aged eighteen, in an act of defiance that had seemed at the time like a defining moment.

Full circle, indeed. She was back in her old pink bedroom in the house in Laurel Lane where she had grown up. The irony of the situation hit her one day in November, when the sun had resolutely hidden behind thick cloud cover all day. From the windows of the house nature itself seemed to mirror her mood – dank, miserable, depressed, and utterly devoid of life or interest. The warm skin colour she had developed during her stay in Nice had faded as surely as though it had never been and with it had faded the memories of her time there. The Museum – her exhibition – *Majik.*

She inhaled softly, trying to recall the hay-mown, lavender scent of his skin, but all she could smell was the air freshener her mother insisted on plugging in downstairs in the hall. The hours she had spent with Majik seemed like a dream now. He had left his mark, though. From his gentle, joyful, carefree loving she had learned important lessons – that she had a beauty all of her own; that giving was a gift to yourself also; and that the skills she possessed could be harnessed and celebrated by others.

Had she learnt those lessons for nothing? Back in Hailesbank, she felt trapped and dull. Her father wielded his helplessness like a weapon to keep his wife and his daughter under his control and that, Daisy realised with a sudden flash of insight that broke through the smog of docile acquiescence, was the ultimate irony. Active and vocal, she had escaped his hold. Slow and voiceless, he was effectively blackmailing her into staying with him.

It would not do. She ran downstairs. Her mother was in the kitchen, preparing supper.

'Can I borrow the car for a bit, Mum?'

'Oh. I suppose so, dear. Why? Supper will be ready shortly.'

'Don't bother about me. I'll grab something while I'm out.'

'Where are you going?' He mother's voice sounded querulous.

No, no no. She would not be subjected to this parental pressure any more. Her mother could manage. Eric was not helpless. She suspected he played on his speechlessness more than he needed to. She had done her bit and it was time to reclaim her life – but first, she had a visit to make.

'Just out,' she said shortly, ignoring Janet's pained expression. 'See you later.'

'Your father ...' She could hear the beginnings of the sentence as she closed the front door behind her. She was glad not to hear the end.

She would go back to France. In the weeks she'd been home, she had worked herself stupid for her parents. She'd spent endless hours trying to talk to her father, encouraging him to speak, running endless little errands for him, ferrying him to and from the physiotherapist, the speech therapist, the doctor, the hospital, and even, one night, to his old golf club where he'd held mumbling but grand court over his former buddies. Her mother, meantime, had begun to rely on her more and more, unable to make the smallest decision without referring to Daisy for approval.

At last Daisy understood that she herself had been a large contributory factor in Jack's departure – she'd been doing the same with him. She had to accept her share of responsibility for what had happened in her life. With the understanding came strength of purpose. She turned on the ignition and put the car into reverse. She would go back to France, but there was someone she had to see before she left. It had been too long.

'Hello, Lizzie.' She didn't call, she simply drove to the cottage and prayed that Lizzie would be in.

Lizzie, standing at the door in a striking assemblage of what Daisy guessed were treasured charity shop finds, was motionless for a second. Daisy just had time to begin to worry that she wasn't welcome, when Lizzie leapt forward with a squeal of delight and hugged her so tightly that she could hardly breathe.

'Daisy, Dizzy, sweetest Diz, hello, hello, hello!' She felt herself being kissed on the cheek and hugged again, then dragged in to the bright, welcoming kitchen with which she was so familiar. 'Dave, come here, look who's arrived!'

From the small front room Daisy could hear the sounds of a newspaper being rustled and folded, a chair moving just slightly off the edge of the rug onto the sanded floor underneath and then a tall, bearded man appeared, his face split into a welcoming smile.

Lizzie moved across to his side and tucked herself under his arm with what appeared to Daisy – oddly – to be shyness. 'Daisy this is Dave. My lodger and –' she craned up at him, smiling, '– the man I love.'

'Hi, Dave.' Daisy might have felt shy herself had Dave not released Lizzie and moved across the small room in two big strides to embrace her in a bear hug that felt cuddly and warm and sweetly comforting all at once.

'I'm – we're – so glad you're here. Sit yourself down, Dais, have a drink, we're going to eat in a mo, do join us, there's plenty, isn't there, Dave?' Lizzie gabbled excitedly.

'Are you sure? I don't want to be in the way.'

'*Silly.* Sit. Now.' Lizzie poured some wine into a glass and handed it to her, then started to set another place at the table.

255

Daisy, overwhelmed by the warmth of her welcome, with pleasure at seeing Lizzie again, with delight that she was still regarded as a friend and feeling at the same time oddly disoriented by the familiarity of her surroundings, burst into tears.

'Hey! What's this?' Lizzie's arms were round her in an instant. Through her tears Daisy was vaguely aware of Dave signalling a 'should I leave?' question and Lizzie motioning him to stay. And then there were tissues and Lizzie squatting in front of her looking concerned and her feeling embarrassed by the unexpected breakdown and then Lizzie remembering something and blurting out, 'Hey Dais, did you hear, Ma Ruby's getting married!'

The shock of the words halted her tears and her embarrassment in their tracks and she could feel her jaw dropping and her eyes widening and she was saying, '*No!*' and Lizzie was laughing and she knew she was back among friends. She blew her nose and wiped her eyes and there wasn't even time to apologise because she just had to ask, 'Who to? When? *Tell* me.'

'Believe it or not, it's the editor of *The Stoneyford Echo.*'

'No! Really? How come?'

'I know. Can you imagine? All those years of rumpy pumpy with Big Angus and never getting anywhere in the marriage stakes, then along comes another editor and sweeps her off her feet.'

'Good thing he's a strong man,' Dave grunted from the sink.

Daisy laughed. 'But how did she ... where did ... I thought she turned down a job at the *Echo.*'

'She did. But their receptionist went off on maternity leave and Dishy Dave persuaded the ed to call her as a stand in and before you know it – bingo!'

Daisy tried to access the filing system in her brain. 'But wait a minute – the editor – what was his name again?'

'Arthur Herring.'

'Something a bit fishy about that,' Dave muttered from the sink.

'Stop it,' commanded Lizzie, laughing.

'Wasn't he married?'

'He was,' Lizzie confirmed, 'but his wife went off with Provost Porter.'

'*No!*'

'You've missed all the fun, Dais, there in France, I'm telling you.'

'So it seems.'

'But you're back and I'll drink to that any day.' She raised her glass towards Daisy. 'Cheers, my dears.'

As their glasses clinked, Daisy remembered her decision to go away again.

Lizzie saw the change and said, 'What?'

'I've got to leave again, Lizzie. I can't stand it at home.'

'I wanted to call you but I wasn't sure – How is he, Dais?'

'Do you know what, he's grim, but not nearly as grim as he makes out. Mum's suffering just as much as he is and if I stay, he'll damage me too. He's using this illness to control us both.'

Lizzie clapped her hands lightly. 'Well done, Daisy! So what'll you do? Go back to France?'

Daisy thought about it. She'd done the hardest thing – turning down Ben's sweet offer – and she knew that she couldn't simply throw away her independence.

'Yes,' she said. 'I'll go back to France.'

As the evening passed in amicable conversation, Daisy wondered whether Lizzie would deal with the long shadow that still lay between them, but it was Dave who, over some very fine honey ice cream, said, 'Have you seen Ben Gillies while you've been here, Daisy?'

Daisy felt the icy sweetness slide down the back of her throat. 'No.'

'I had a pint with him the other day.'

'How is he?'

In the weeks since she'd been back in Hailesbank, Daisy had kept her head down, doing what she had to do, thinking about the future and gathering all the resolution she possessed to break away from Laurel Lane and her parents once more.

'He didn't say much, but I'd place an odds-on bet that he's not a happy man.'

'I'm sorry to hear that.' The ice cream didn't taste so sweet now. Daisy laid down her spoon.

'He was throwing pebbles from the beach into the sea as if the devil was behind him.'

'Oh.' Daisy closed her eyes, pictured the scene, felt a wave of sadness. 'Is he working?'

'Very much so. He's got more writing commissions than he can handle. But hey, the guy's back at home, living with his folks. I don't think that's where he wanted to be.'

Nor me, thought Daisy dismally. Ben could hardly blame her though – he could live anywhere he liked, couldn't he? 'Did he ask about me?' she ventured.

'Actually no.'

Daisy shoved back her chair and lifted her glass. 'What the hell. To friends,' she said, keeping the toast unspecified.

She stayed another hour, enjoying the company. Around ten she switched on her mobile to call her mother. It rang at once. 'You have messages.'

The first had been left at seven. 'Daisy love, any chance you could get home? Dad's being a bit difficult. Thanks.'

The second call had been made about twenty minutes later. 'Daisy dear, I wish I could reach you. If you get this message, please call as soon as you can. Oh dear, what shall I do?' There was a pause. Daisy could hear noises in the background. 'Have to go. Call me!'

The third call, and the most alarming, had been left at eight thirty. 'Daisy?' The anguish in her mother's voice was way beyond mild concern. 'Call me darling, please call me, as soon as you can. It's urgent. Please Daisy, something awful's happened.'

'Jeez,' she muttered.

'Something up?' Lizzie asked, pouring Daisy a coffee.

'Mum. She sounds panicky.' She dialled Laurel Lane. Her mother answered at once.

'Hi Mum, what's up?' She had a feeling that the small bubble of calm she had been enjoying was about to be popped.

'It's awful, Daisy, just awful. You've got to come home quickly – but not too quickly, take care, darling, please take care, but get here as fast as you can …' There was a choked sob and her voice trailed off.

Something had happened with her father, thought Daisy. Had he had another stroke? A heart attack? Fallen? 'What is it? Is it Dad?'

'Noooo,' Janet sounded frantic. 'It's … I can hardly … oh Daisy … it's too awful ' She was gabbling, incoherent, hysterical. 'It's Kath Gillies,' she managed to get out at last, 'Kath –' There was another sob and the next time she spoke her voice sounded thick and strangulated. 'Oh darling, she's dead!'

Chapter Three

The tale was simple but tragic. Eric Irvine, in a fit of profound irritation at some repeated failure to communicate his meaning to his wife, had grown increasingly violent. Janet, frightened and unable to cope, had phoned her best friend and strongest support, Kath Gillies. Daisy gleaned these facts when, barely twenty minutes later, she pushed open the front door to find her mother still sobbing into a sheaf of sodden tissues.

'You weren't around, Daisy, I did try to reach you, so I phoned Kath and asked if she could come over. She said she'd be round at once, but she didn't arrive. It's only a ten-minute drive from their place and I thought she must have been held up by something so I waited half an hour then called again. Martin answered and told me that she'd left right after I'd called.'

She was shaking and there wasn't a vestige of colour in her face. Her father, who must have taken in the news, sat subdued and silent in his chair next to the fire. His face seemed to be sagging even more than usual and his eyes were dull.

'It's all right, Mum, take it easy. Here,' Daisy quickly fixed her mother a small brandy and handed it to her.

Janet took a small sip, spluttered, and found in the neat spirits the strength to go on. 'I started to get really worried. So did Martin. Then just as I was on the phone, I could hear his doorbell ring. He put the phone down but I could hear voices in the background, then there was this terrible cry, like a wounded bear or something and I was shouting down the phone, "Martin! Martin! Martin! What's happened? Tell me!"'

The brandy in the little glass was being shaken so much that it threatened to swill over the rim so Daisy eased it out of her mother's quivering hands and set it back down on the side table.

'I was just going to put the phone down and get in your father's car and drive round myself, never mind having to leave your father alone for half an hour, when Ben came on the phone.'

Daisy could hear Ben's steady voice in her head, picture his dark burnt-sugar eyes. The impressions were so strong that she felt almost as if he was in the room with her. Her hand went up to her heart in a swift, involuntary movement. It was as if she was connecting to him in some invisible way, feeling his pain. 'What? What did he say, Mum?'

The tears were flowing freely down Janet's face. Daisy watched numbly as small rivers formed on the dry, papery cheeks and glistened in the harsh glare of the overhead light. When she spoke, her mother's voice was thick, choking, stifled, almost unrecognisable. 'He said, "Janet? It's the police."' She gasped for air then stuttered, '"There's … there's been an accident. It looks as though it might have been caused by a young lad racing round the blind corner down near Mains village, though it's too early to say. It's bad news, I'm afraid."'

Now she was sobbing and her next words were incoherent. From the corner of the room, came a deep, guttural noise. For a minute, Daisy couldn't work out what it was. Then she realised.

It was her father, weeping.

There are times when you feel as though you are holding the fabric of your life together with the flimsiest of threads; when the smallest of tugs in any direction will rend it apart to reveal the rawness of the skin beneath. Yet you have to cling to the hope that the stitches will hold, that somehow you will walk through the dark days with your delicate covering intact so that somehow, sometime, on the far side, you will be able to mend the rips and slowly, carefully, patch together a new garment to wear into the future.

That week, that was how Daisy felt. Each day was an agony. Janet could do nothing but go over and over and over the incident, full of remorse and self-condemnation. 'I shouldn't have called her. I should have managed myself.'

Nothing Daisy could say seemed to ease her guilt. Her mother was like the walking dead, barely functioning. She spent a fair part of each day in tears. She needed to recreate her remorse again and again, desperately seeking a way through it. Only time would heal that pain, Daisy's instinct told her, but in the meantime she had to take on most of the caring, cooking, cleaning, and shopping and many other chores that were necessary to get her parents through the day. On top of it all, she carried her own guilt. If she'd had her phone on ... if she'd checked back earlier ... if she hadn't been so self centred and headed out in the first place. She carried out her chores like an automaton, the thoughts circling in her head. If only she had ... if only she hadn't –

It was pointless. The fact is, she had gone out. She hadn't had her mobile on. If her mother had been more capable, she could have dealt with the situation without having to call on Kath. It had been sheer bad timing that Kath had been driving round that blind corner at the exact moment that the boy racer had swerved into the centre of the road from the other direction.

She spoke to Ben, briefly, the day after the accident, a short, formal conversation. She expressed her sorrow, wished it could be different. Was there anything she could do and when was the funeral? Ben sounded strained but his voice was level. Thank you. No, nothing. The funeral is on Tuesday next week, in St Andrews Church. She left it at that for now. For the moment every ounce of energy she had was being poured into the many things she had to do at Laurel Lane.

To compound the evils of the week, Daisy found herself in the wrong place at the wrong time on the Saturday morning. Leaving her mother in charge for a brief hour, she allowed herself a quick trawl round the shops on the High Street for something suitable to wear for the funeral. She was just ten yards from the car when a wedding party emerged from the Registry Office. It was Jack Hedderwick and Iris Swithinbank. *Iris Hedderwick* now, she supposed.

She stopped dead. A small crowd had gathered to watch the bride emerge. She'd be more noticeable if she moved than if she stayed where she was, almost hidden behind a large woman and her equally obese friend. Iris looked radiant. As for Jack – Daisy scanned her erstwhile lover dispassionately. She felt detached from the scene, as if she were watching a movie screen rather than real life. Jack looked just as attractive as he had on the day she'd met him but she felt absolutely nothing for him. Her heart felt empty, scoured out, raw but at the same time numb, past pain. In the scale of things, in the face of Kath's death, the wedding was insignificant. Perhaps her embarrassment the night she'd attempted to throw herself back at Jack had acted like a weed-killer, eradicating the roots of her misplaced feelings. Perhaps distance had put things in perspective. Maybe the delightful hours spent making love with Majik had liberated her from the shackles of the past, or maybe Ben's declaration of his feelings for her had sown itself somewhere in her being and was germinating under the surface, simply waiting for sunshine.

There were cheers and flashbulbs and the first drops of rain from a sky that threatened much more. In front of her, the large women started to move off. Keeping pace with them on the kerb side, she successfully avoided being spotted. Once, she would have killed to be by Jack's side, in this place. It had taken a great length of time, but at last she could say with complete honesty that she was glad she wasn't.

'Thank you for your kind wishes.'

'Thank you.'

'You've been very kind. Everyone has been.'

'I'm so pleased you came. Thank you.'

Daisy could hear the phrases repeated over and over in front of her as she waited to leave the church after the funeral. Martin Gillies, his hair now pure white, looked gaunt, but managed to smile at every mourner who had turned out – and the large church had been full. By his side stood Ben. She'd seen him earlier, of course. He'd gone to the lectern and given a speech of such bravery and such humour that it had broken her heart.

'My mother –' his voice cracked a fraction before he

managed to gather himself and go on. 'My mother would have loved to be here. She always enjoyed a good party.'

She didn't hear much after that, just saw the head held high and a brightness in the eyes that looked most unnatural. He was balancing, she thought, on the edge of a knife.

Her father was there, in a wheelchair, his head lolling to the side, his mouth drooping. Janet, getting through the days with the aid of sedatives and sleeping pills, was robotic. Daisy waited until the church was almost empty before steering them to the door.

'So kind of you to come.'

Hearing Martin's words, Janet buckled and started to collapse. He caught her, put a firm hand under her elbow, pulled her close. Daisy watched as her mother clung to him for support. She and her mother, she thought, they'd always allowed themselves to be subordinated by her father's rough will. She looked at the scene around her. There was a new story now and the people told it through the way they were arranged – Martin clinging to Janet. Her father, slack-limbed and helpless. Ben, his feet planted wide to give himself the strongest possible base, his usual good colour drained by exhaustion. They were all victims now.

'Daisy.'

One word. One word, spoken so softly that she barely caught it. One word that held a plea she knew he would never express in any other way. Turning, she slipped her arm round his waist and put her head against his chest. They were in a long tunnel and she saw no light at the end of it. Ben's heart was beating sluggishly. She could feel the thud, thud, thud of it against her ear and wondered, wretchedly, if he was warm enough on this chill November day in his thin suit and crisp white shirt.

His arms rose hesitantly and locked round her. In the dark of the tunnel, a small glow flickered.

Chapter Four

Ben was not a man given to high drama. In the course of his thirty-two years he'd had his share of ups and downs, of jobs done well, of failures, of girls won and lost, of pride swollen or battered, of feelings bruised, and great times enjoyed. For the most part, he coasted through it all, learned whatever lessons he could, and moved on, secure in his conviction that whatever cards life dealt him, he could handle. He was not ambitious, but he was confident in his abilities. Girlfriends had been plentiful enough to keep him happy.

Falling for Daisy Irvine had been a mistake. He understood that now. He'd been chasing a dream, probably on the rebound from Martina. He had allowed something about her familiarity, from their childhood friendship, to draw him in and make him feel as if she was the right woman for him. It had all been illusory. He'd travelled half across Europe, laid himself open for her, and he'd been knocked back. Well, it was done. Over before it had started. When she'd put her arms round him after the funeral service, he understood that there had been nothing in the least bit romantic about the gesture.

To be frank, Ben thought as he sat in his room on the third floor of his parents' home – his *father's* home – he couldn't cope with it now if she did harbour feelings for him because for the first time in his life, Ben felt as if he had been dealt a hand that was unplayable. In the cold, clear light of a mid-November day, he could see almost as far as the sea. Perhaps he should put on his boots and walk. Walking was about the only thing that brought him any relief at the moment. He found himself walking about ten or twelve miles a day. He could feel the flesh melting off him. Bones he'd never known he had were beginning to appear. He was making an acquaintance with his own skeleton. The idea fascinated him for a moment, then passed. Thinking about skeletons was too difficult.

He stood, stretched, turned round, ruffled his hands through his hair. He should stay in and work. His laptop sat on the small desk he'd placed under the window, where Nefertiti used to stand. He missed Nef. When he'd gifted the dummy to Lizzie, he'd been on the move, full of optimism about what lay in front of him. It had been the right thing to do. Yet she would have been a comforting presence here now, unanswering, uncritical, just *there*. His mother had loved to dress her.

His mother.

Ben stared at the screen of the laptop. He had two articles to complete and he had to make up his mind about whether to take on another commission from the travel publisher. Russia. A couple of weeks ago, he'd have leapt at the opportunity, but now he had to think about his father. In any case, since the accident, making any kind of decision was completely beyond the bounds of possibility. All he could see was mangled metal and sightless eyes. The swift brutality of it haunted him. It was so unjust. His mother had been a good person, a warm, loving, funny, generous person who had lost her life trying to help someone else.

He felt adrift. His hands went through his hair again, leaving it standing on end in a mad way. He slumped down again on his chair and buried his face in his hands. He felt the loss of his mother not like a dull ache but like a searing pain. Memories crowded in. Memories from far back – a face close to his, smiling, mouthing sweet babyish endearments; the perfume from a sweater as his face pressed into her chest in the midst of some playful hug; playing cricket in the garden, his mother running and laughing; her love of gossip, her many kindnesses; the sound of her laughter, the laughter he would never hear again.

He couldn't bear it.

'Ben?' There was a knocking at his door. His father's voice barely penetrated into his torpid brain. 'You've got a visitor.'

He swung round on his chair, his mind about a minute behind the words. He had to work. Things were waiting for his attention. Articles. Decisions. He had to walk. His body needed him to walk. He had to write. That was what he did. He was a writer. But he had to walk something out of his system. Work. Write. Walk. Work. Write. Walk. What? What did he have to do? A visitor? Finally, the word snaked past his defence system. He stood up. His jeans slipped downwards, loose around his hips. He tugged vaguely at them as the door opened.

'Hi Ben.' Daisy Irvine stood in a shaft of sunshine, her dark hair shot with rust as the light sparked off it. She was steady and sweet and dearly familiar and Ben felt a rush of feeling flood into what a second before had been an arid desert. But he couldn't move.

'Are you hugging?'

He heard the words, little more than a whisper, and found his lips framing the response. 'Are you asking?'

'I'm asking.'

'Then I'm hugging.'

It wasn't sudden passion. She wasn't declaring undying love for him. She wasn't, Ben realised, offering anything other than friendship – but that, for now, was enough. More than enough. It was the dearest, most precious thing she could have given him. Love? He couldn't have dealt with that. He wouldn't have trusted it. He wouldn't have had any faith in his own feelings, lying as they did in the shadow of death.

The hug went on a long time. Minutes. He was grateful, to the core of his being, for her presence there, for the solid *realness* of her.

At length they moved apart and sat, as they had once before, on the floor.

'You've lost weight.'

'I'm not eating much. Plus, I'm walking a lot.'

'How's Martin? I thought he looked good, considering.'

Ben and his father didn't talk about Kath. It was a man thing, he supposed. They drank together a lot. They talked about other matters, like the football and whether Martin should enter the competition at his golf club or not and the prospects for Scotland in the Six Nations rugby. They marvelled at how quickly the kitchen got into disarray and puzzled at the dial of the washing machine and were astonished when the washing came out blue. It had never happened before. They didn't think to make a shopping list before heading to the supermarket and found they had forgotten several essentials but had a great range of bread to choose from – bread that would turn green long before they were able to eat it all. 'Considering. I suppose. Yes.'

'Are you working?' She nodded toward his laptop.

'Trying. I'm not –' he hesitated, then confessed, 'My mind doesn't seem to be very focused. I keep thinking about –' It seemed like a weakness to say it.

Daisy finished for him, gently, 'Thinking about your mother. It's all right, Ben. It's not bad to feel bad. We all mourn her, but you were a *part* of her. She made you, she loved you in a way no one else ever has or ever will.'

The lump in Ben's chest felt like lead, heavy and poisonous.

'You'll always think about her. She'll never leave you, but in time it won't hurt and you'll only remember the good times, not the times you argued or got cross with each other or said things to each other you didn't mean to say.'

He stared at her. How did she know?

'So what's your deadline?'

His mind was drifting everywhere – to a row he'd had with his mother when they'd told him the family was moving to London; to how his father was coping and whether he should be finding strength from somewhere to give him more support; to the feature he was trying to write on an alternative therapy he'd been researching; to Daisy and her amazing intuition.

'Ben? Deadline?' She reached forward and took his hand in hers. He liked the feel of her hand. It was warm and small and very smooth. He curled his fingers round her palm.

'Deadline? Yesterday, I think.'

'And how's it going?'

'It's not really going at all. I've done all the research, I just have to pull it together.'

'You'll do it though.'

He shrugged. 'Maybe.'

'*Ben.* This is your job. Your livelihood. You can't let it slip. You mustn't. You have to separate the grief part of your life from the work part.'

'Is that possible?'

She looked at him squarely. 'Yes. I've done it. And if I can do it, you can too.'

He stared at her. How did he know what she'd been through? Dizzy Dais, with her sad, unrequited passion for Jack Hedderwick. He thought she'd been running away when she'd fled to Nice, but she must have understood that she was not fleeing, she was simply seeking a cure, because right now, in the face of his inexpressible weakness, she seemed to him like a tower of strength.

'Can't you?' she repeated, giving the hand entwined with his a gentle shake.

His mouth twitched into the smallest of smiles. 'I can try,' he said.

Chapter Five

'It's like *Four Weddings and a Funeral*,' Lizzie hissed as they stood, muffled in wool and sporting jaunty hats, waiting for the appearance of Sharon Eddy from the back of the church.

'Shhh,' whispered Daisy, though she was unable to resist smiling. It was all too true. First there had been Jack and Iris – she'd stumbled on that wedding quite by accident, but it had been real enough. Then there had been the grim occasion of Kath Gillies's funeral, here in this very church just a few weeks ago. Last week Ruby Spence had married Arthur Herring in a small ceremony in the Town Hall. All the old crowd had been there – Sharon and Cosmo, in the throes of preparation for their own big day, Dishy Dave with a new girlfriend in tow, Chantelle, Murdoch Darling, as cynical as ever but looking far more relaxed, Jay, now on the ascendancy and with Amelia by his side – and Ben, of course.

He'd been reluctant to go. 'I only knew her for a little while. And anyway ...'

'You're coming. I need you.' Daisy said firmly. Since the visit to Ben's house, when she'd taken her courage in both hands and risked a snub, she had taken on the role of prop and support for Ben. It was the most extraordinary turnabout. From earlier that year, when she'd been a dithering, forgetful, indecisive girl, lacking in confidence in her abilities and her attractiveness, she had gained some self assurance.

Not that it was all straightforward – she still had to decide her future. The job was waiting for her in Nice, but Madame Prenier wouldn't hold it open indefinitely. She had days when the old, familiar panic returned. How would she break free from Laurel Lane? Having once made the decision to leave, how

273

could she abandon her parents now?

With every question, though, there came either an answer or a feeling of optimism. She *would* leave Laurel Lane, and soon. Her mother *would* get stronger – without Daisy there, or Kath, she would build self reliance, because she would have to. As for a job, she had managed to support herself in the past, so she would do so again, end of story. It would happen.

Music struck up. Daisy turned her head and watched the entrance of the bride. Sharon, her face veiled, her train held by four pageboys, attended by six bridesmaids, leaned on her father's arm and began the long walk to the altar. Daisy leaned over to Lizzie and whispered in her ear, 'It *will* be Four Weddings when you and Dave get hitched.'

'Piss off,' Lizzie hissed back. But she looked pleased.

Weddings can be lavish but dull, conducted on a shoestring but joyous, they can be pretentious, or simple, or anything you want them to be. If she'd been asked to guess what kind of event the marriage of Sharon Eddy and Sir Cosmo Fleming would be, Daisy would have come down on the side of flamboyant – not because of Sir Cosmo, but because she would have put money on Sharon being unable to resist scale, gaudiness, and all the trimmings imaginable. But despite the numerous bridesmaids and pageboys (all cousins, nieces, great nieces or nephews, or other relatives on the Fleming side, apparently), the wedding turned out to be delightfully down to earth and Daisy was pleased to be proved wrong. Sharon had already submerged herself in Cosmo's lifestyle and become more country gentry than the country gentry – right down to embracing shabby chic with fervour.

Fleming House stood in extensive parkland and although the house drained money and was in constant need of repair, it did boast a sizeable ballroom, which was where they now headed for the reception. When they reached the top of the chipped stone steps that led up to the thick double doors into the vaulted hallway, they joined the queue to meet the newlyweds. Sharon – now Lady Fleming – was luminous in ivory, her blonde hair swept up under the Fleming family tiara, her dress, Daisy learned later, a Chanel classic worn by Lady Fleming at her own wedding in 1957.

'You look fab,' Daisy said, leaning across acres of creamy lace to embrace Sharon's nipped-in waist and kiss her glowing cheeks.

'Thanks, Dais. Thanks for coming – after I ... you know ... I'm sorry.' Sharon's emerald green eyes were bright with tears. 'Still friends?' she asked tentatively as the queue built up behind them.

'Of course,' said Daisy, surprised.

'Ain't she lovely, my bride?' Cosmo broke in, beaming, his face ruddy, his normally tousled brown hair gelled into submission. At his feet lay two of his Labradors, decorated for the occasion with cream beribboned collars. The third – Gem? – was nudging his way between Cosmo's legs.

'Very,' Daisy agreed, hugging him.

'Thank heaven the boy's married someone at last,' grunted Sir Cosmo's indefatigable mother, resplendent in purple and leaning on a silver-topped cane.

'You must be very proud,' muttered Ben, following close behind Daisy.

'Proud. Hah! At least the boy's not gay. I'd begun to wonder,' she declaimed in a loud voice as Cosmo's face grew, if that were possible, even redder.

They escaped, trying to suppress their giggles. 'Shar's going to have her work cut out for her,' said Ben as they lifted whisky and ginger ales from a tray offered by a youth Daisy recognised as one of the bar staff in The Duke of Atholl.

'Bet you she's got the old witch sussed,' answered Daisy, hunting for something to eat. There were no posh canapés, though, just bowls of nuts and crisps to dig into, while instead of a string quartet, Daisy recognised a local folk group, looking distinctly not dressed to kill. She looked at Ben, Ben looked at her, and they both laughed.

Daisy hadn't seen him smile for a month. The thinness of his face twisted something in her heart and a longing to hug him overwhelmed her. She quelled it. She had probably used up all permissable hugs recently.

An hour and four whiskies later, the photographs were at last over. There was to be no banquet, it seemed. Instead, small pots of steaming hot shepherd's pie appeared, with red plastic scoops.

'Different,' mused Daisy, tucking in.

'Nursery food,' said Ben. 'Bet you Cossers chose this.'

'Cost effective too,' Daisy reflected uncharitably.

And then talking became impossible as the ceilidh band struck up and the dancing started. They watched from an alcove as kilts swayed and swung, attractively raffish. Ben leaned over and bawled something into her ear.

'What?' She cupped her hand and leaned closer to catch his words.

'I said, do you want to get married?'

She looked at him, stunned. 'Are you asking?'

He shook his head, then moved his mouth to within an inch of her head and shouted, 'Nah. This isn't for me. Not yet awhile anyway.'

'Nor me,' she shouted back. She meant it. The last thing she wanted was urban tedium. She'd just begun to discover that life could be exciting.

'I thought all women dreamed of a big white wedding,' he yelled.

She shook her head vehemently in denial. It was impossible to talk above the noise of the band and the whoops from the dancers. Behind them, a waiter was hovering at the entrance to the ballroom with another tray of small shepherd's pies.

'I'm ravenous, Diz,' said Ben, spotting it, 'How about you?' Without waiting for an answer, he reached for the tray and lifted the whole thing out of the waiter's hands. The boy stared after them, astonished as, shrieking with laughter, they scurried into the large orangery that led off the grand entrance hall and collapsed on some green-painted wicker furniture.

'Here.' Ben handed her another pot and scoop. She ate the small portion of shepherd's pie, then reached for another.

Breakfast had been many hours ago and she'd forgotten to eat at lunchtime. They chomped their way through a full quarter of the tray before the edge of their hunger was blunted and Ben put his hands on his stomach and sighed contentedly.

'Full?'

He shook his head. 'Not yet. Just resting. Shit, I should've grabbed some drinks.'

'There was a tray on the chest in the hall. I think the waiter abandoned it.'

'Give me a sec, then, I'll fetch.'

He returned seconds later with the whole tray. 'Well spotted.'

'*Ben!*'

'What?' He affected a look of innocence. 'It's a wedding, for heaven's sake. We hung around for hours while all those bloody photos were taken, this is the least they can do for us. Cheers.' He lifted a glass and toasted her. 'To whisky and pies. And friends.'

'Friends.'

They gazed at each other in silence. The music from the ballroom was distant enough to make talking possible. Daisy felt wonderfully at peace and stronger than she had ever felt in her life. That morning, she had told her mother that she was going back to France. Instead of provoking the dramatics she had anticipated, Janet had been understanding and even encouraging. 'Go, Daisy love. You're right. You have a life of your own to live. Your Dad and I will manage.'

Bizarrely, Kath's death appeared to have unlocked something in Janet. Now that she didn't have her friend to call on, perhaps she had realised that she had to find the strength to manage on her own. Even Eric, unusually subdued, had simply lifted Daisy's hand to his lips and kissed it – and with that one simple signal he had unshackled his daughter. She had been wonderfully, miraculously released. She could go back to France and carry on with her new life.

In the half-light of the orangery, a row of tea lights had been placed on the low sill. They flickered softly in the draught from the door, throwing a dancing light onto Ben's thin face as he closed his eyes and sat motionless. He was a picture of suffering and it came to Daisy, as it had so often over the past weeks, that she couldn't bear to see it, that she longed to be able to mend him. She sat very still, using all the power of her mind to try to reach his. What was he thinking? Was there a space in his life for her or had she closed that door for ever? To be in charge of her own life meant so much to her, yet the thought of leaving him was like a sharp pain. In the half shadows of the room, she wrestled with her thoughts.

Ben broke the silence first. As the music crashed to a halt in the ballroom amid laughter and whoops and applause, he opened his eyes and said, 'Couldn't have got through the last couple of weeks without you, Diz.' He looked down, obviously realised he was still clutching an empty pie pot, and tossed it onto the tray. 'Thanks.'

She found words. 'I've been glad to help,' she said and wondered if he could possibly realise how much she meant it. The small space between them seemed like a million miles – and yet she *had* to reach out across the abyss and make him understand what she was only just beginning to understand herself.

Above them, tall ferns waved gently and the scent of lilies was strong in the air. Deep inside Daisy, something twisted and stilled and all her doubts resolved into a sharp focus of certainty. She had been terribly wrong. The feelings she had for him were not just feelings of friendship, nor were they an empty passion, not to be trusted. They were real and warm and loving, deeper and stronger than anything she had known or dreamt of.

Independence? What would that be worth if she didn't have Ben in her life? Looking at his fatigued features, it felt as though she had loved him for ever. She clenched her hands into fists without being aware of it, her mouth twisting and working into a thousand different shapes.

'You remember Nice,' she said at last, her tentativeness like a crucifixion. Ben's gaze was burning a hole in her soul. 'About what you said –'

What do you call it when you hold the camera shutter open for a long time, letting the light in to reveal the tiniest specks of dust in the very darkest corners? Maximum exposure. That's how I feel right now. I've opened the core of my being to maximum exposure and let you see the dust. Please tell me it's been worth it.

'Maximum exposure. That's how you described it. I panicked, Ben.' Her hands were still balled tight, but her voice had steadied. 'All my life, it seemed to me, I had let myself be regulated by others. My father reined me in, managed me, undermined my sense of myself. Jack too, in a different way. I couldn't let that happen again. I needed to feel that I had a life of my choice.'

Still he was watching her. Still he didn't respond. She ploughed on. 'And then it happened all over again. I allowed myself to be drawn back home. My *duty* –' she grimaced at the word, '– my duty to my parents held me as tightly as ever.'

There was clapping and cheering. She remembered dimly that they were at a wedding – but the only reality was in this room, here, with Ben. She drew a deep breath. The only risk was *not* saying it.

'I love you, Ben. I have for a long time. I just didn't know it.'

She saw his head go back a fraction, but his face didn't change. Had she made another mistake? She had to trust her judgement now.

'These past weeks, you needed me. In the worst of all possible situations, the one good thing that came out of it – for me at least – was that I felt I was able to help you. I could give you strength. I was needed. I was an equal part of a relationship. I liked that feeling Ben. I'm sorry for the reason for it, but I liked the fact that you needed me.

'Now I've stepped in front of the camera, if you like. I'm not hiding. I've just opened myself to maximum exposure too.' She smiled at him, but she was trembling violently. 'I love you, Ben. That's the dust in my corners.'

In the distance, she could hear the music starting up for

279

another dance. There were whoops as the first chord was struck. *He-euch!* Was he never going to say anything? Uncertainty crept into her mind. She hadn't rehearsed this. She hadn't planned anything. She had, quite simply, shown how vulnerable she was, just as he had in Nice. She had rebuffed him then. Was he going to do the same to her now?

The amber eyes were unreadable. There was something in the depths of the gaze she couldn't quite fathom. He was still protecting himself from all emotion. He wasn't ready for this.

She started to stand. 'I'm sorry—'

It was all she managed to say before she felt her hands being taken in his. She turned towards him. The veil in front of his eyes had cleared.

'I've been thinking about Russia,' he said, pulling her back down into her chair. She could feel the wicker digging roughly into the backs of her knees.

'Russia?'

'I've been offered another commission. More food, more farmers, more real people. I was going to turn it down, but I guess if I could persuade a photographer to come with me, I might consider it.'

'A photographer?'

'Well not any photographer, obviously. I'd pick a ditsy, adorable, infuriating one who is maybe just beginning to understand that loving someone doesn't have to be serfdom.'

The dimness inside her skull cleared slowly and her lips began to curl into a soft smile. 'Are you asking?'

'I'm asking.'

They were two naked souls, soft, vulnerable, loving. The smile turned into a little laugh and she realised that her heart was pounding.

'Then I'm coming to Russia with you.'

The kiss went on for ever. She felt his lips on hers, softly at first, then more warmly, more passionately, and so familiar that it felt as though this moment had happened a hundred sweet times before and would happen a thousand times more.

There was more applause, but it seemed closer. She drew her

head away from Ben's, just an inch, the furthest she could bear to be apart from him, and out of the corner of her eye she saw that Lizzie and Dave were standing there, clapping.

'Four weddings?' Lizzie was saying, laughing.

She looked at Ben. He gazed back.

'No more weddings,' they groaned in unison.

Daisy felt Ben's hand curling round hers, warm and familiar. It was a grasp that asked for strength as well as lent it. She smiled at him and she smiled at Lizzie. She was replete with hot pies and love.

Giving is a gift to yourself also.

Face the Wind and Fly

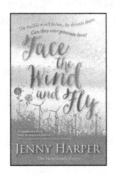

She builds wind farms, he detests them. Can they ever generate love?

After fifteen happy years of marriage, Kate Courtenay discovers that her charismatic novelist husband is spending more and more of his time with a young fan. She throws herself into her work, a controversial wind farm that's stirring up tempers in the local community. Sparks fly when she goes head to head against its most outspoken opponent, local gardener Ibsen Brown – a man with a past of his own. But a scheme for a local community garden brings the sparring-partners together, producing the sort of electricity that threatens to short-circuit the whole system.

Loving Susie

She thought she knew her husband, but he's been keeping a secret ... about her.

Scottish politician Susie Wallace is under pressure. She risks censure from her Party for her passionate and outspoken views on arts funding. A charity she's involved with runs into difficulties. And a certain journalist seems to have it in for her.

Susie stumbles across some information that rocks her world but not, apparently, her husband's – Archie has been in on this particular secret for thirty years. Now Susie wonders if she can trust him at all. Soon, unemployed son Jonathan and successful daughter Mannie begin to feel the fallout too, fracturing the family and leaving Susie increasingly isolated.

Troubled by mounting pressure from her family, her Party and the Press, Susie goes into hiding. The Party needs her back for a crucial vote, but more importantly, Archie knows he needs to find his wife quickly if they are to rebuild their relationship and reunite the family.

The Heartlands Series

Jenny Harper

For more information about **Jenny Harper**

and other **Accent Press** titles

please visit

www.accentpress.co.uk

http://www.jennyharperauthor.co.uk